STICK AND STONE
ON THE GO

BETH FERRY
KRISTEN CELLA

CLARION BOOKS
Imprints of HARPERCOLLINS*Publishers*

HARPER
alley

CONTENTS

STICK AND STONE
AND THE CAVE

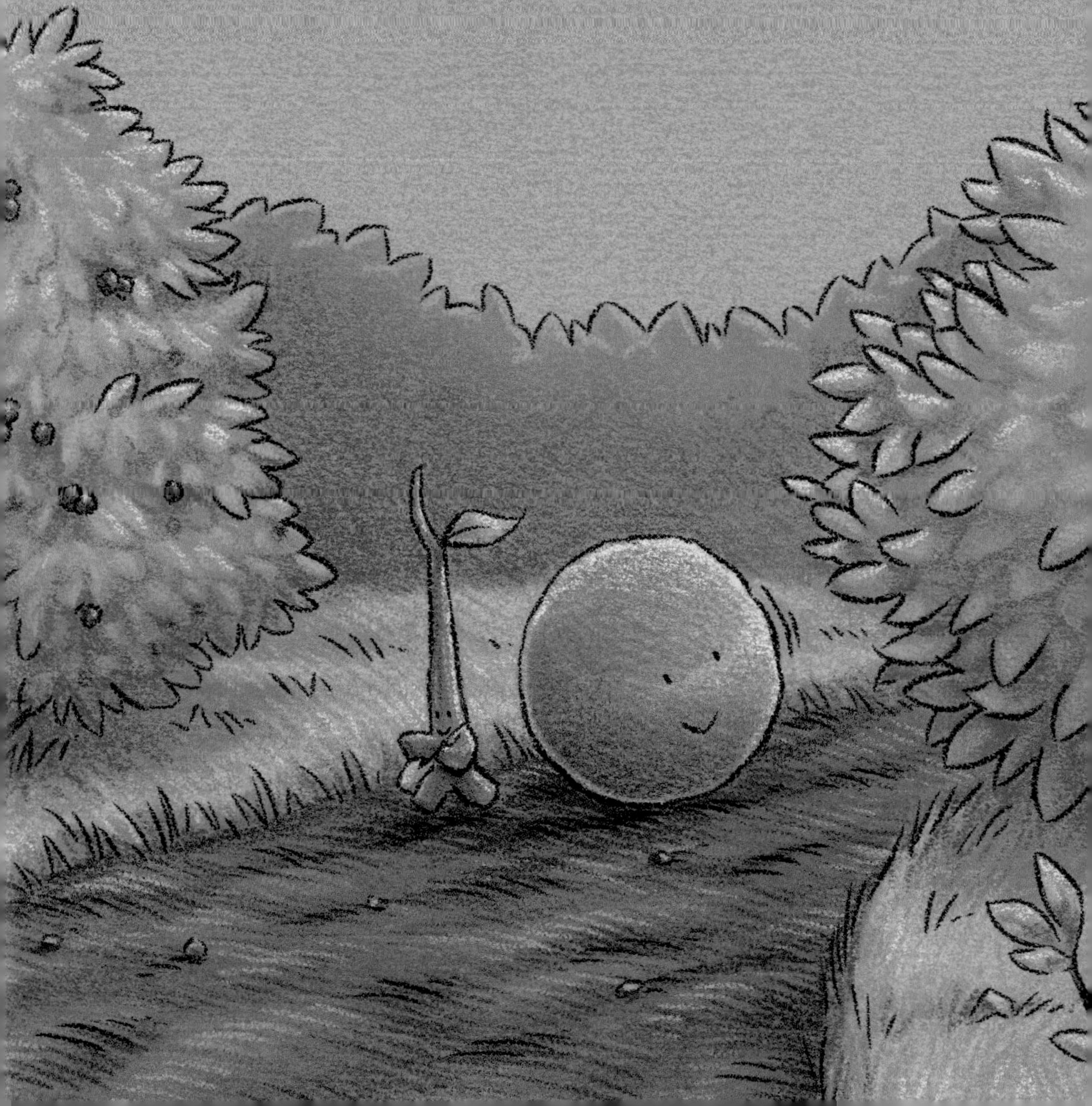

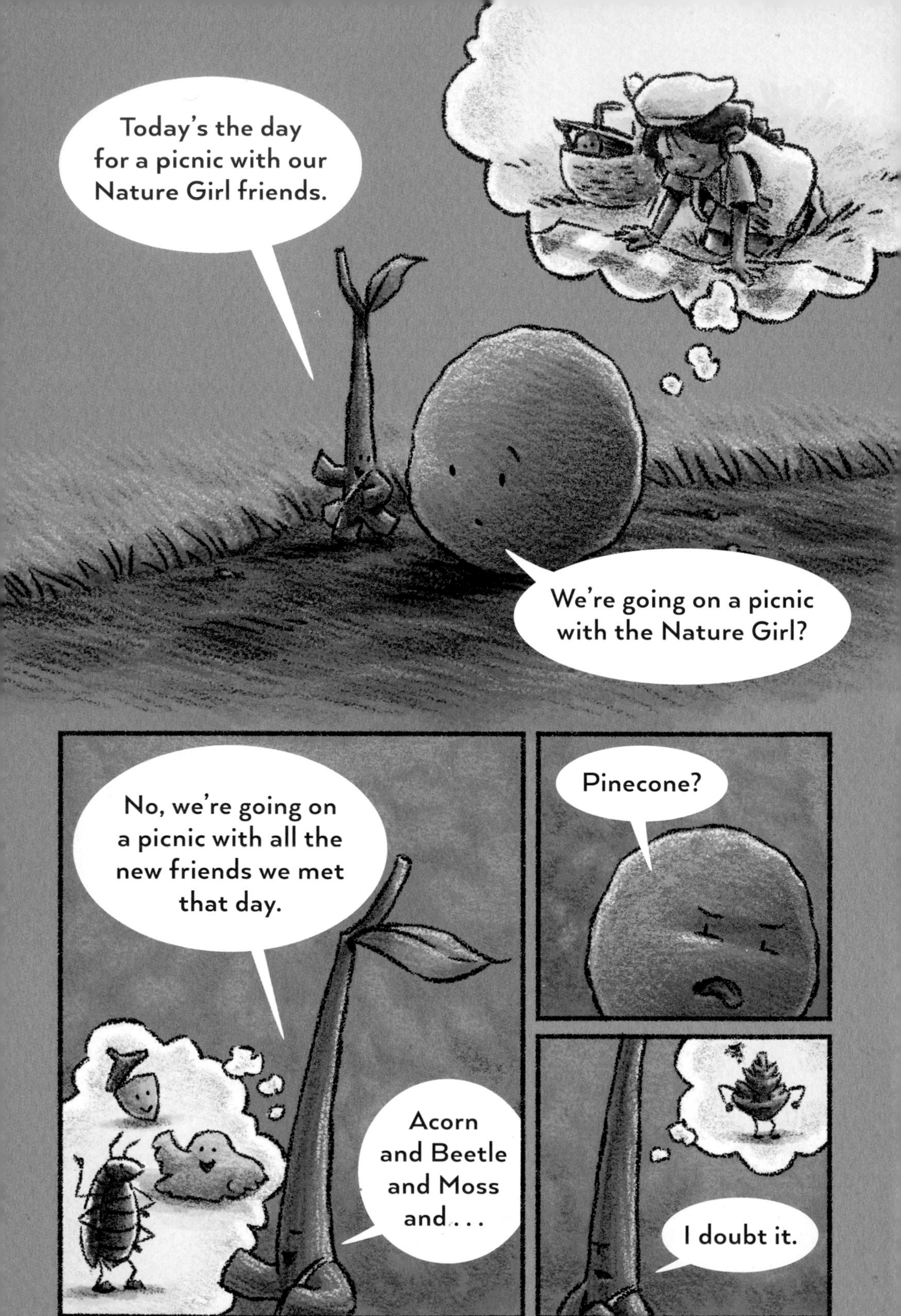
Today's the day for a picnic with our Nature Girl friends.
We're going on a picnic with the Nature Girl?
No, we're going on a picnic with all the new friends we met that day.
Acorn and Beetle and Moss and . . .
Pinecone?
I doubt it.

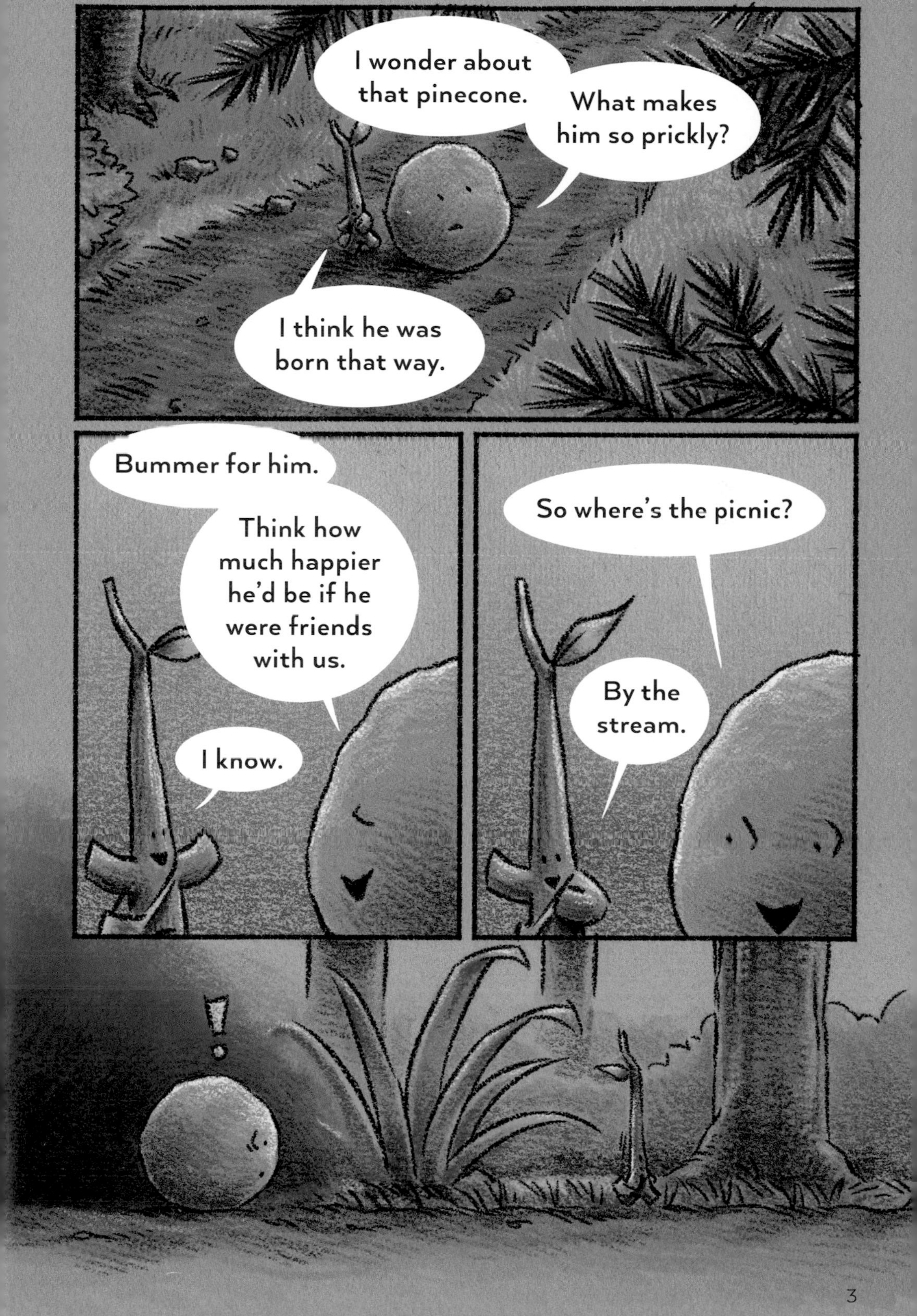
I wonder about that pinecone.
What makes him so prickly?
I think he was born that way.
Bummer for him.
Think how much happier he'd be if he were friends with us.
I know.
So where's the picnic?
By the stream.
!

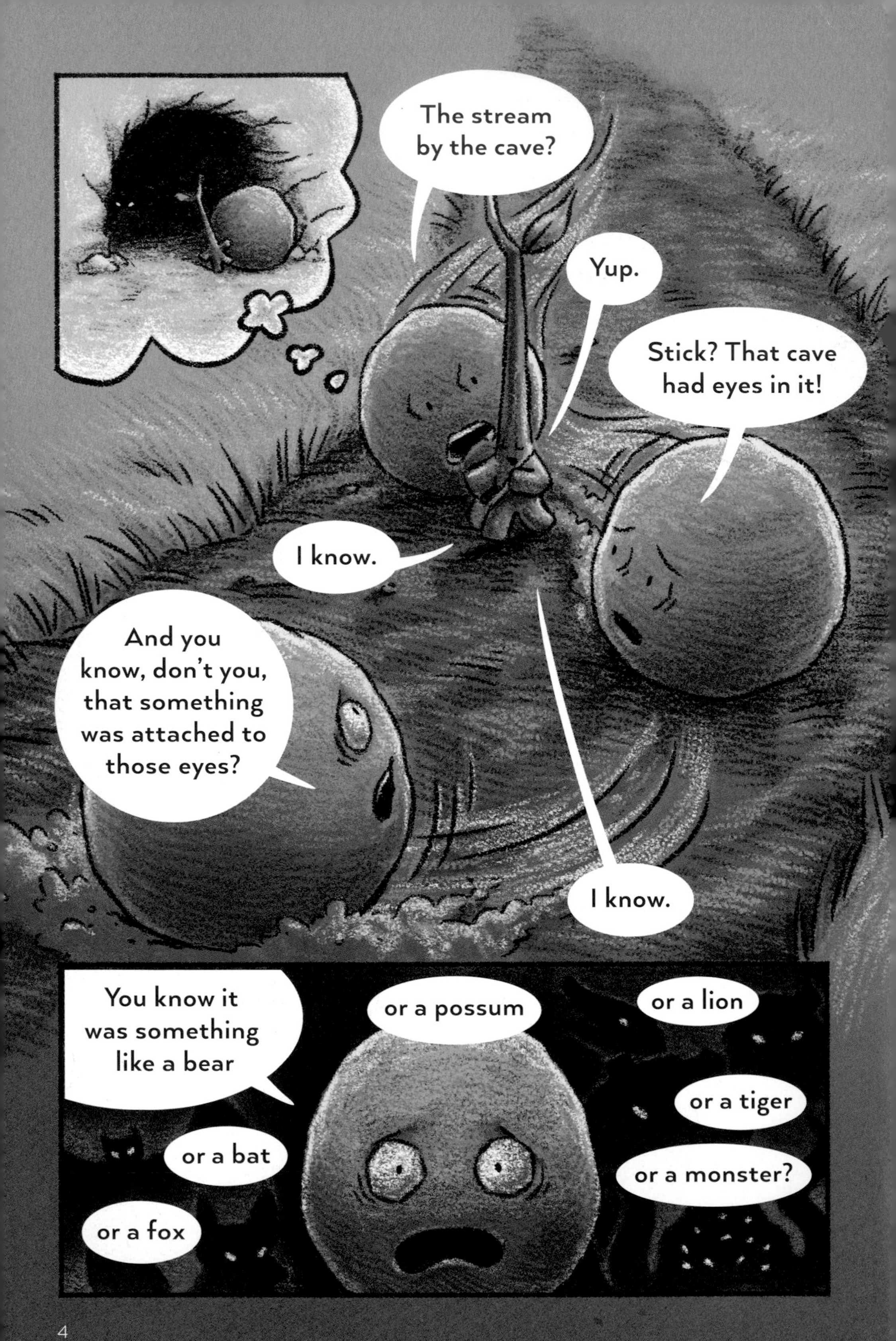
The stream
by the cave?
Yup.
Stick? That cave
had eyes in it!
I know.
And you
know, don't you,
that something
was attached to
those eyes?
I know.
You know it
was something
like a bear
or a possum
or a lion
or a tiger
or a bat
or a monster?
or a fox

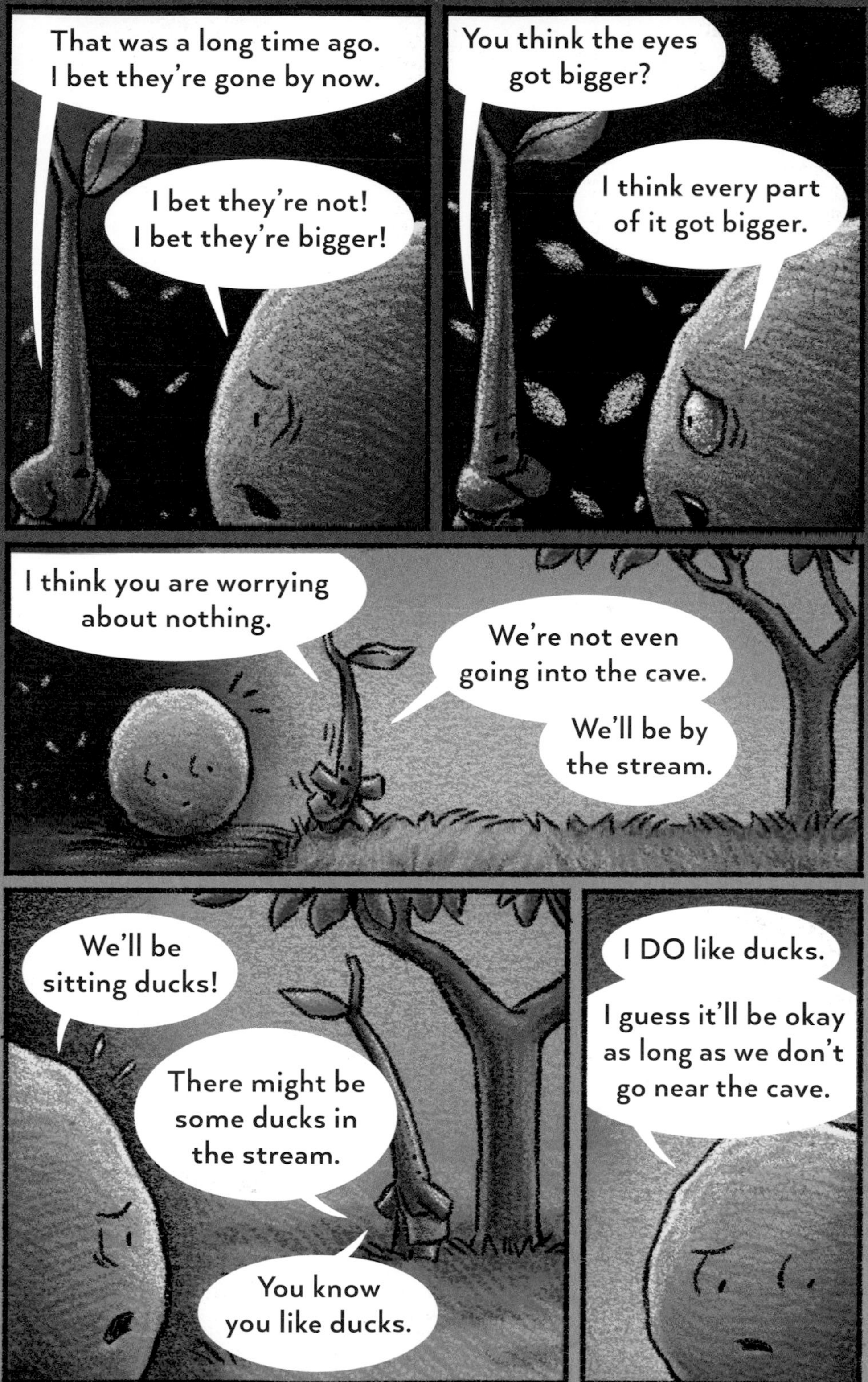
That was a long time ago. I bet they're gone by now.
I bet they're not! I bet they're bigger!
You think the eyes got bigger?
I think every part of it got bigger.
I think you are worrying about nothing.
We're not even going into the cave.
We'll be by the stream.
We'll be sitting ducks!
There might be some ducks in the stream.
You know you like ducks.
I DO like ducks.
I guess it'll be okay as long as we don't go near the cave.

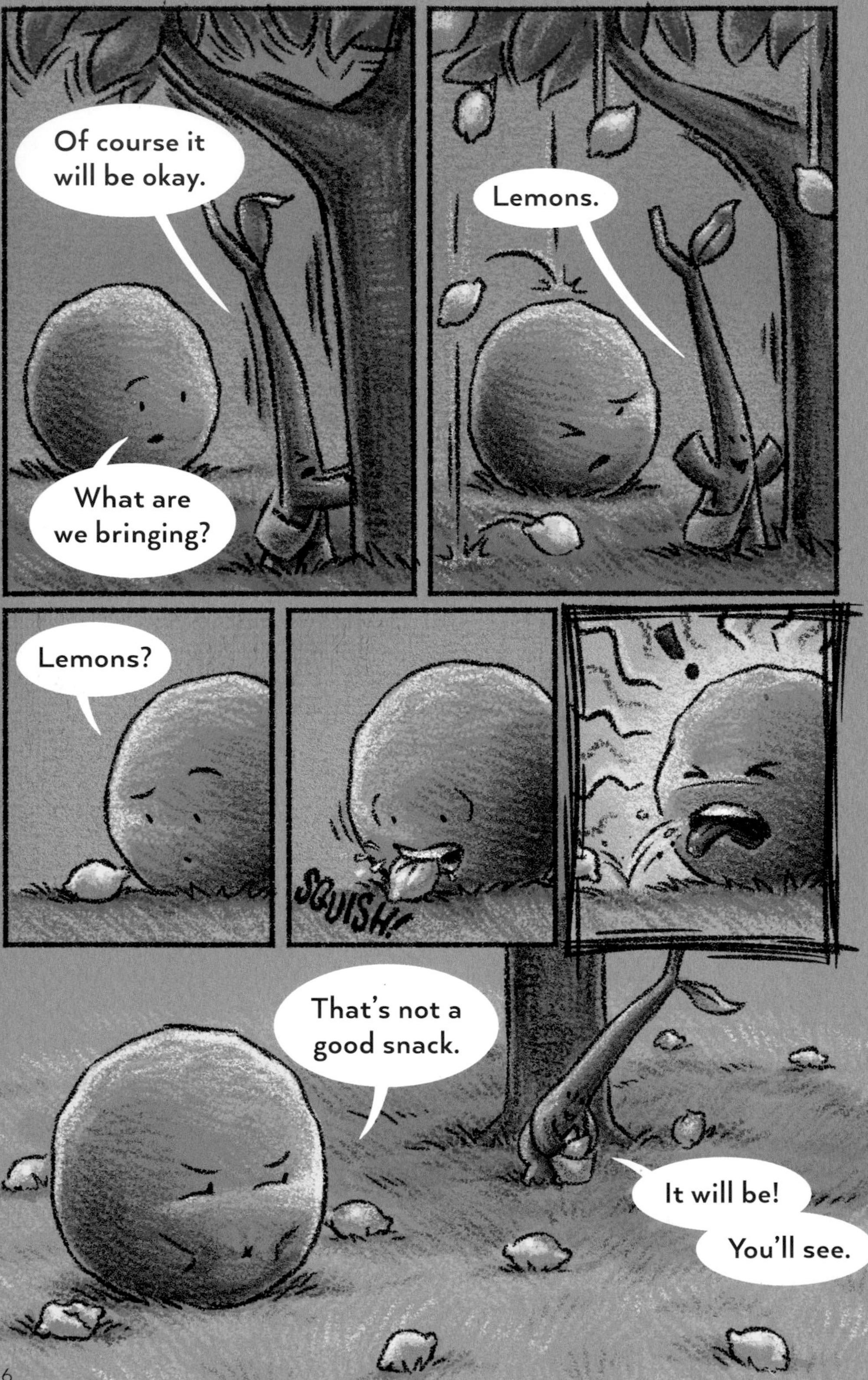
Of course it will be okay.
What are we bringing?
Lemons.
Lemons?
SQUISH!
That's not a good snack.
It will be!
You'll see.

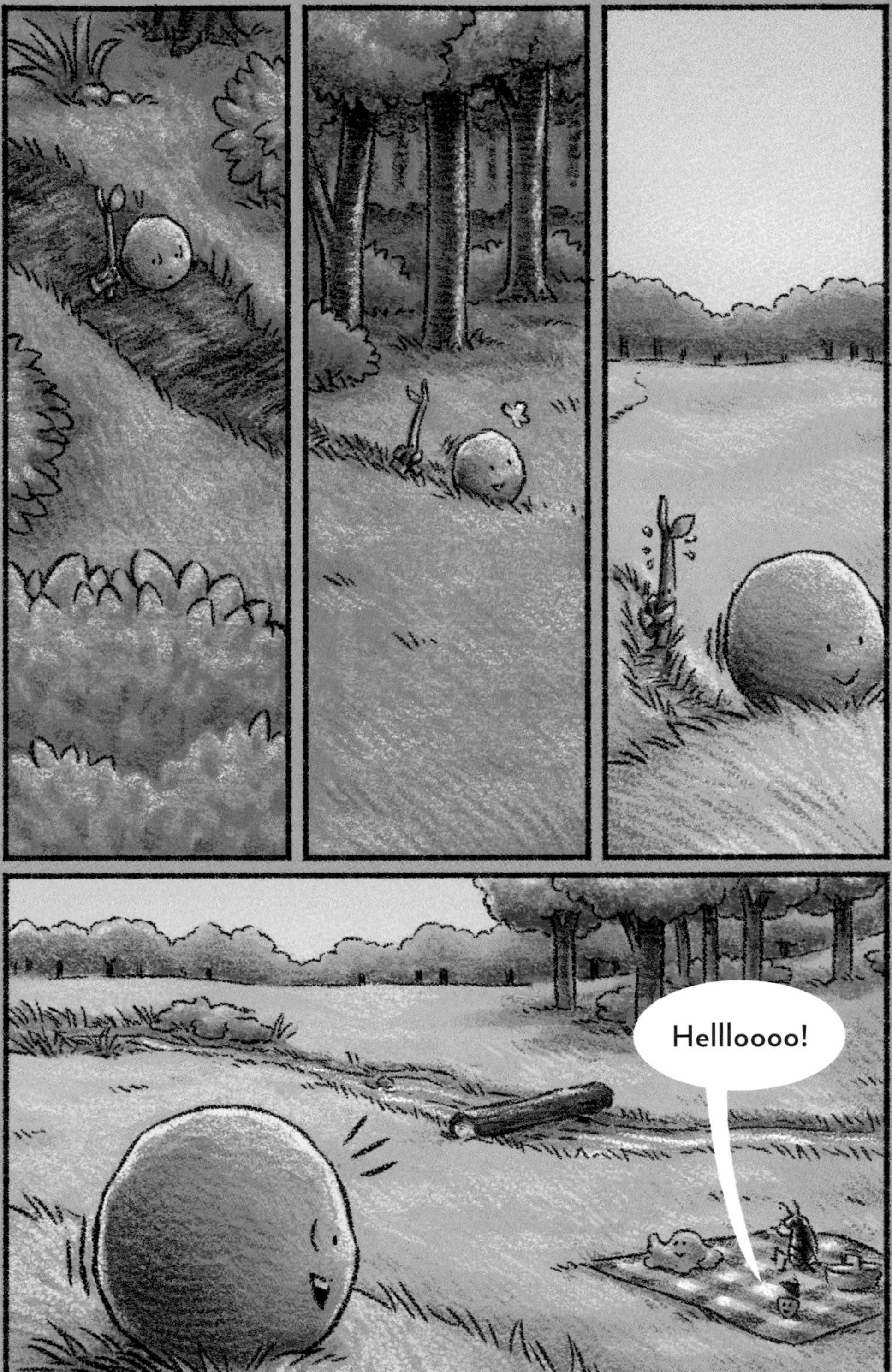
Hellloooo!

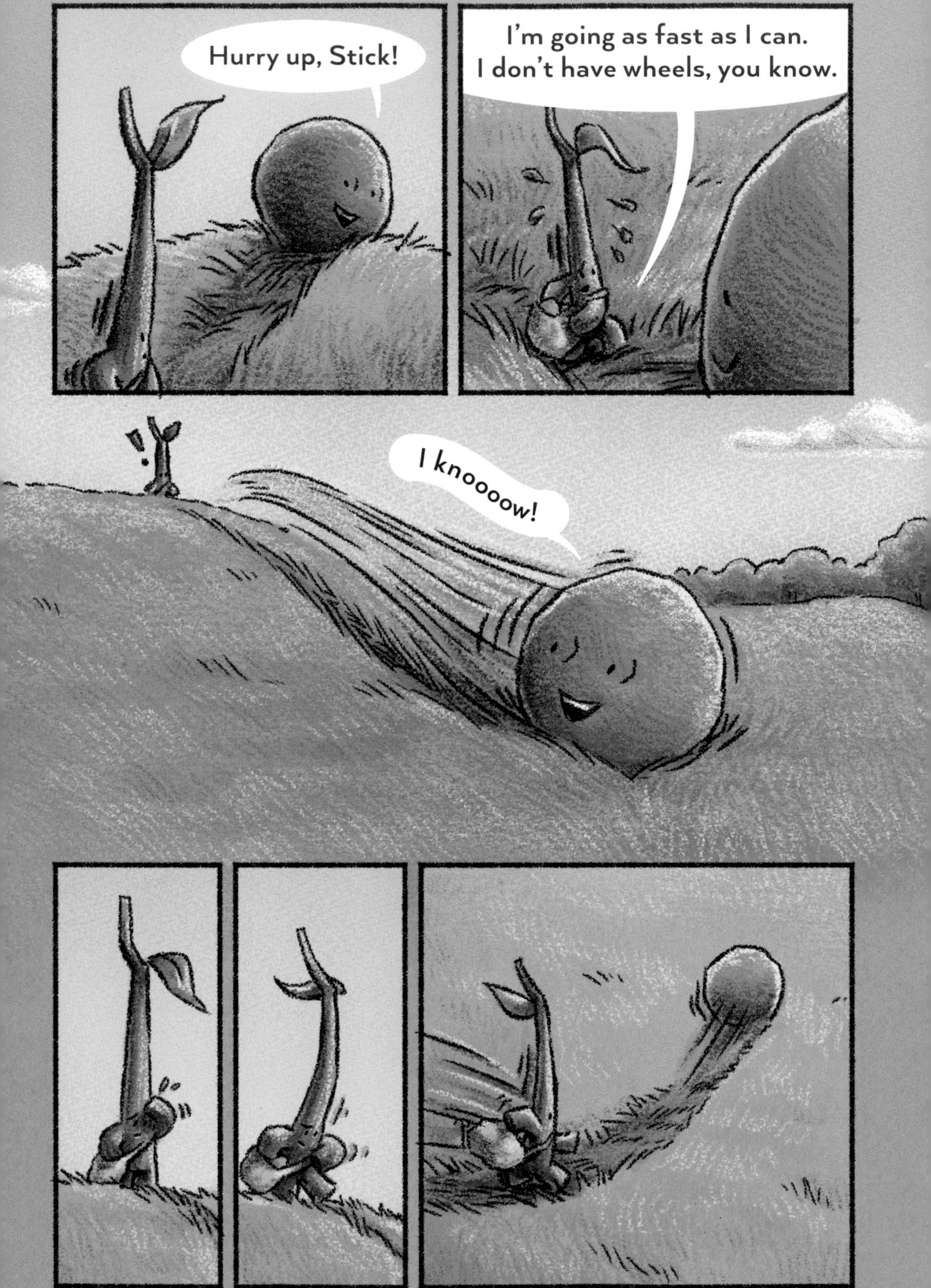
Hurry up, Stick!
I'm going as fast as I can. I don't have wheels, you know.
I knooooow!

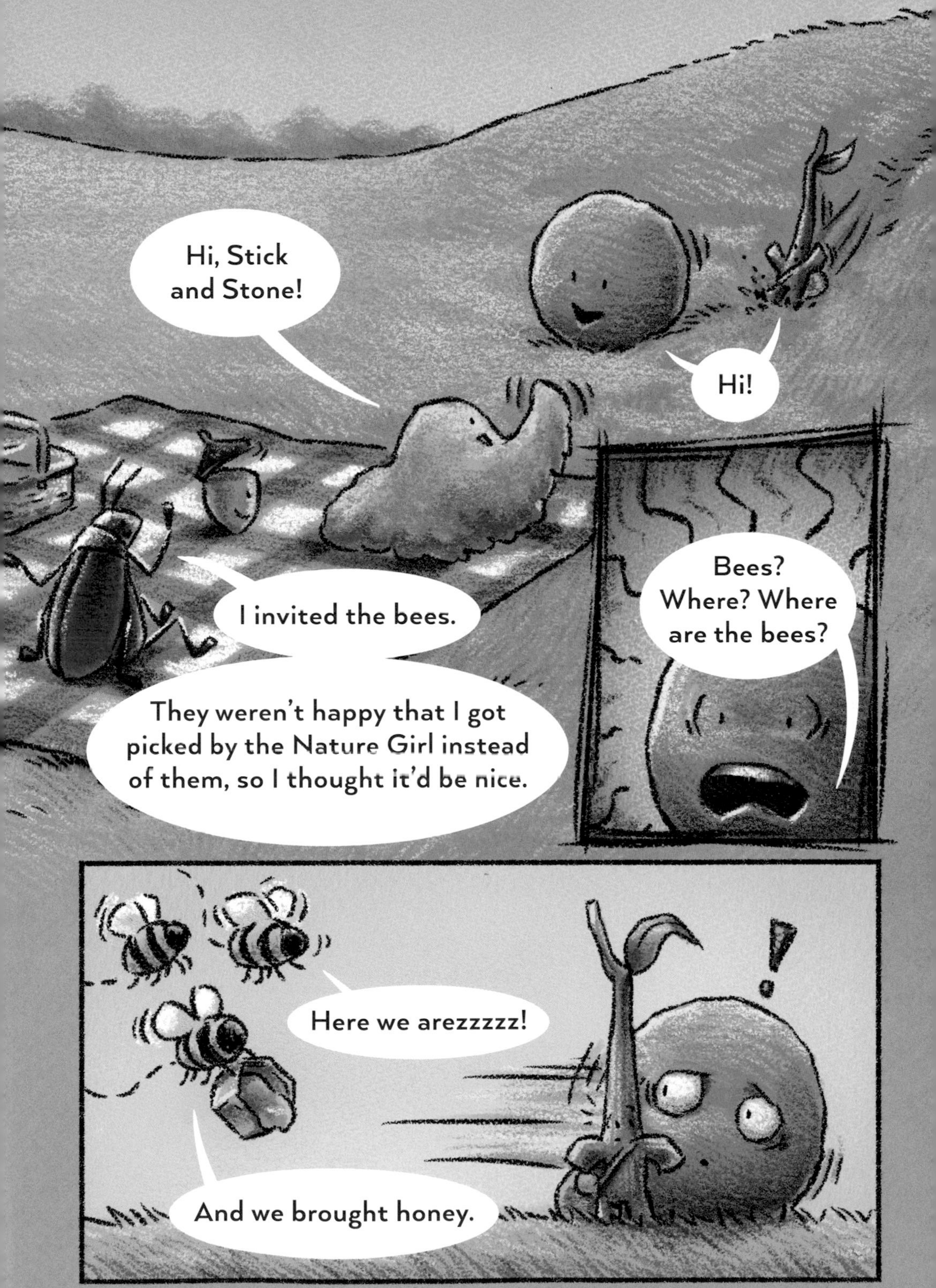
Hi, Stick and Stone!
Hi!
I invited the bees.
They weren't happy that I got picked by the Nature Girl instead of them, so I thought it'd be nice.
Bees? Where? Where are the bees?
!
Here we arezzzzz!
And we brought honey.

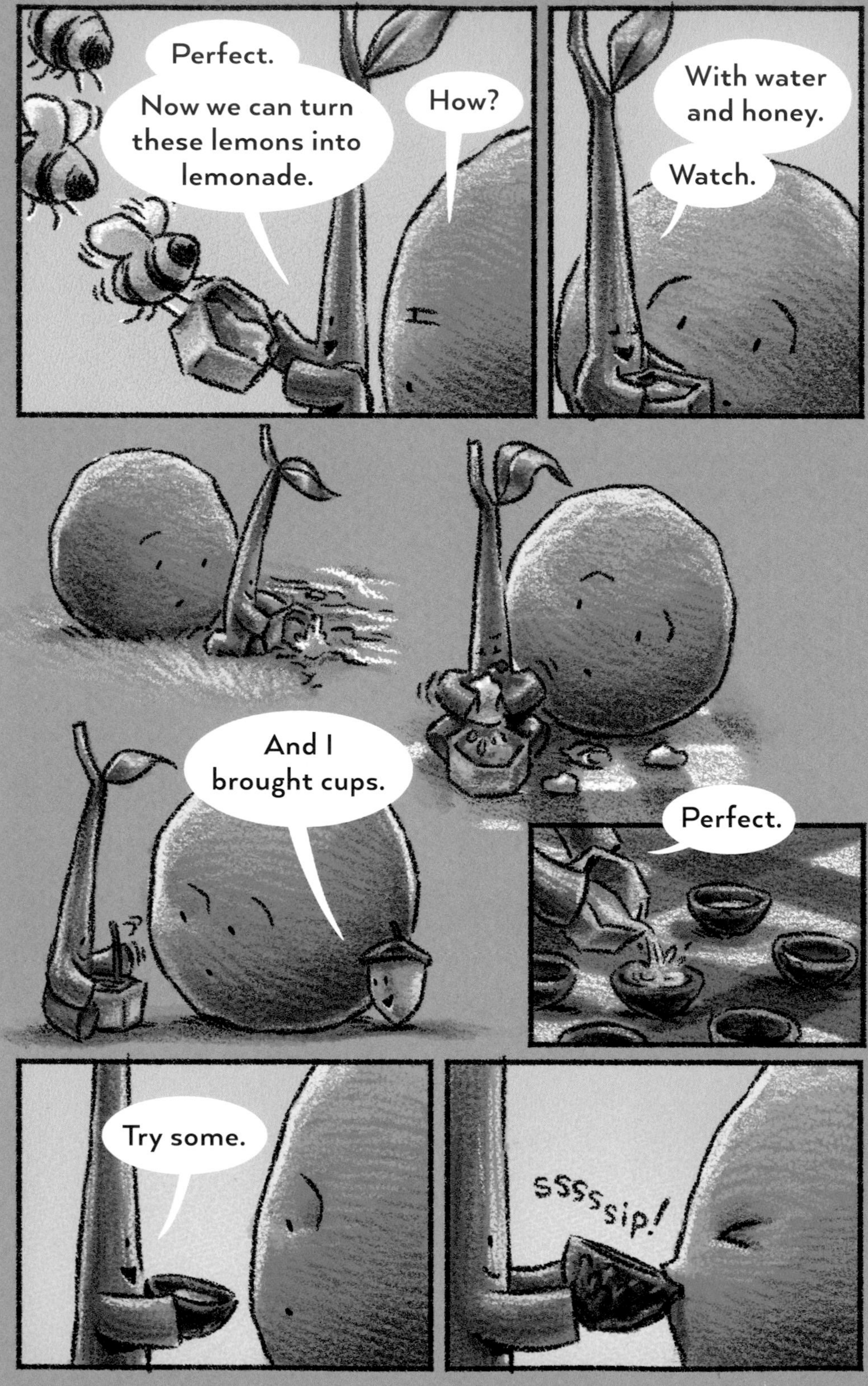
Perfect.
Now we can turn these lemons into lemonade.
How?
With water and honey.
Watch.
And I brought cups.
Perfect.
Try some.
SSSSsip!

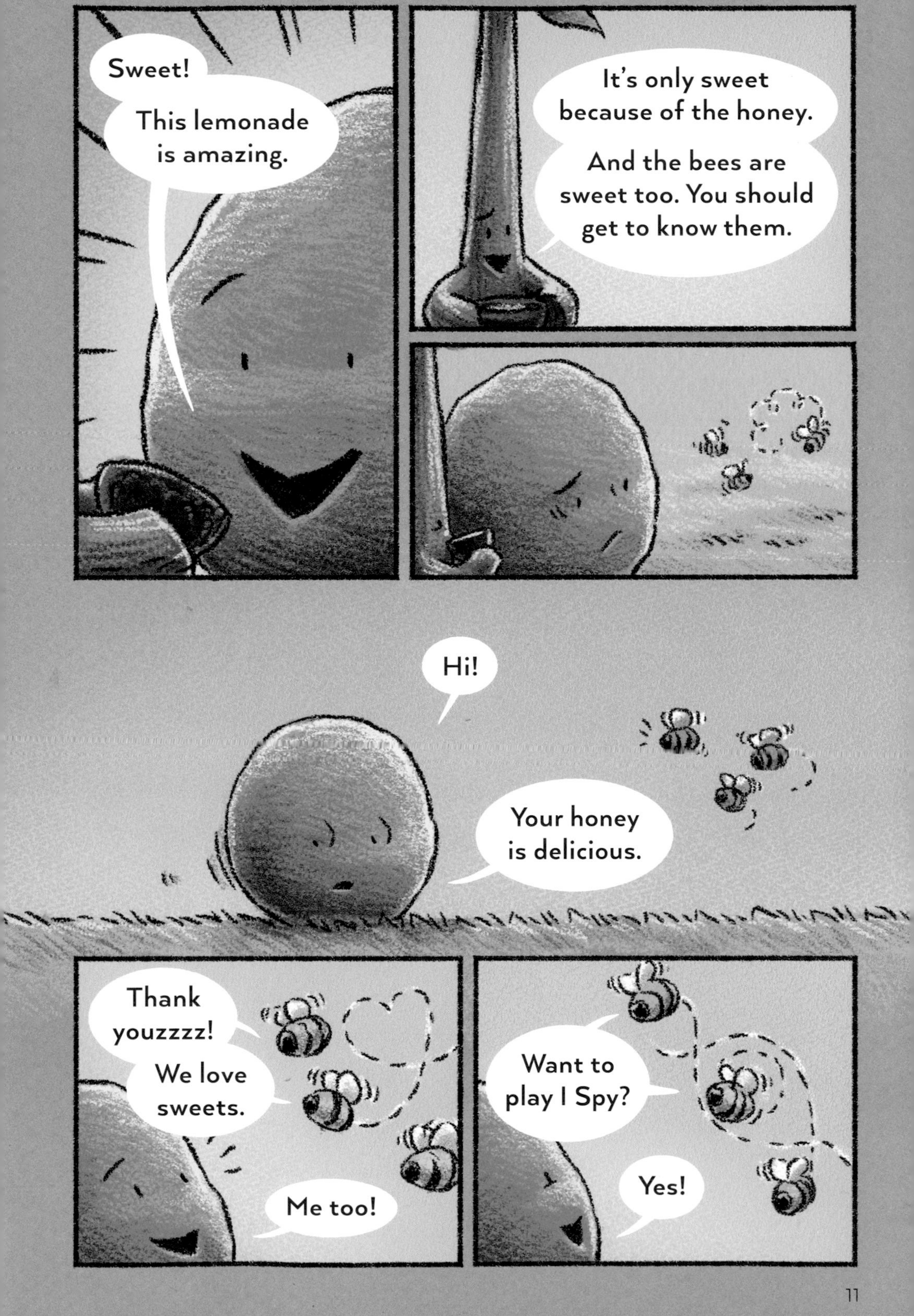
Sweet!
This lemonade is amazing.
It's only sweet because of the honey.
And the bees are sweet too. You should get to know them.
Hi!
Your honey is delicious.
Thank youzzzz!
We love sweets.
Me too!
Want to play I Spy?
Yes!

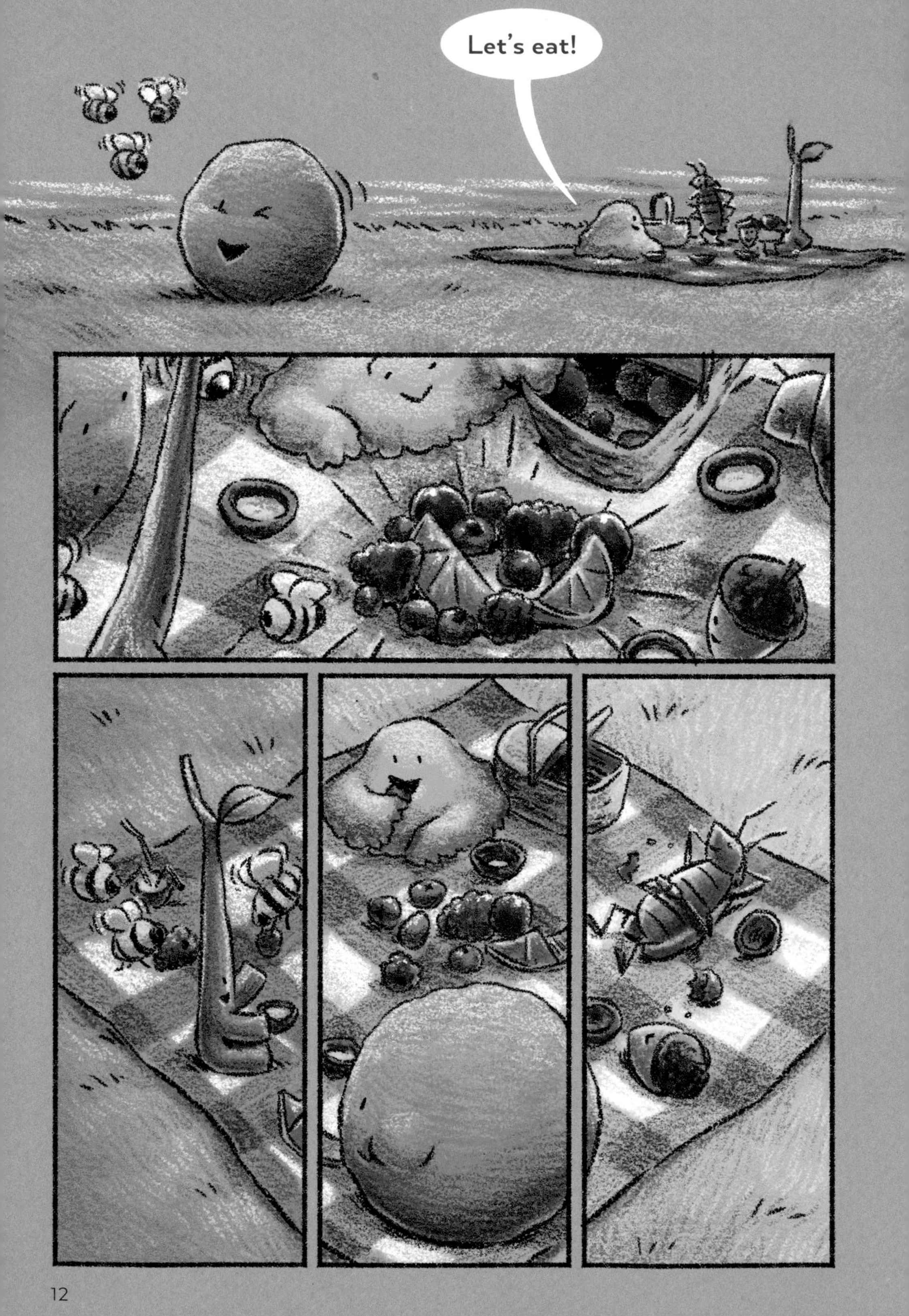
Let's eat!

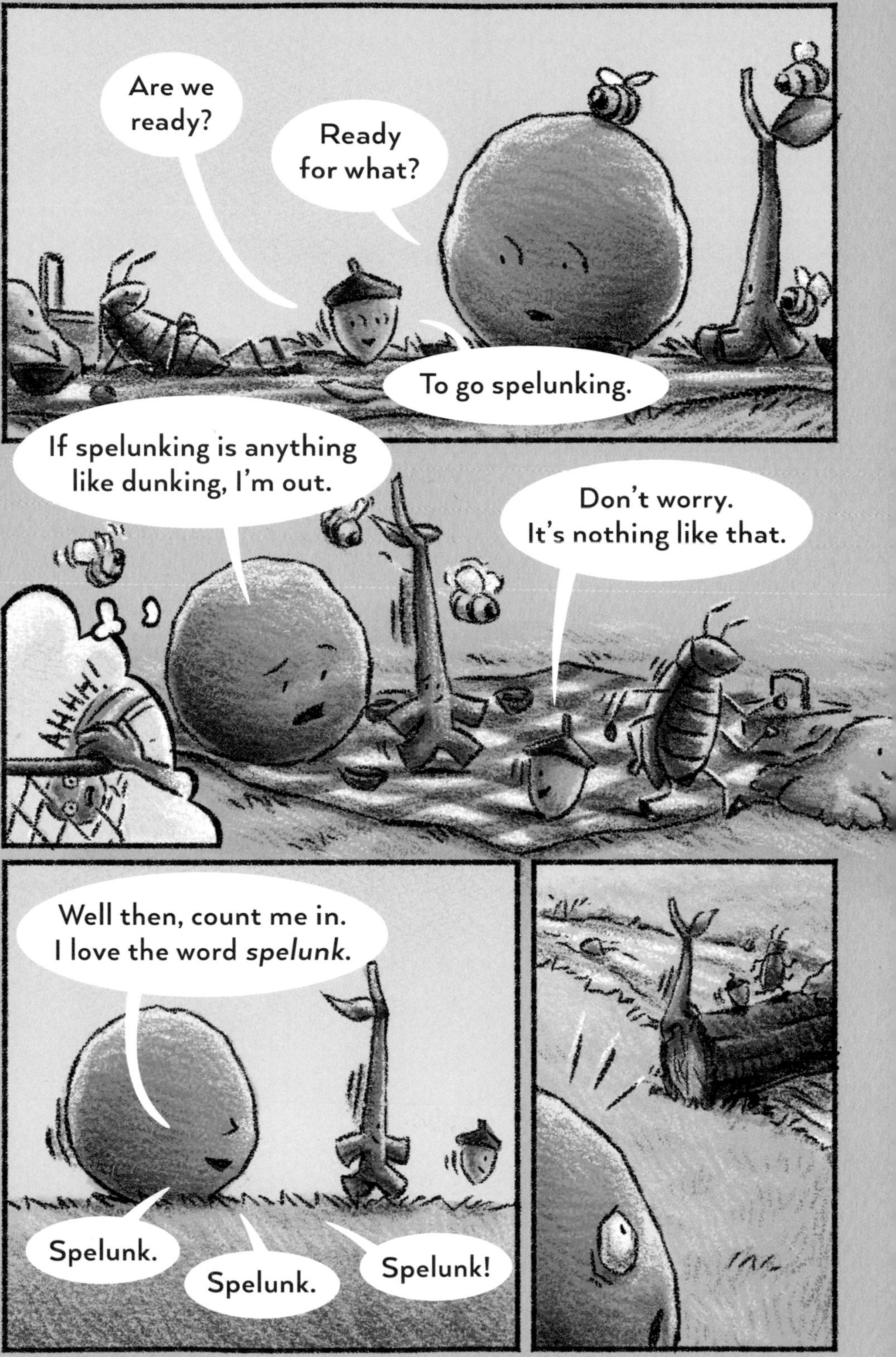
Are we ready?
Ready for what?
To go spelunking.
If spelunking is anything like dunking, I'm out.
AHHHH!
Don't worry. It's nothing like that.
Well then, count me in. I love the word *spelunk*.
Spelunk.
Spelunk.
Spelunk!

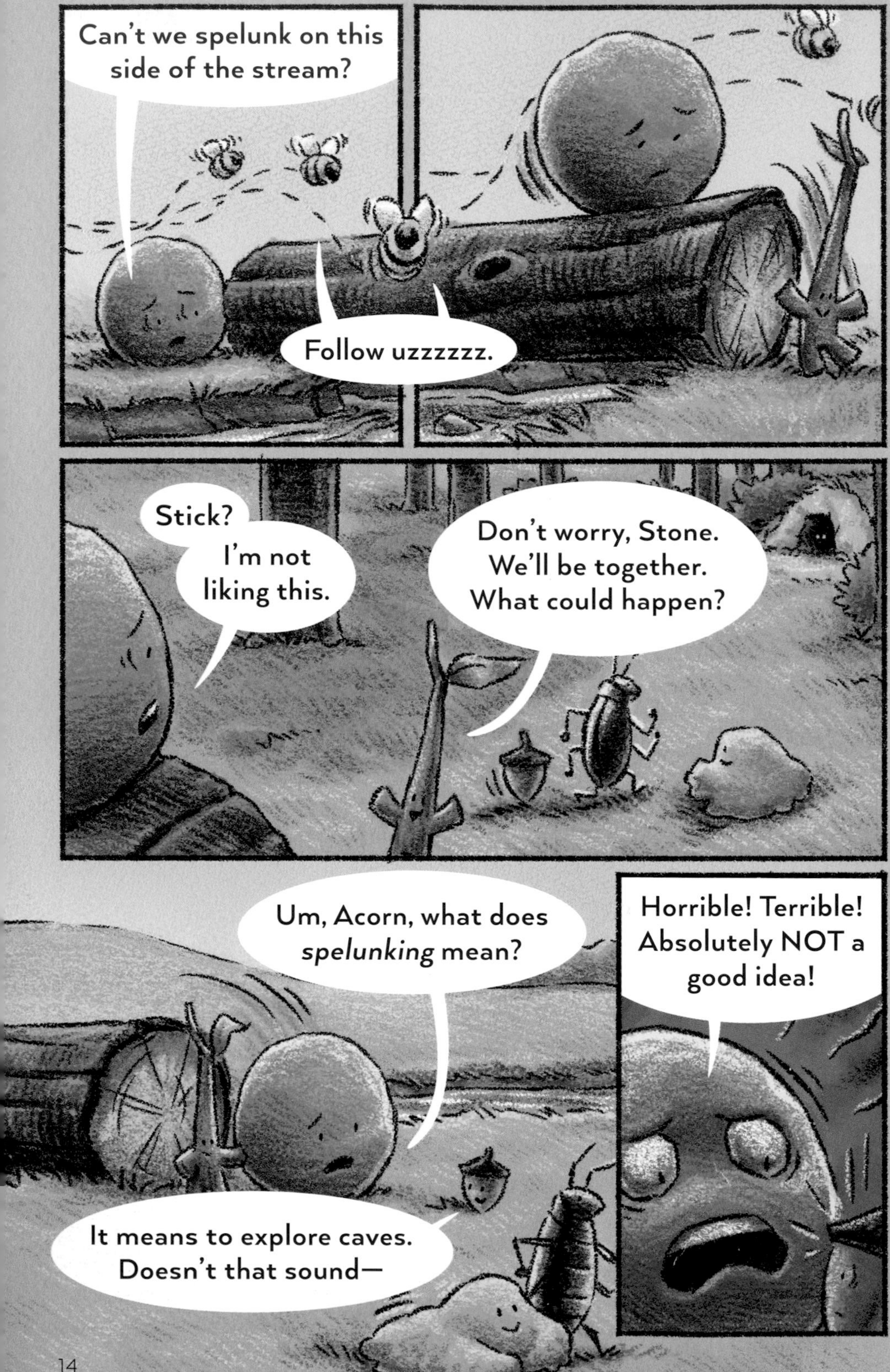
Can't we spelunk on this side of the stream?
Follow uzzzzzz.
Stick?
I'm not liking this.
Don't worry, Stone. We'll be together. What could happen?
Um, Acorn, what does *spelunking* mean?
It means to explore caves. Doesn't that sound—
Horrible! Terrible! Absolutely NOT a good idea!

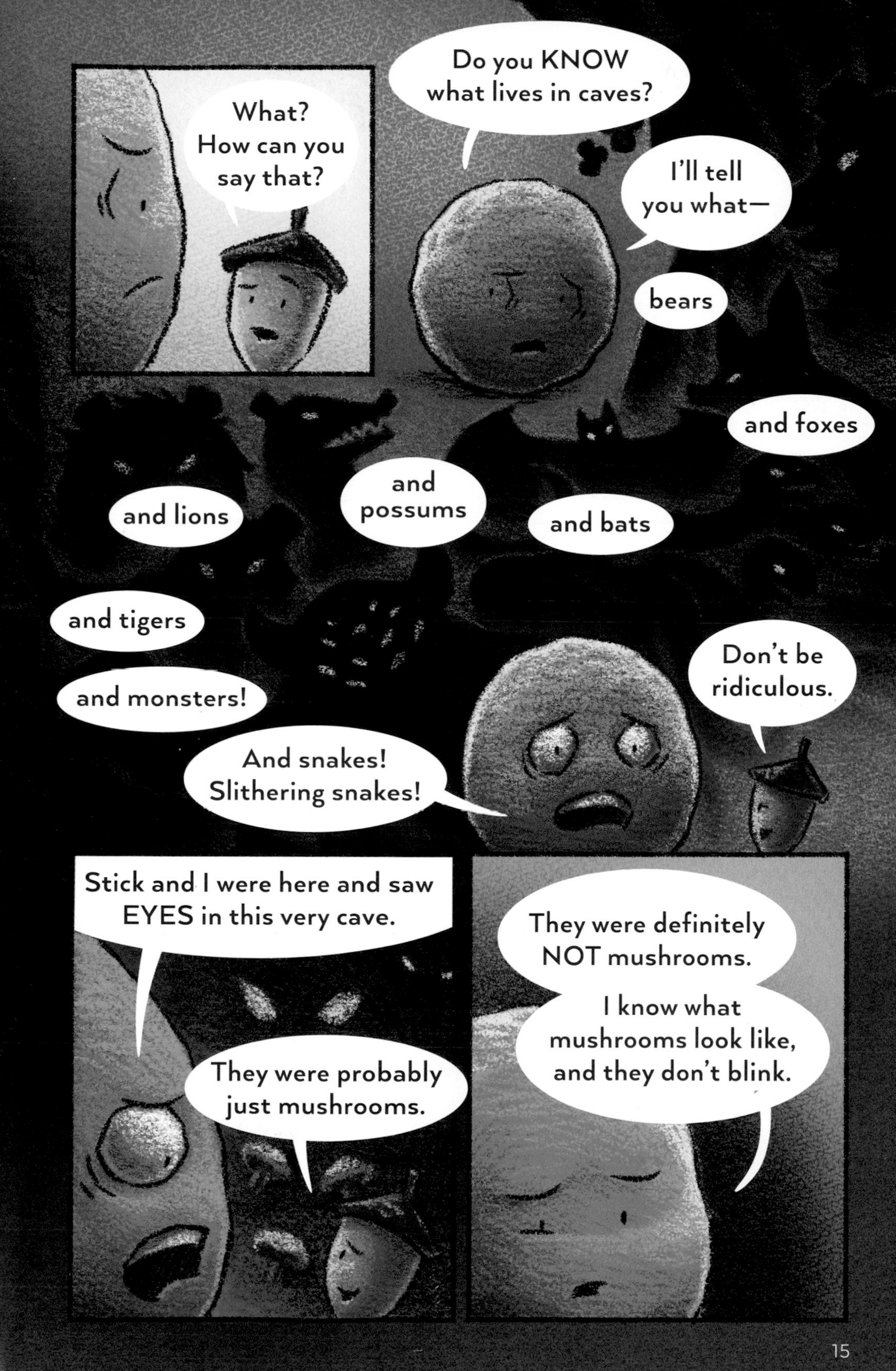
What? How can you say that?
Do you KNOW what lives in caves?
I'll tell you what—
bears
and foxes
and lions
and possums
and bats
and tigers
and monsters!
Don't be ridiculous.
And snakes! Slithering snakes!
Stick and I were here and saw EYES in this very cave.
They were probably just mushrooms.
They were definitely NOT mushrooms.
I know what mushrooms look like, and they don't blink.

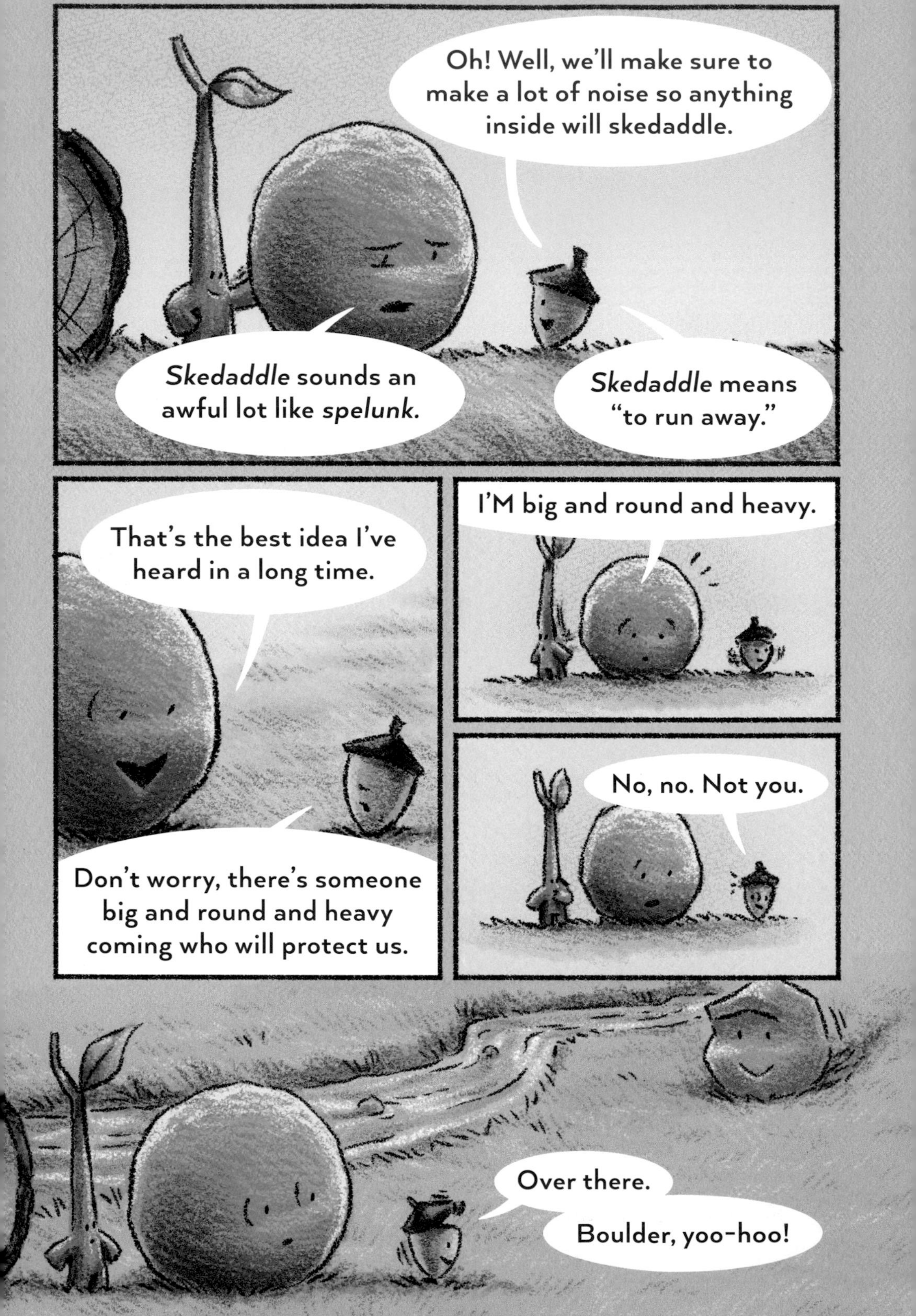
Oh! Well, we'll make sure to make a lot of noise so anything inside will skedaddle.
Skedaddle sounds an awful lot like *spelunk*.
Skedaddle means "to run away."
That's the best idea I've heard in a long time.
Don't worry, there's someone big and round and heavy coming who will protect us.
I'M big and round and heavy.
No, no. Not you.
Over there.
Boulder, yoo-hoo!

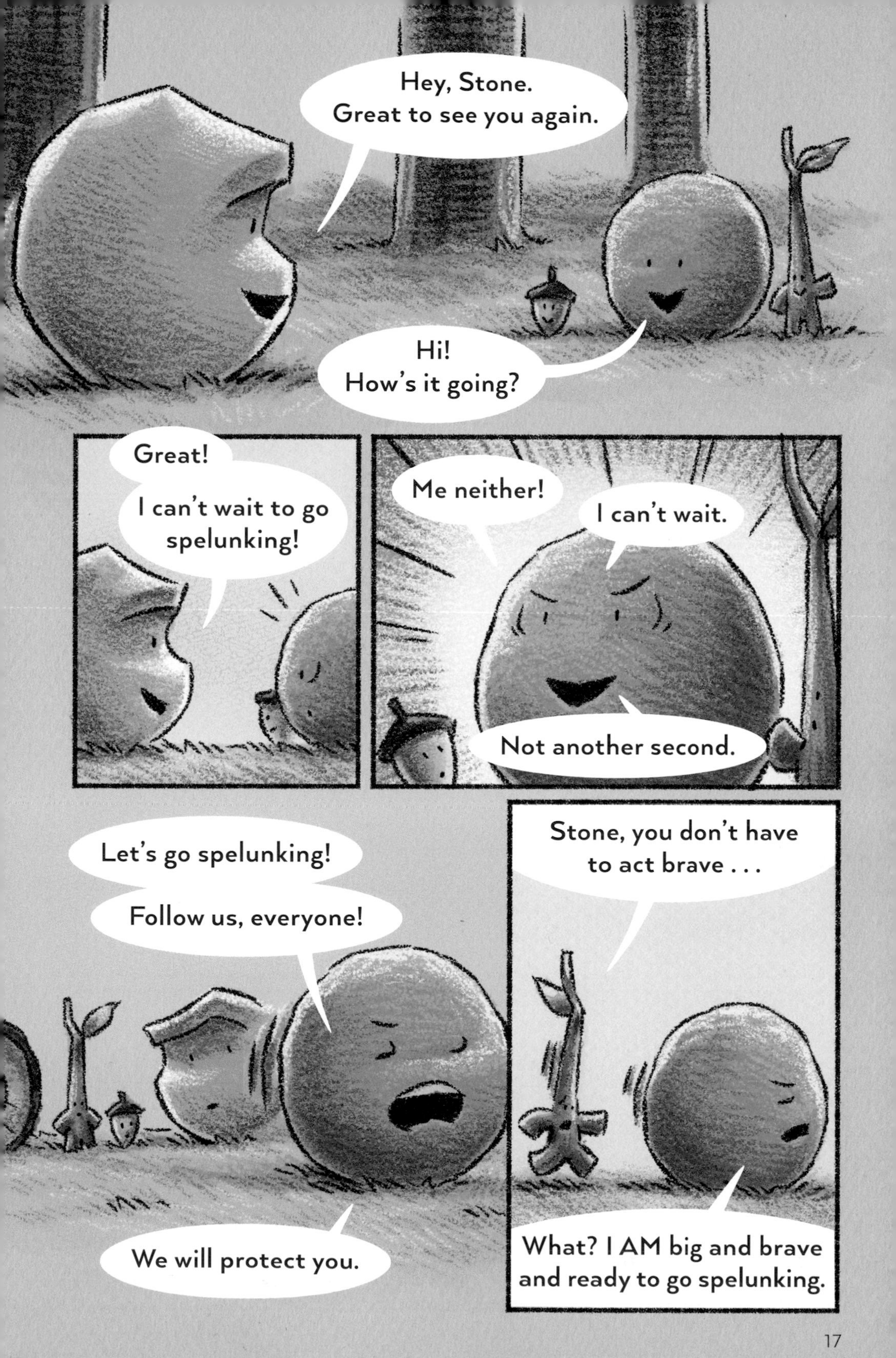
Hey, Stone.
Great to see you again.
Hi!
How's it going?
Great!
I can't wait to go spelunking!
Me neither!
I can't wait.
Not another second.
Let's go spelunking!
Follow us, everyone!
We will protect you.
Stone, you don't have to act brave . . .
What? I AM big and brave and ready to go spelunking.

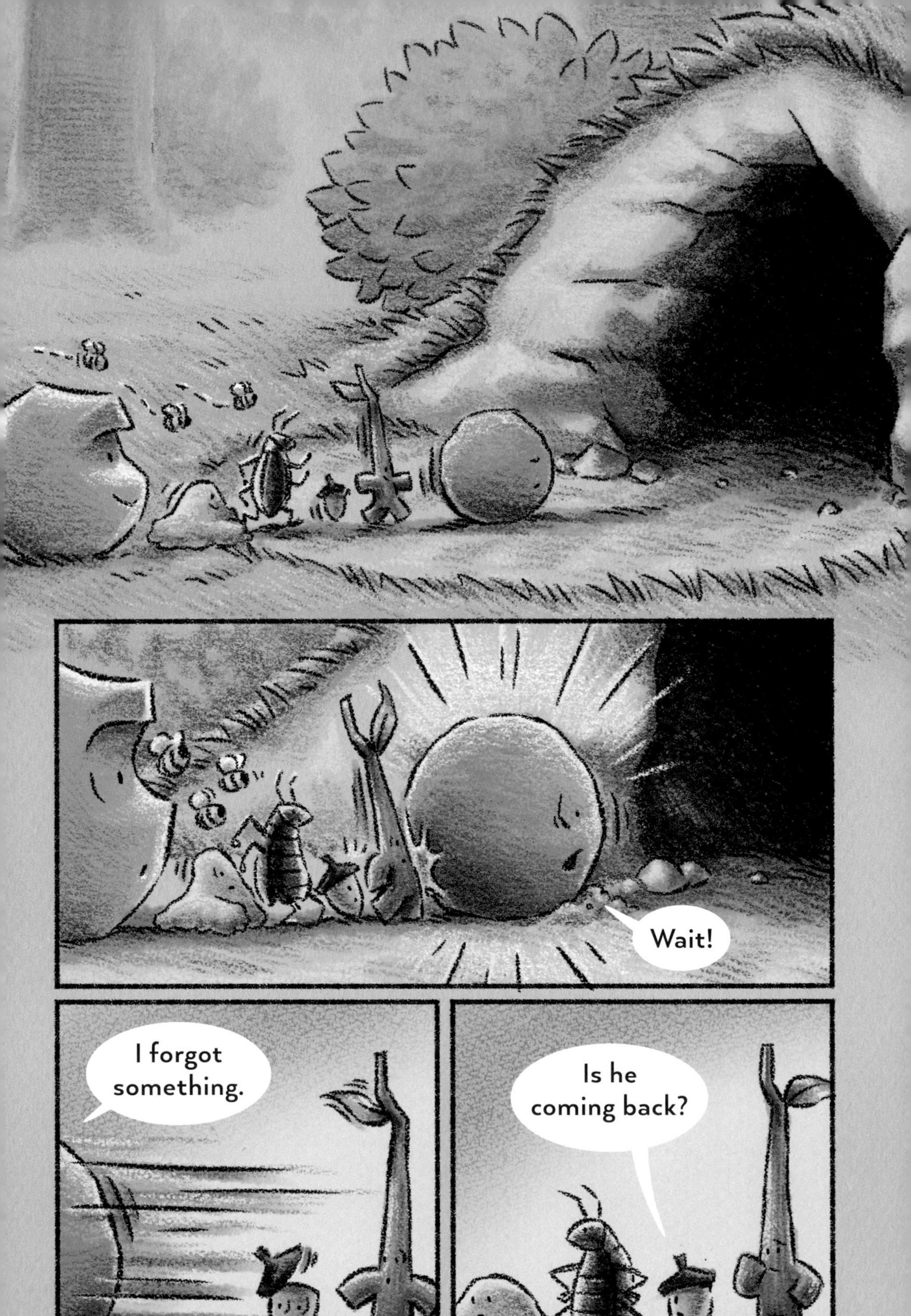
Wait!
I forgot something.
Is he coming back?

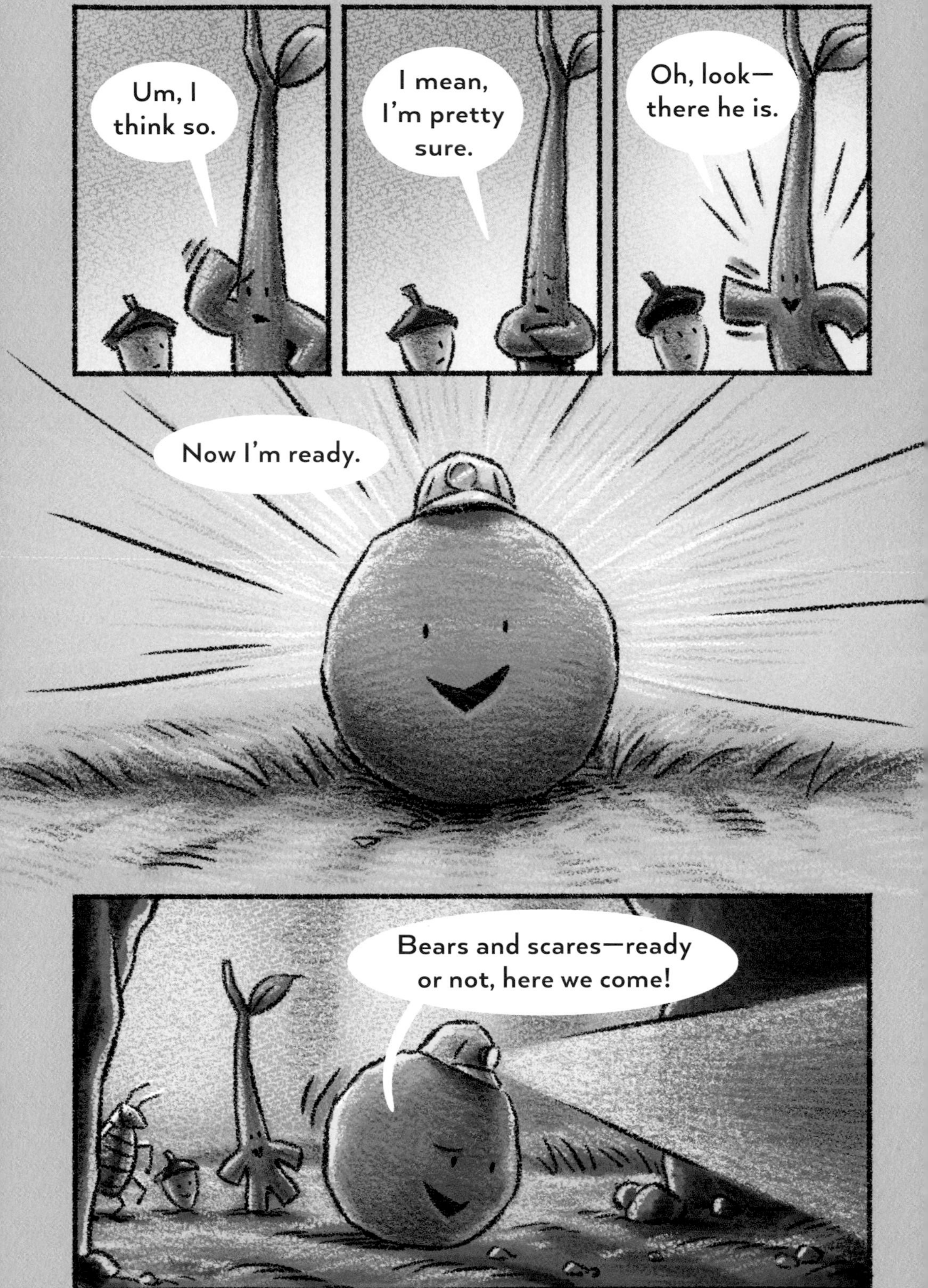
Um, I think so.
I mean, I'm pretty sure.
Oh, look—there he is.
Now I'm ready.
Bears and scares—ready or not, here we come!

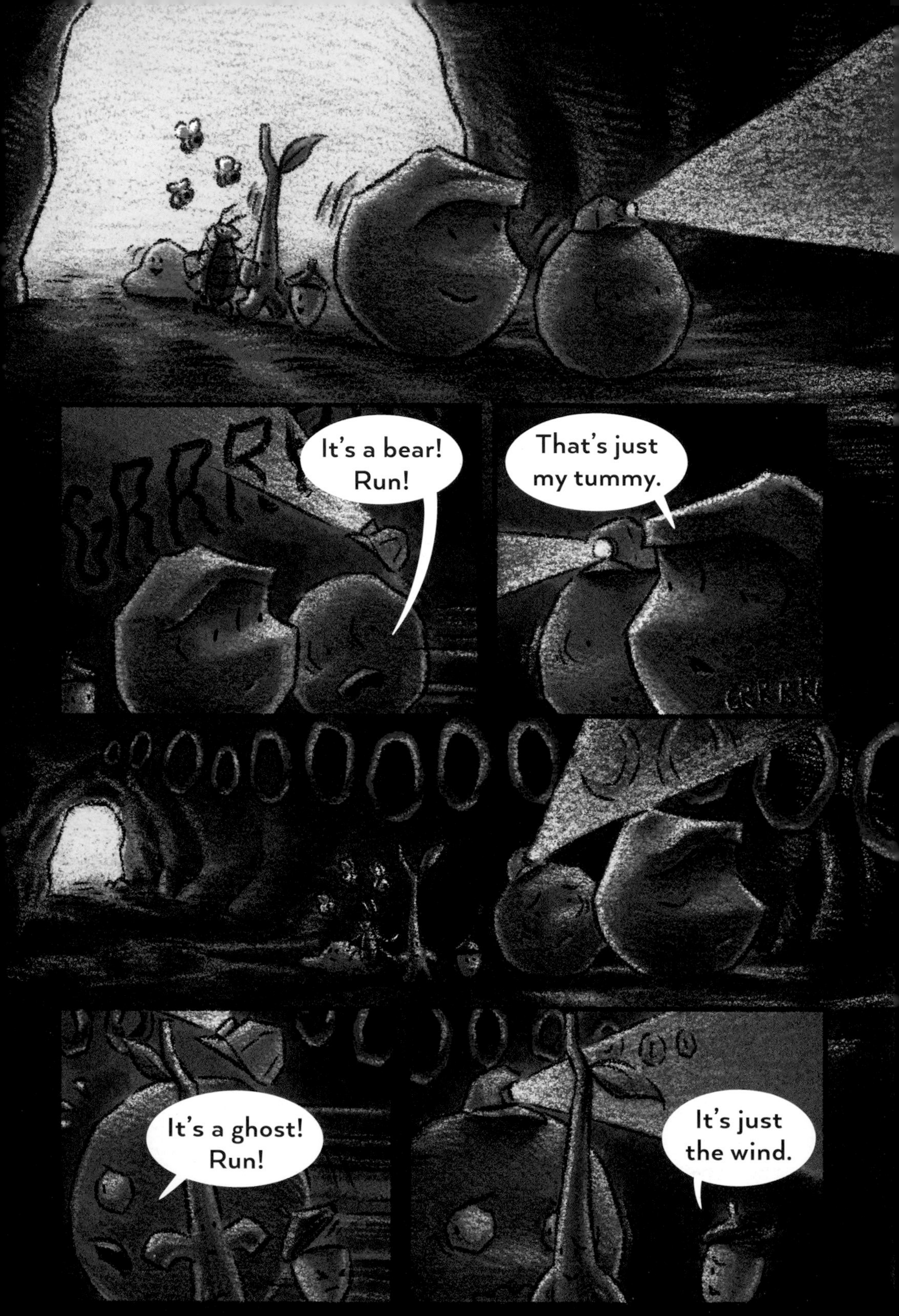
GRRR
It's a bear! Run!
That's just my tummy.
GRRR
It's a ghost! Run!
It's just the wind.

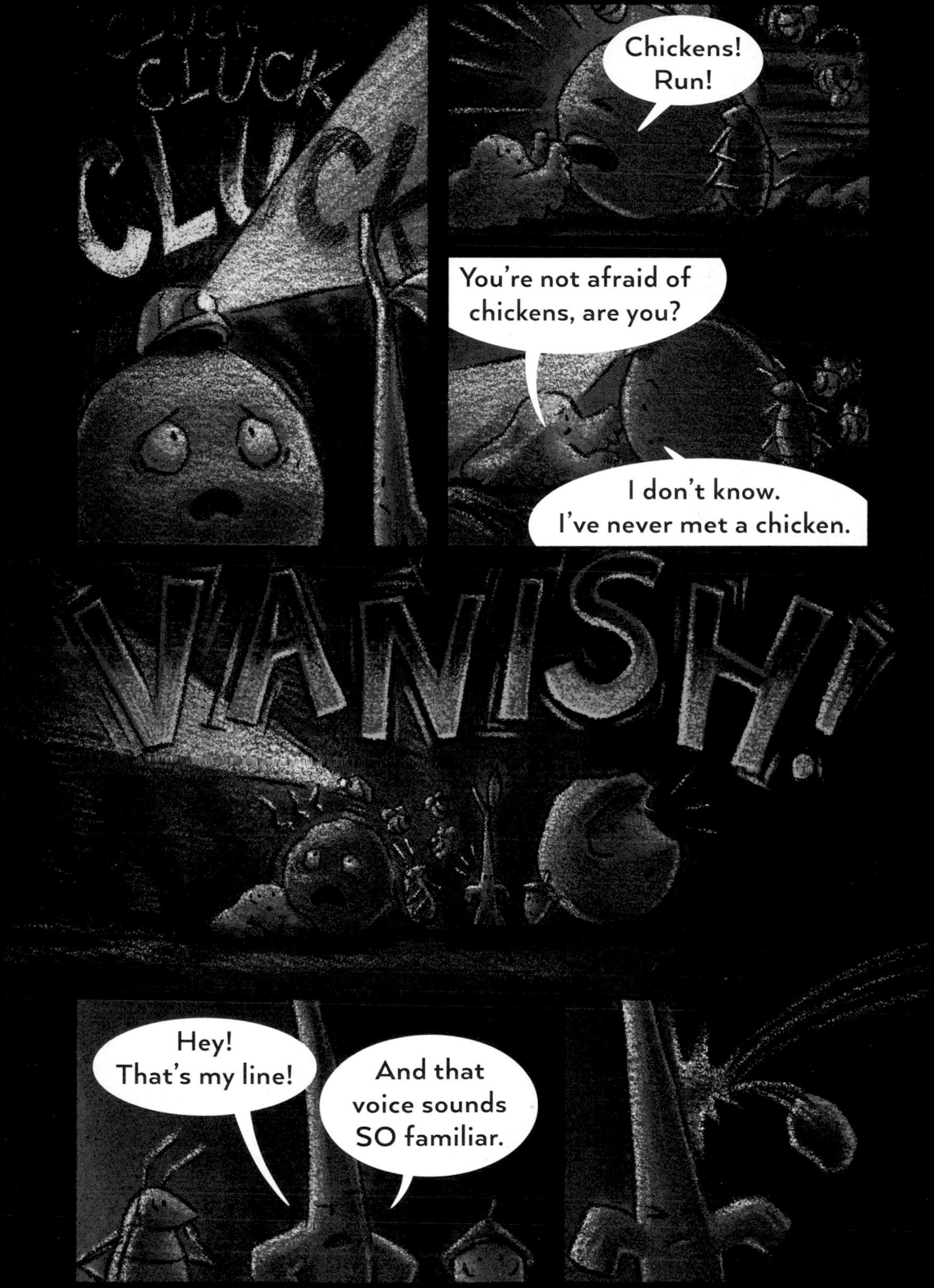
CLUCK
CLUCK
Chickens! Run!
You're not afraid of chickens, are you?
I don't know. I've never met a chicken.
VANISH!
Hey! That's my line!
And that voice sounds SO familiar.

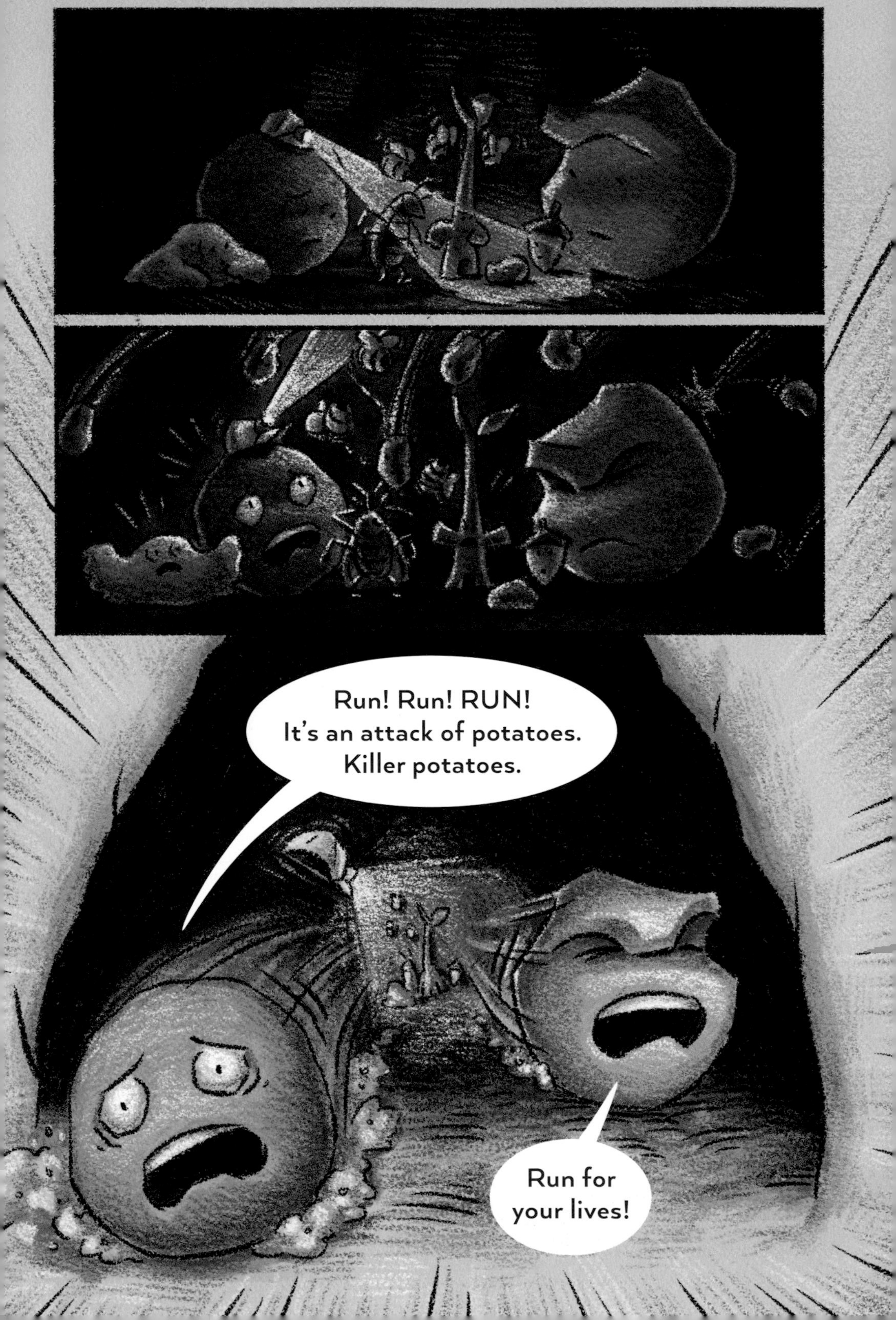
Run! Run! RUN!
It's an attack of potatoes.
Killer potatoes.
Run for
your lives!

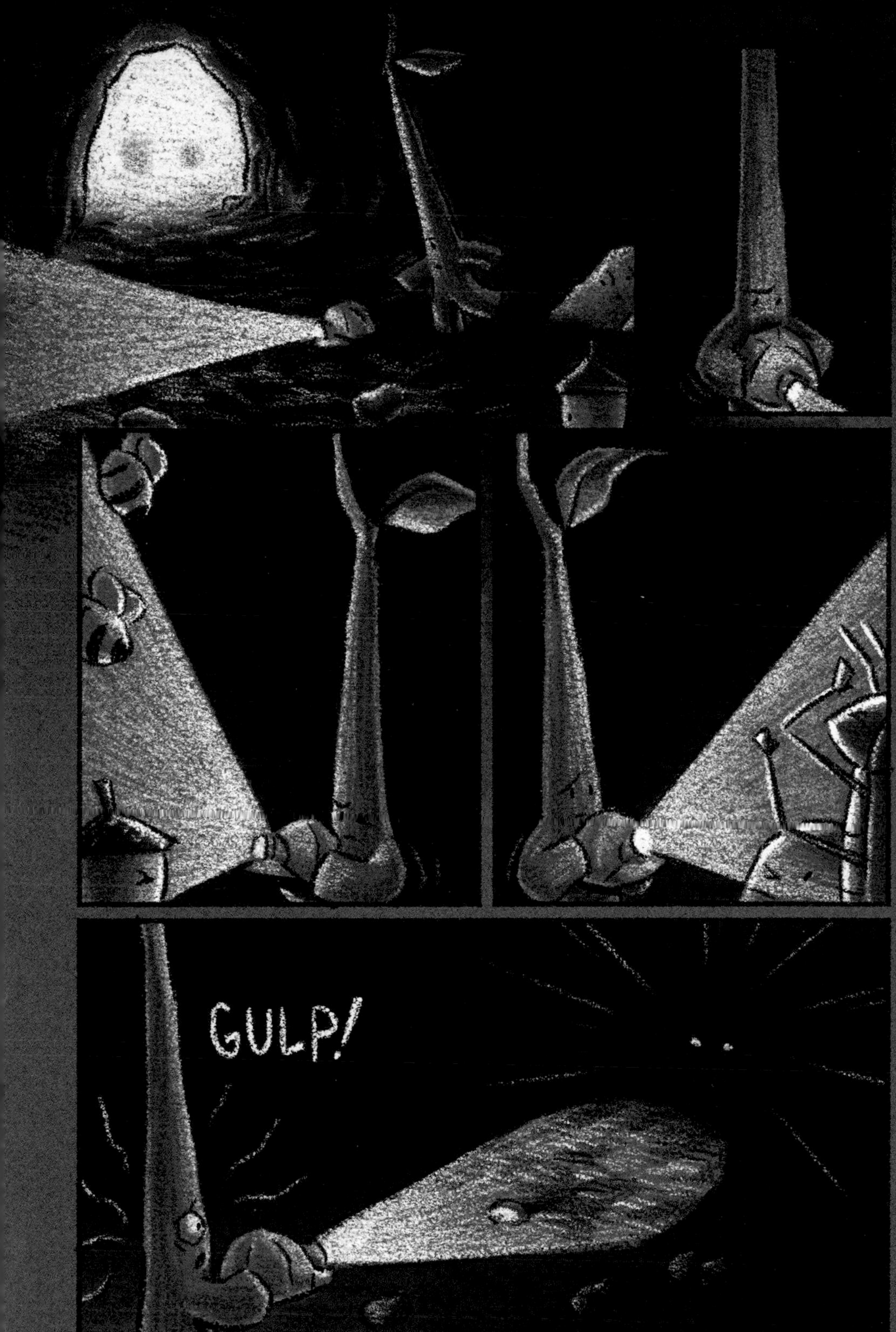
GULP!

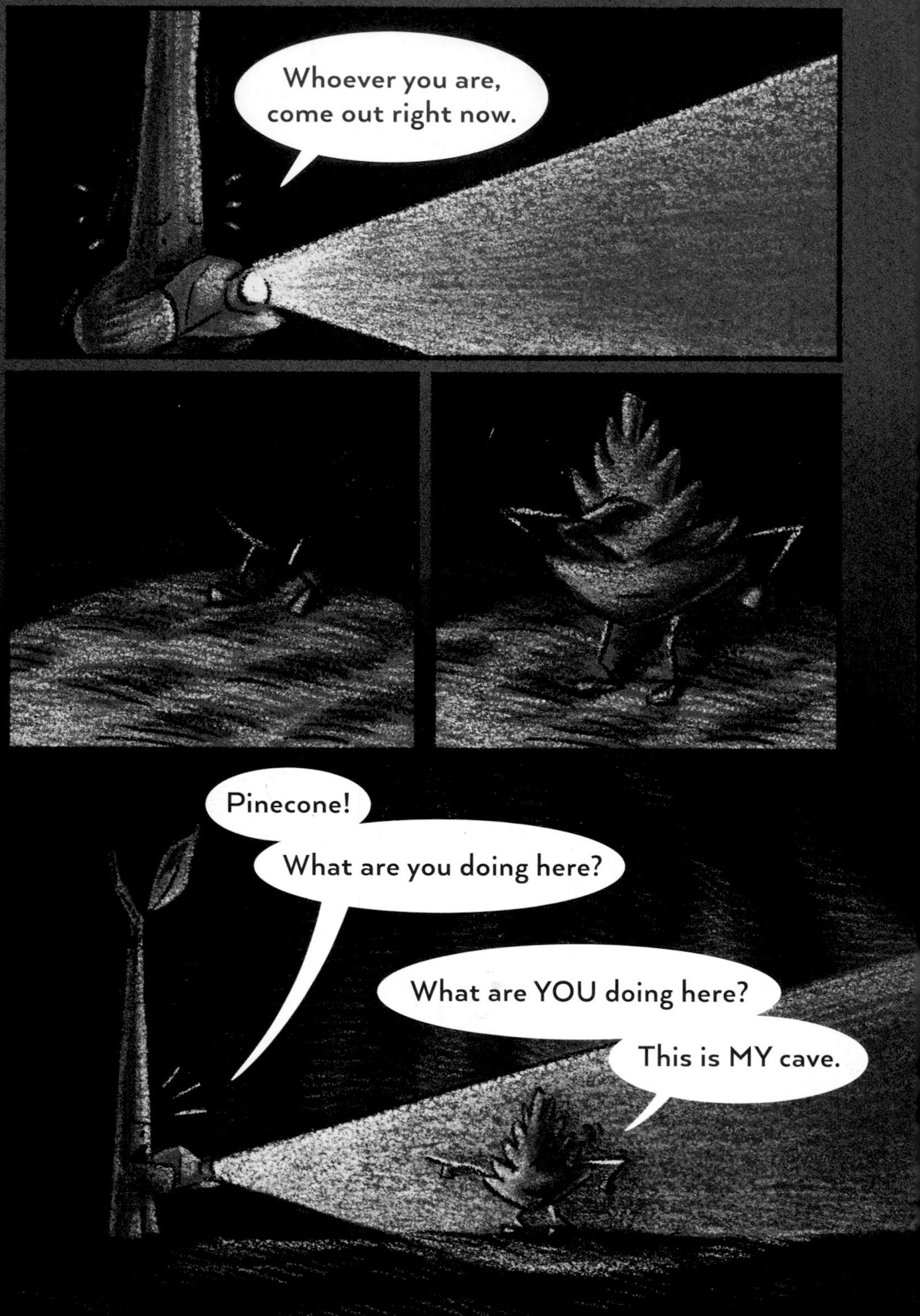
Whoever you are,
come out right now.
Pinecone!
What are you doing here?
What are YOU doing here?
This is MY cave.

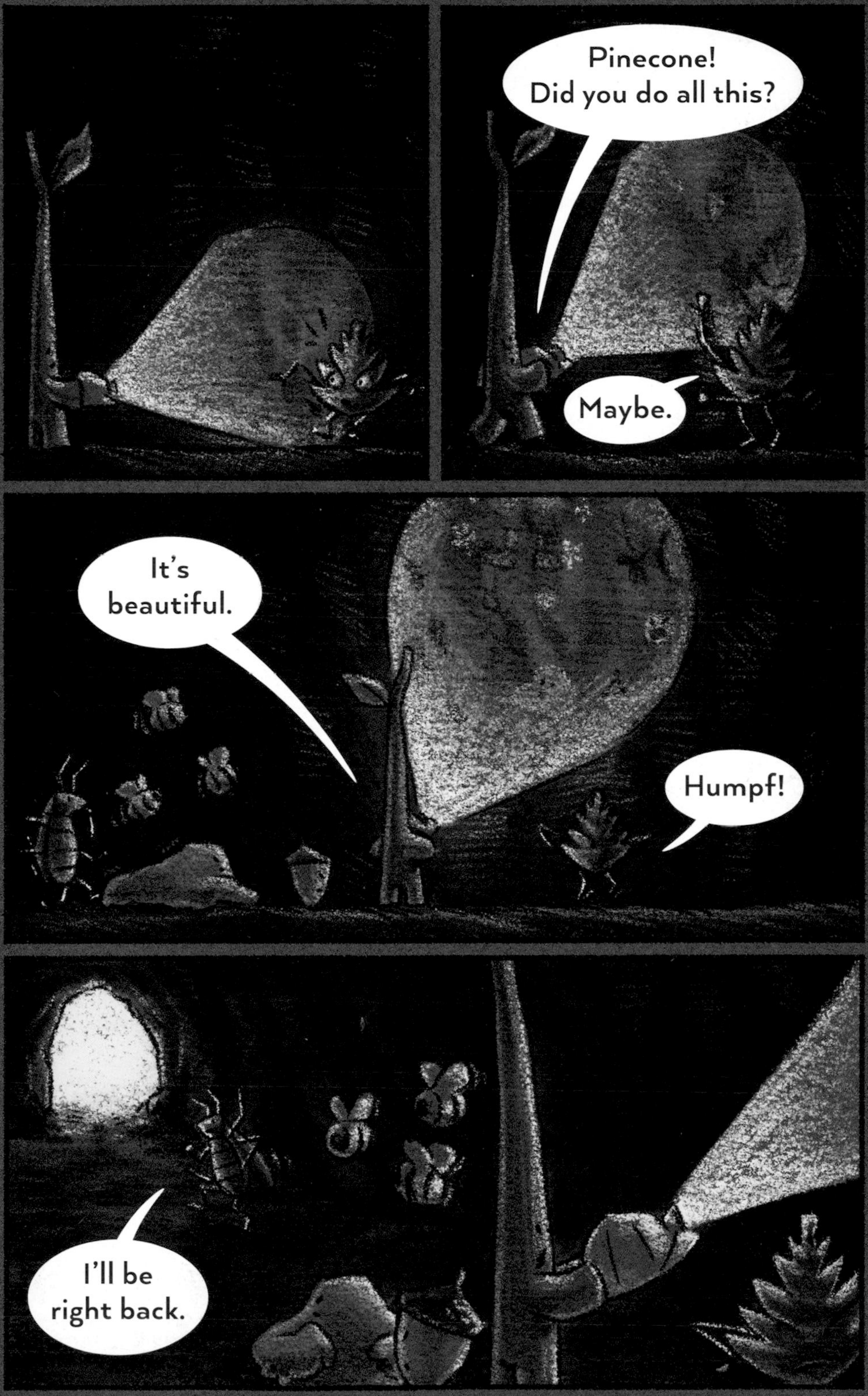
Pinecone!
Did you do all this?
Maybe.
It's beautiful.
Humpf!
I'll be right back.

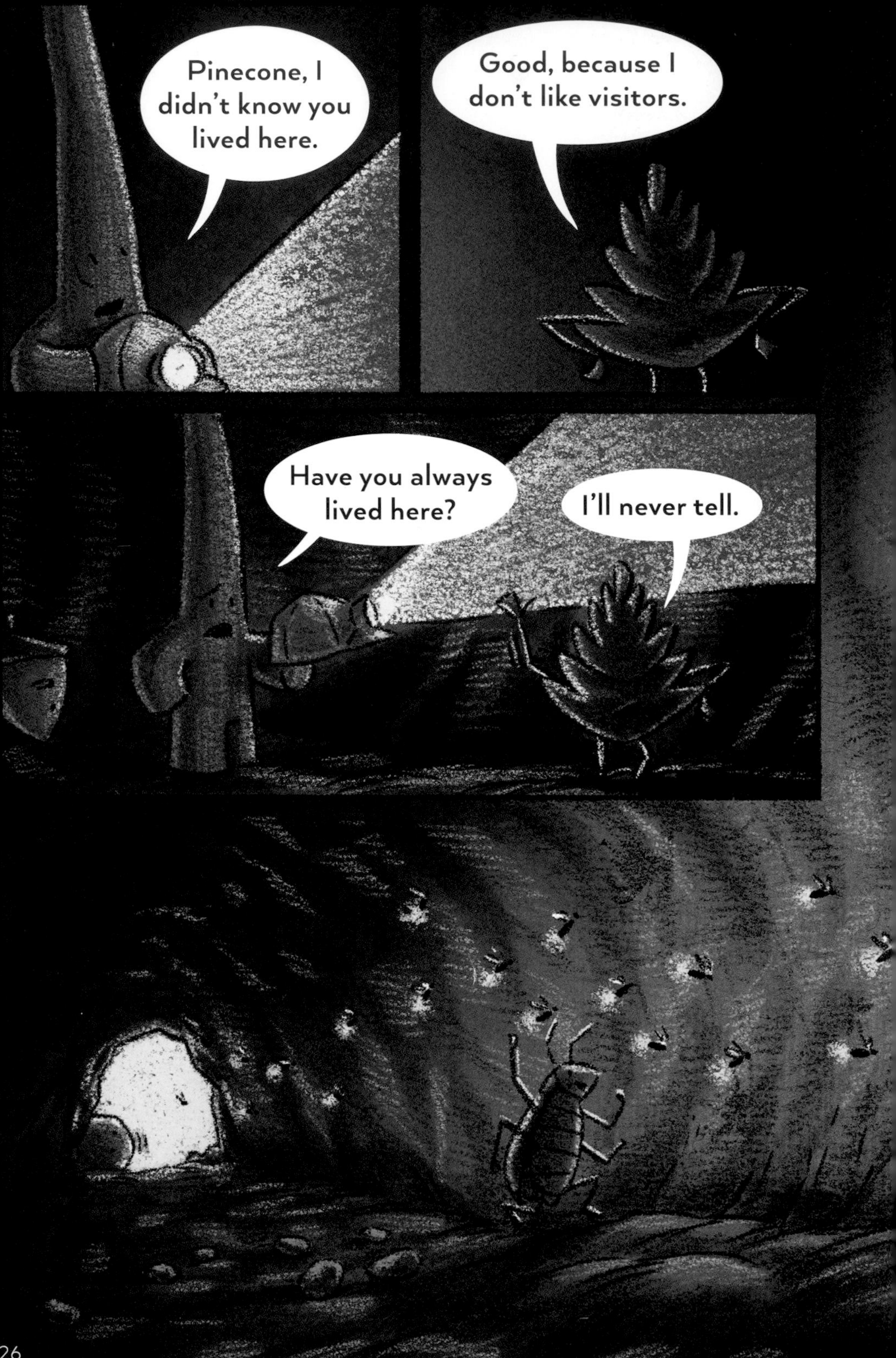
Pinecone, I didn't know you lived here.
Good, because I don't like visitors.
Have you always lived here?
I'll never tell.

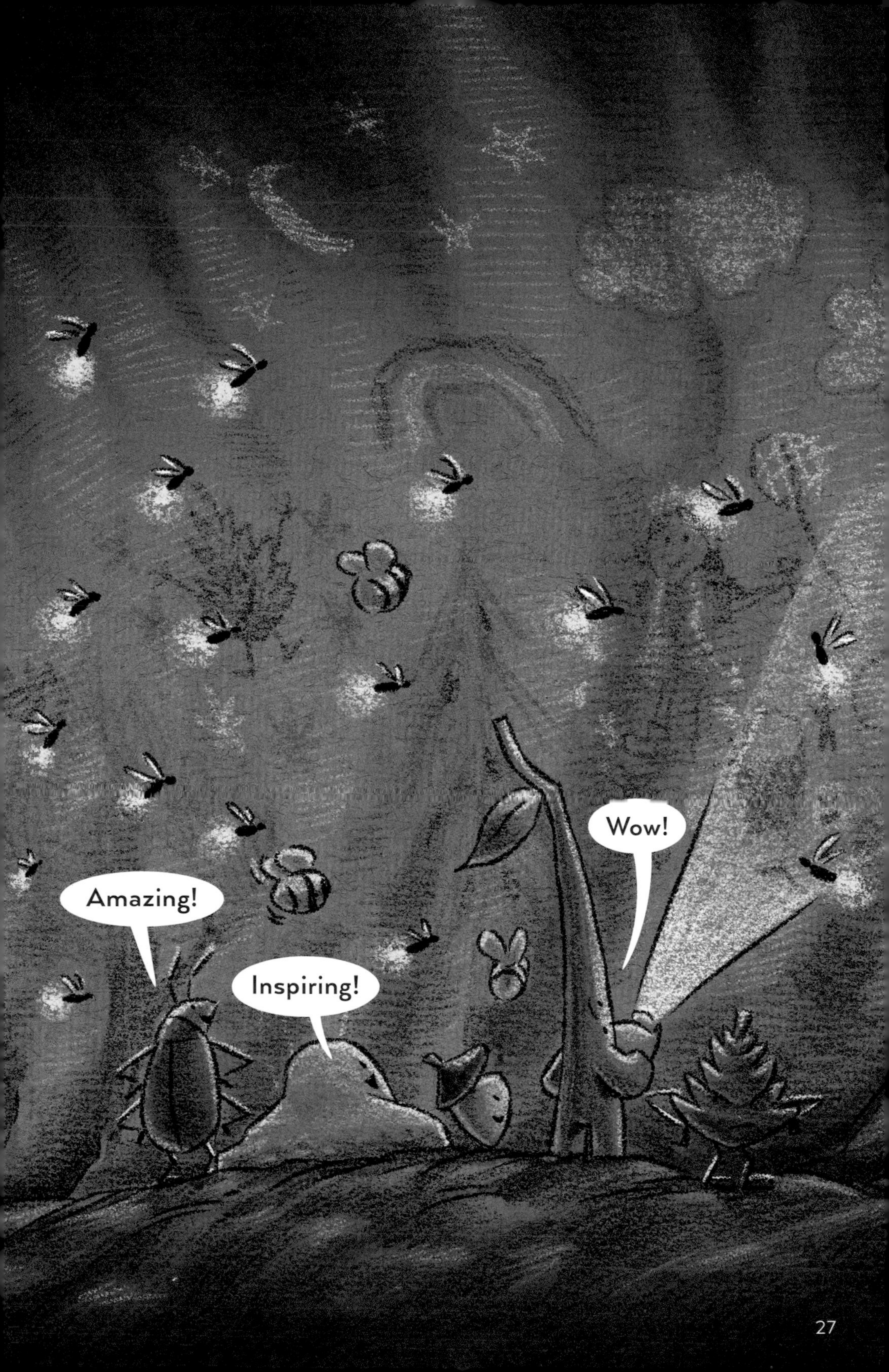
Amazing!
Inspiring!
Wow!

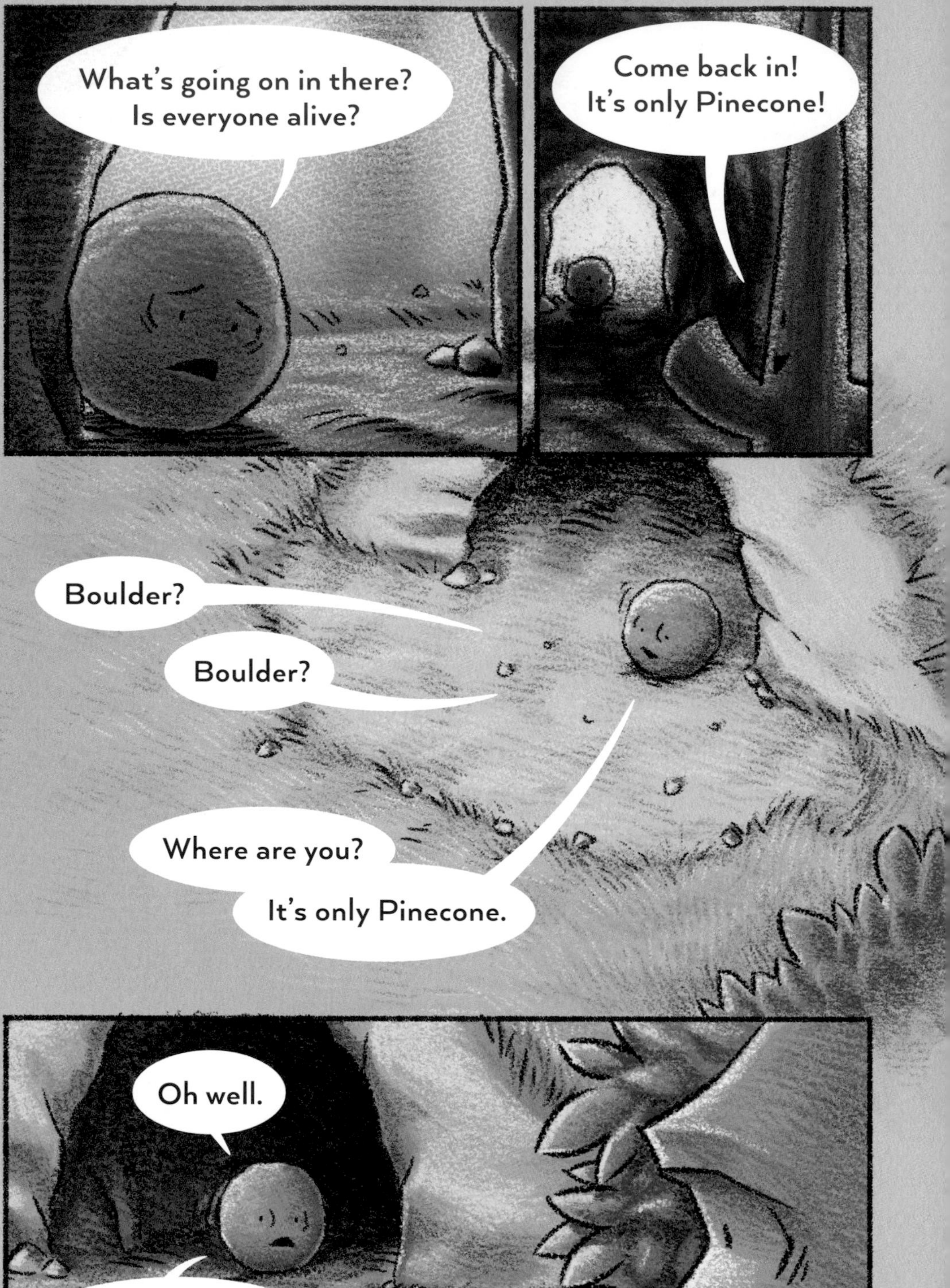
What's going on in there?
Is everyone alive?
Come back in!
It's only Pinecone!
Boulder?
Boulder?
Where are you?
It's only Pinecone.
Oh well.
I'm going back in!

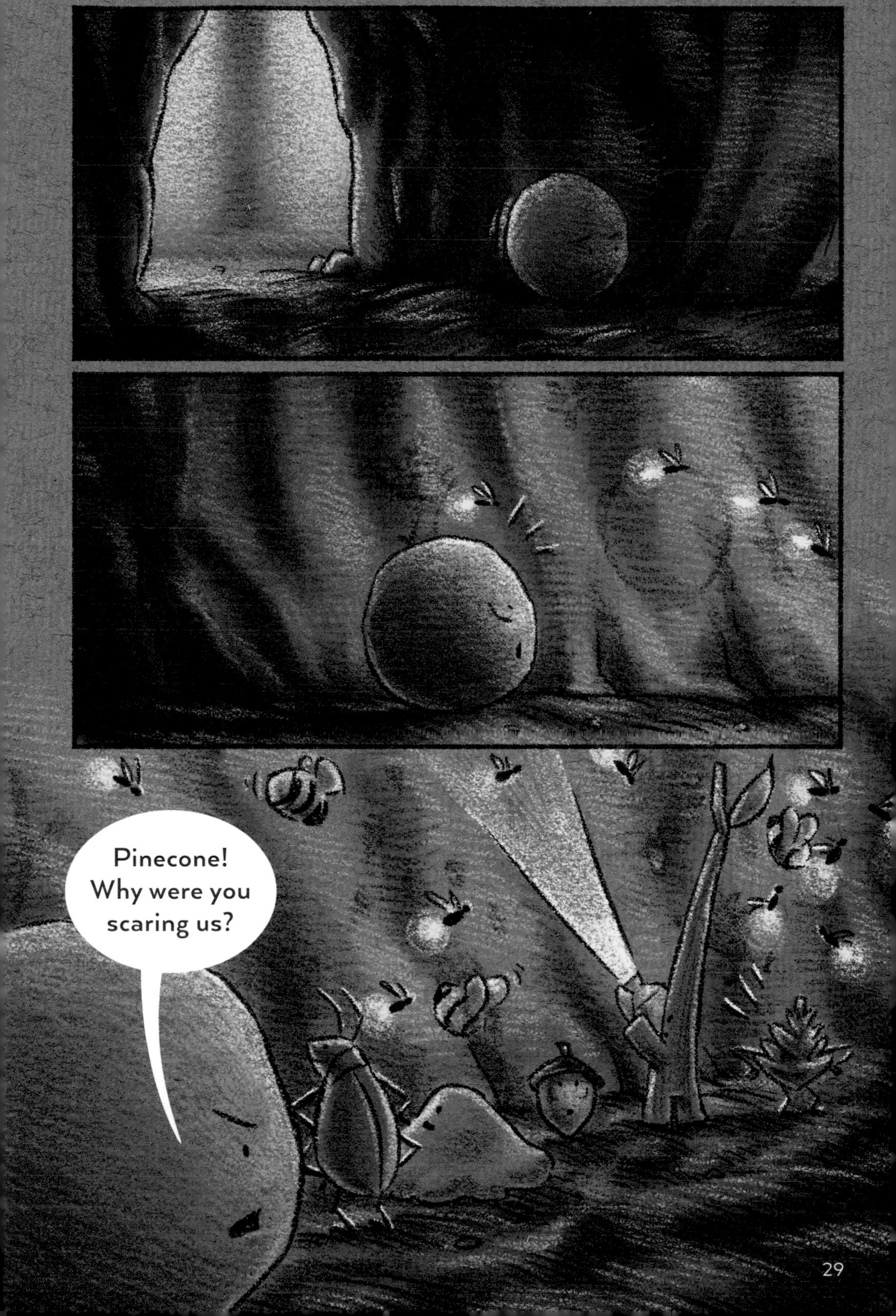
Pinecone! Why were you scaring us?

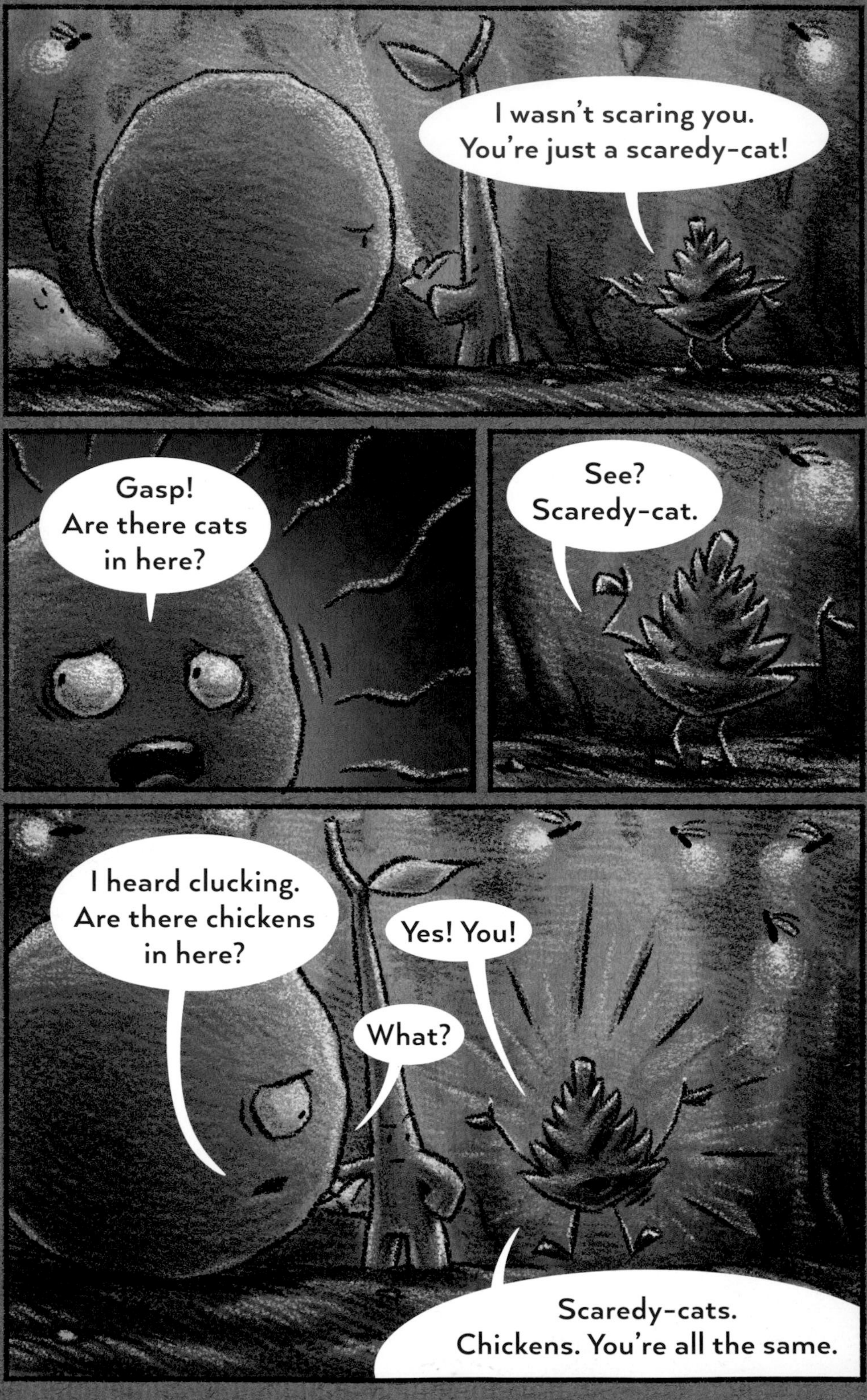
I wasn't scaring you.
You're just a scaredy-cat!
Gasp!
Are there cats
in here?
See?
Scaredy-cat.
I heard clucking.
Are there chickens
in here?
Yes! You!
What?
Scaredy-cats.
Chickens. You're all the same.

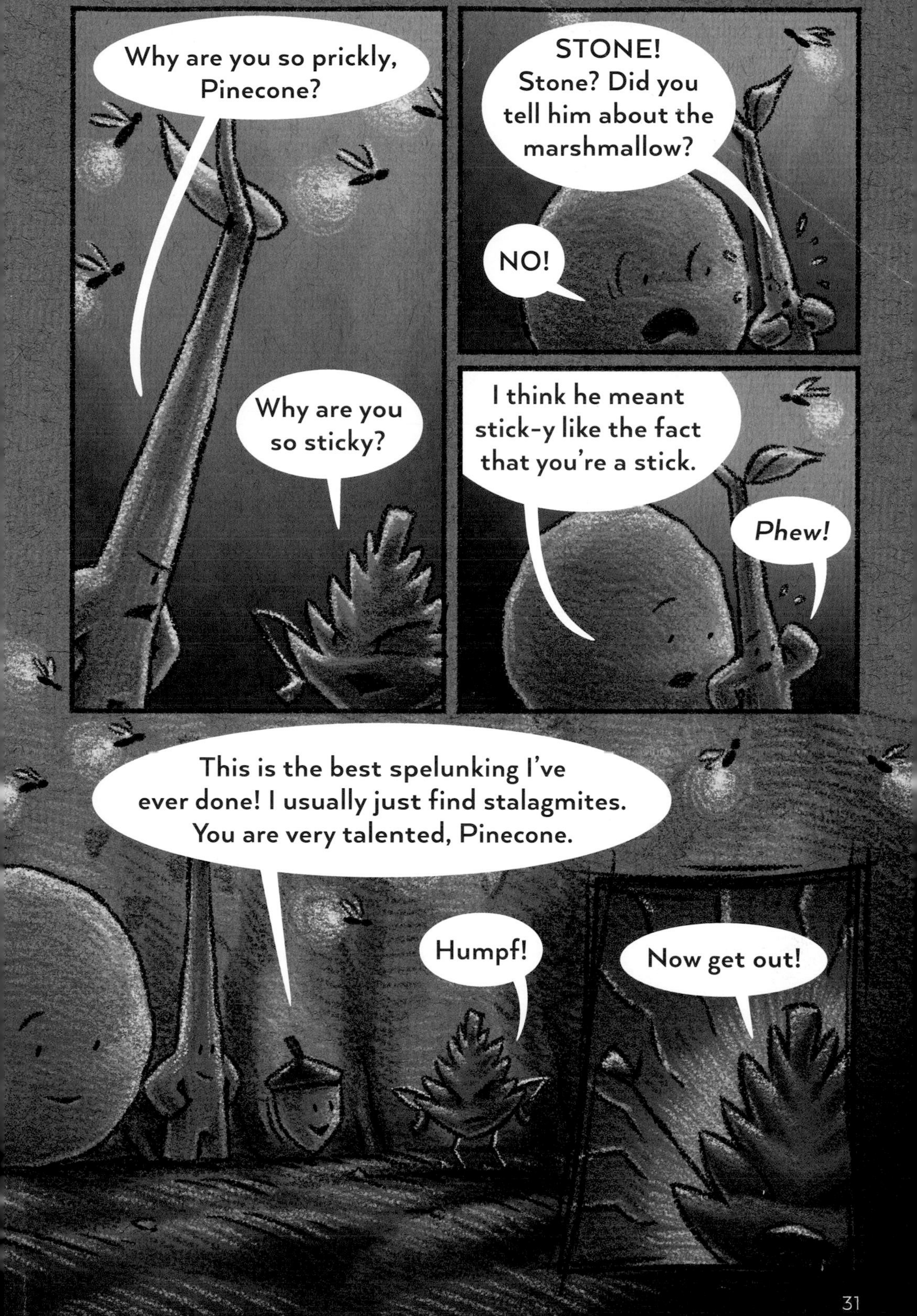
Why are you so prickly, Pinecone?
Why are you so sticky?
STONE! Stone? Did you tell him about the marshmallow?
NO!
I think he meant stick-y like the fact that you're a stick.
Phew!
This is the best spelunking I've ever done! I usually just find stalagmites. You are very talented, Pinecone.
Humpf!
Now get out!

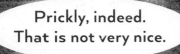

Prickly, indeed.
That is not very nice.

Well, it's not very nice
to barge in to someone's art
studio uninvited.

We didn't know it was
your art studio.

Well, now you know,
so now you should go!

Fine! We can tell when
we're not wanted.

Are you sure?
You're still here.

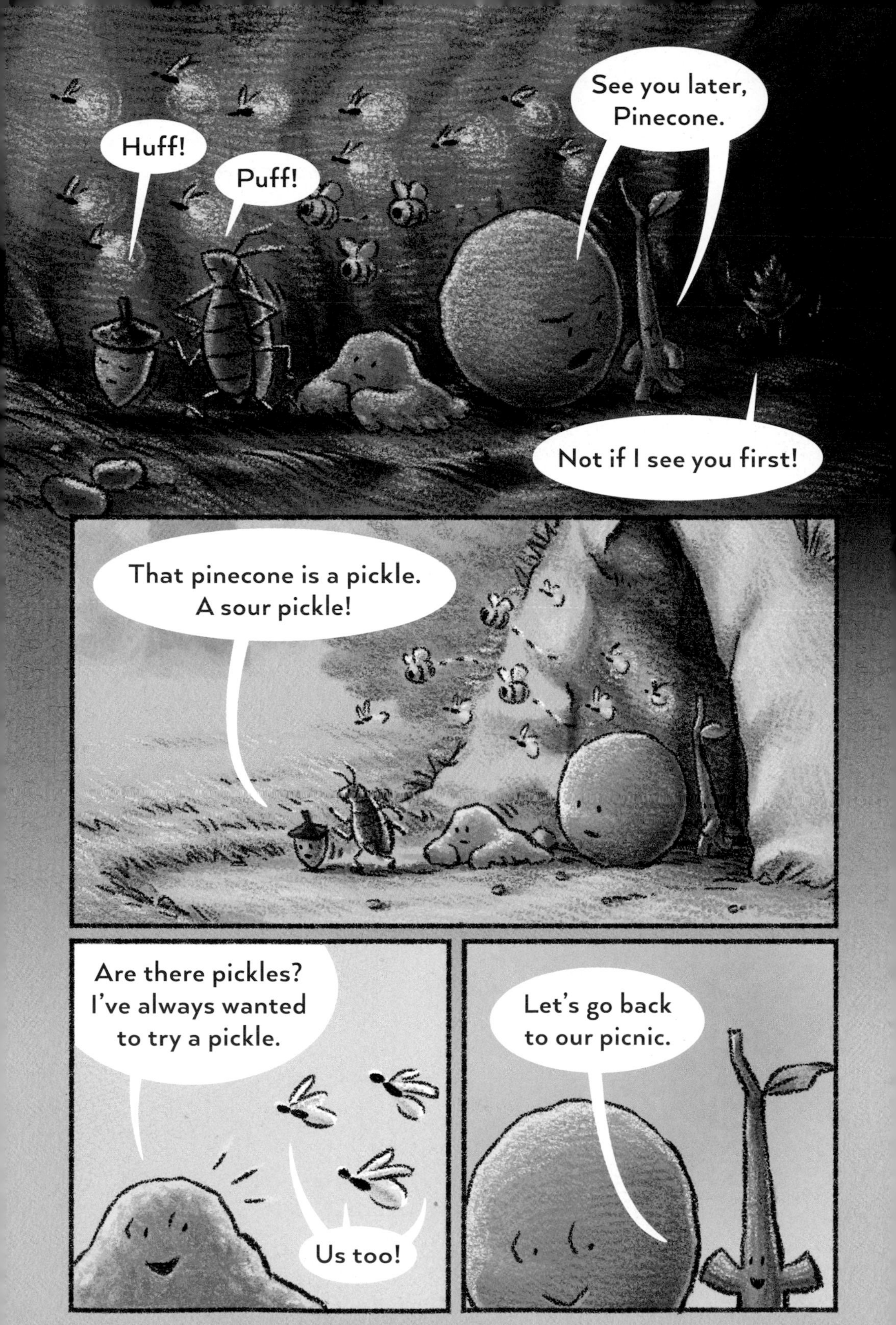
Huff!
Puff!
See you later, Pinecone.
Not if I see you first!
That pinecone is a pickle. A sour pickle!
Are there pickles? I've always wanted to try a pickle.
Us too!
Let's go back to our picnic.

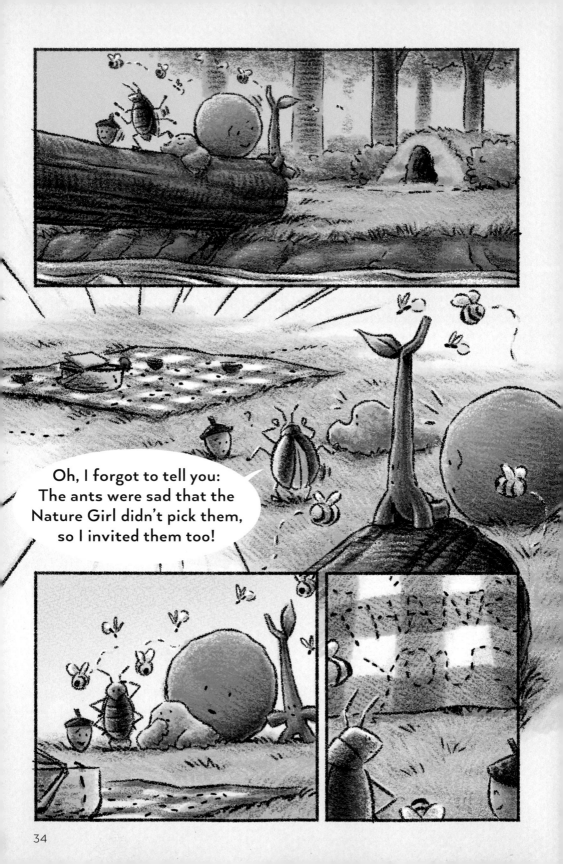

Oh, I forgot to tell you:
The ants were sad that the
Nature Girl didn't pick them,
so I invited them too!

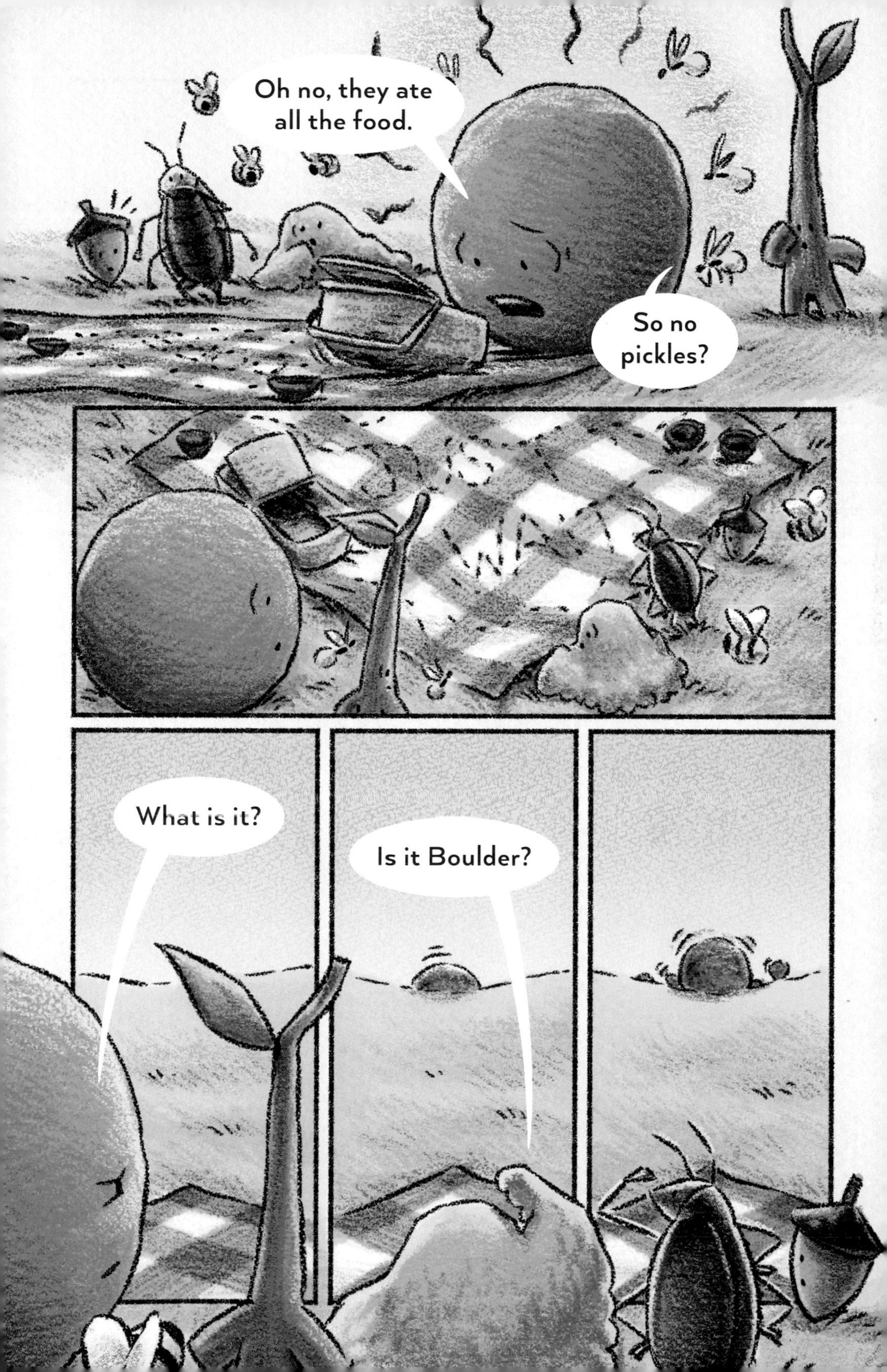
Oh no, they ate all the food.
So no pickles?
What is it?
Is it Boulder?

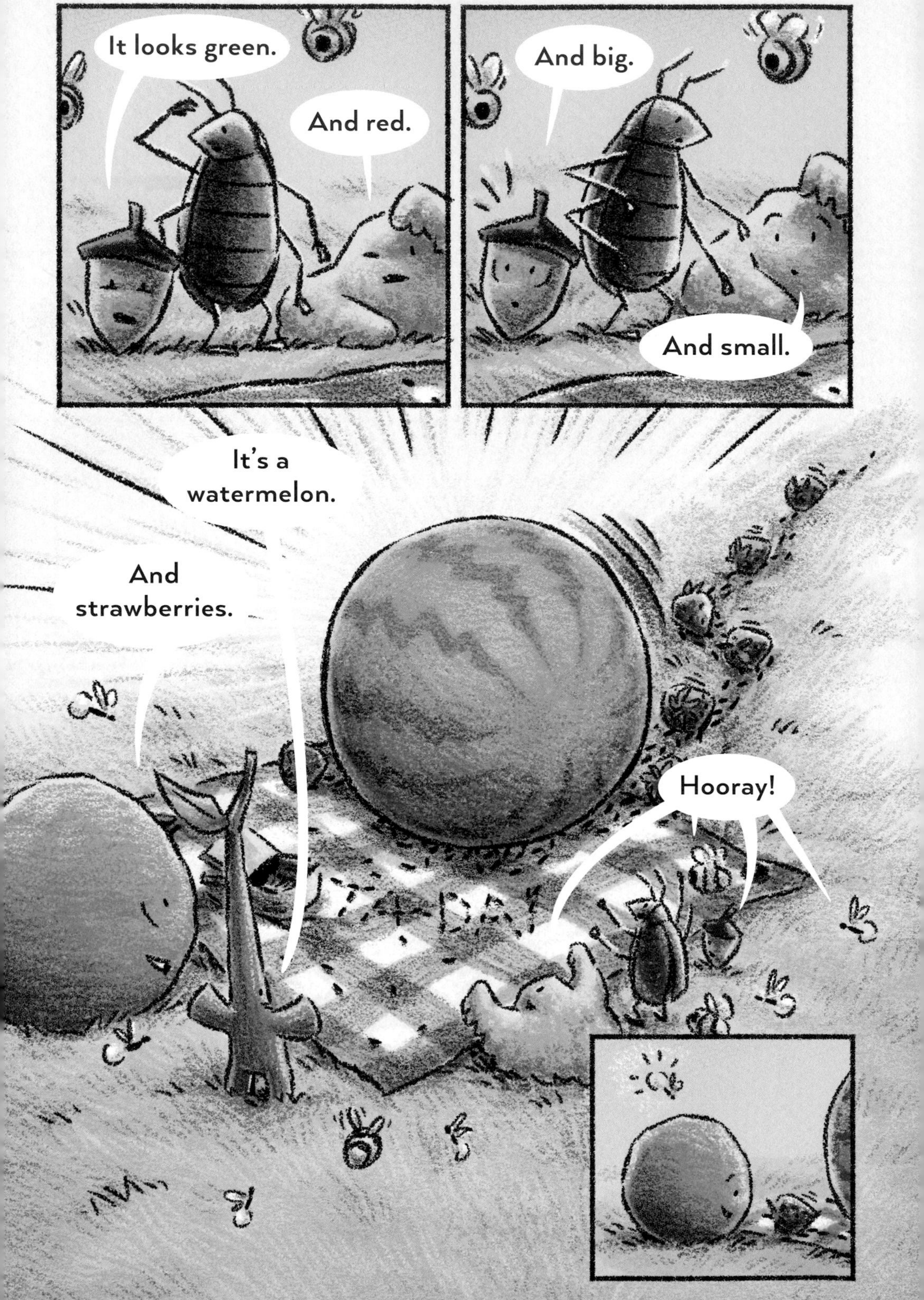
It looks green.
And red.
And big.
And small.
It's a watermelon.
And strawberries.
Hooray!

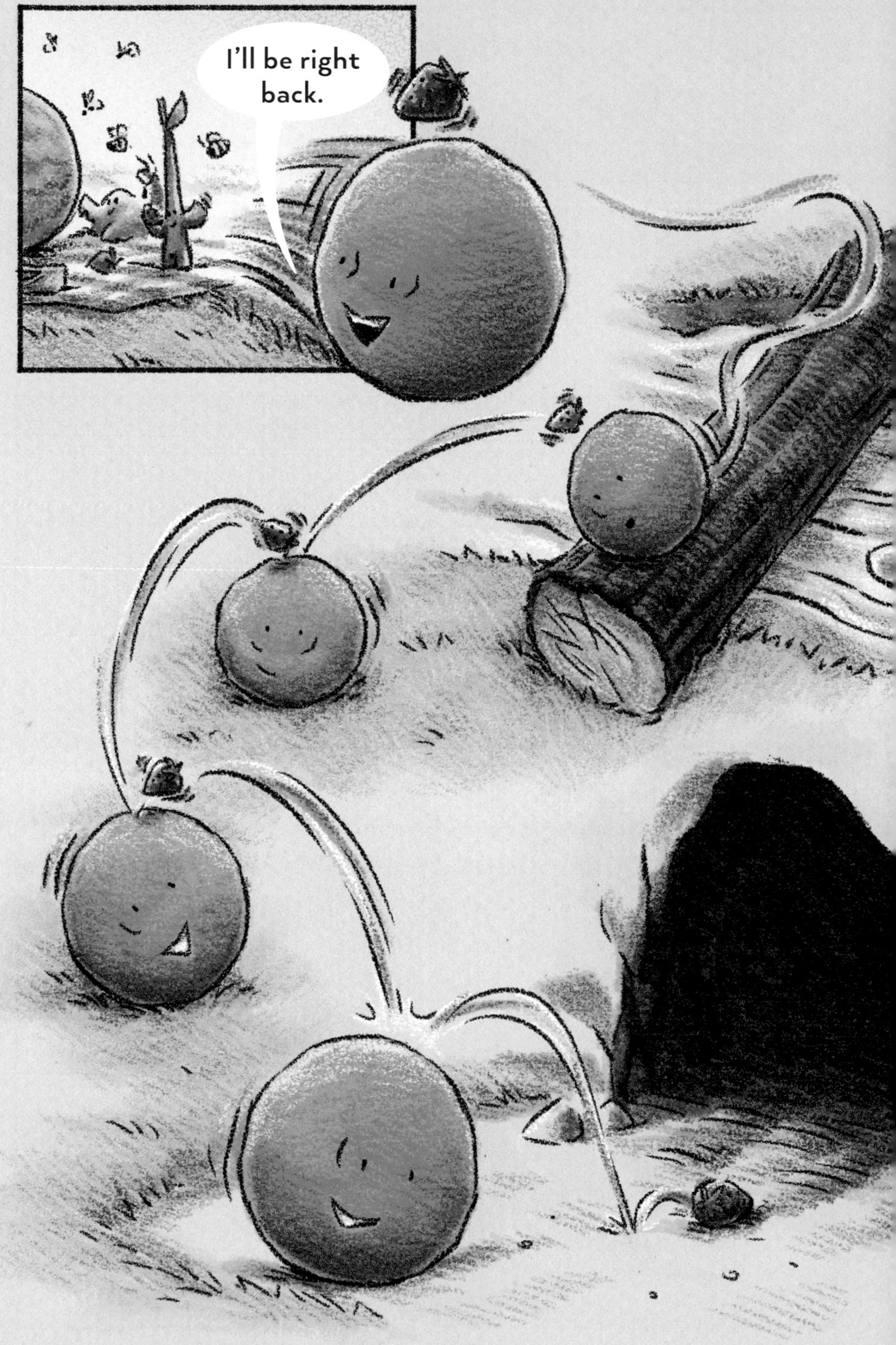
I'll be right back.

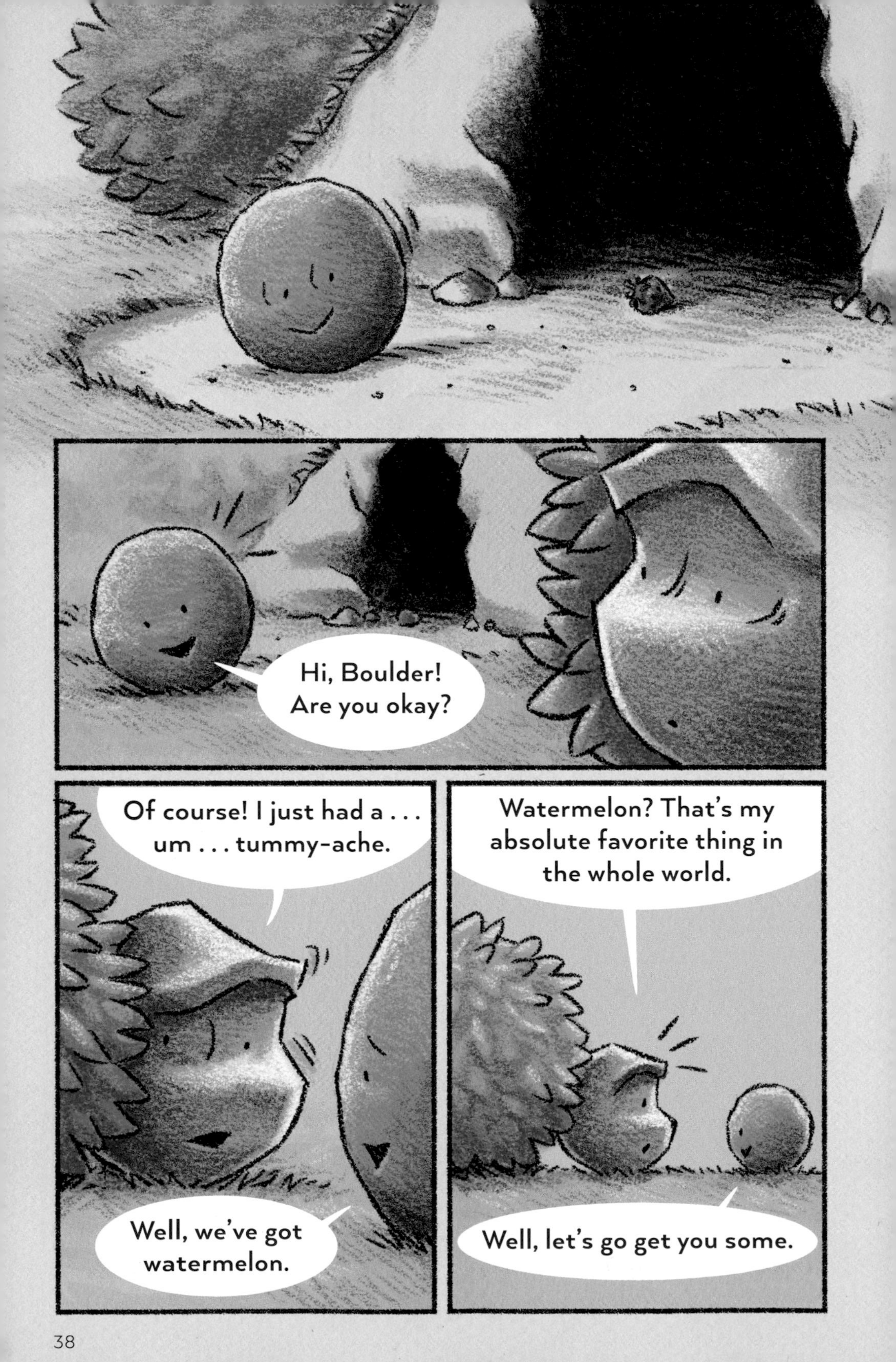
Hi, Boulder! Are you okay?
Of course! I just had a . . . um . . . tummy-ache.
Well, we've got watermelon.
Watermelon? That's my absolute favorite thing in the whole world.
Well, let's go get you some.

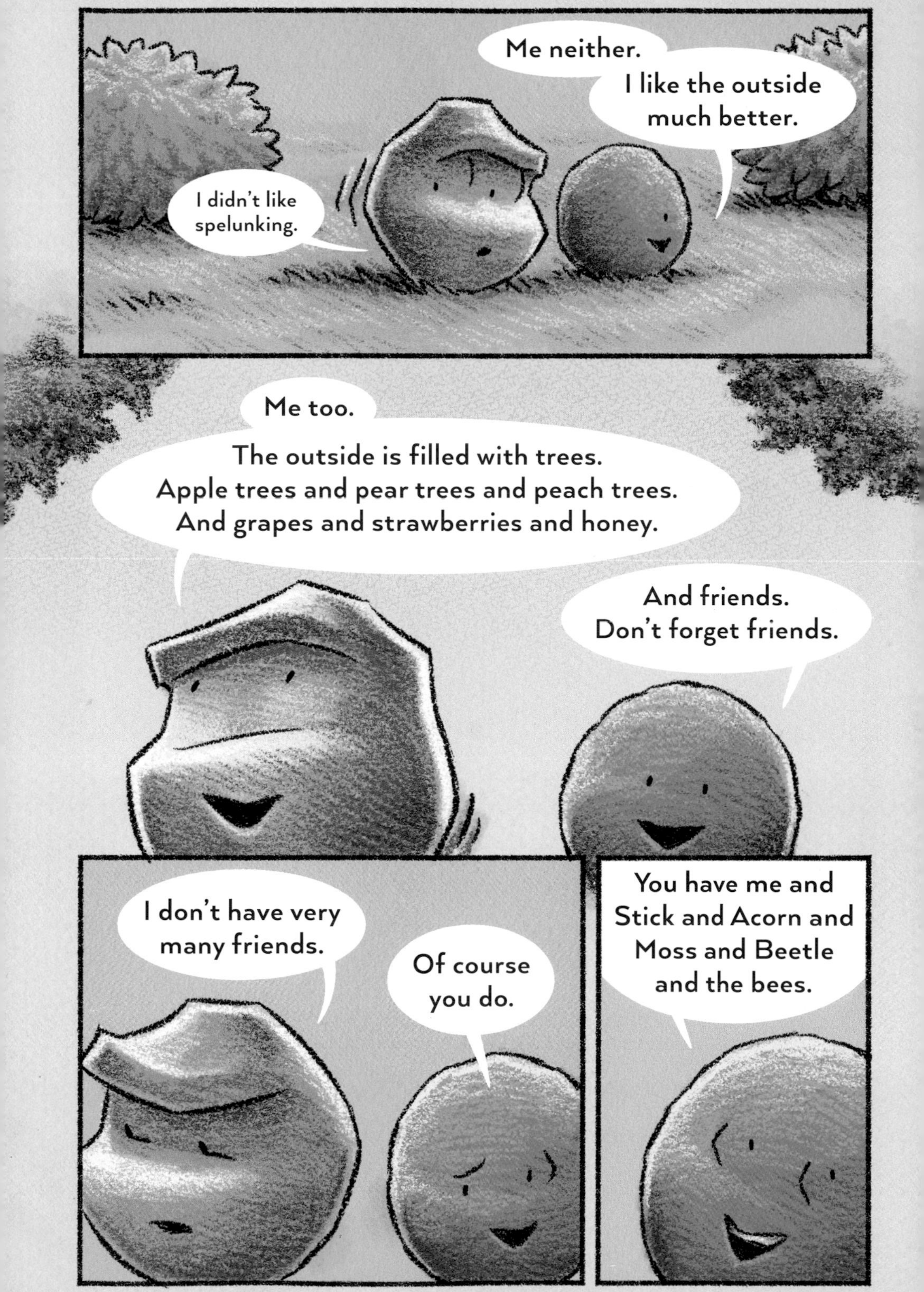
I didn't like spelunking.
Me neither.
I like the outside much better.
Me too.
The outside is filled with trees. Apple trees and pear trees and peach trees. And grapes and strawberries and honey.
And friends. Don't forget friends.
I don't have very many friends.
Of course you do.
You have me and Stick and Acorn and Moss and Beetle and the bees.

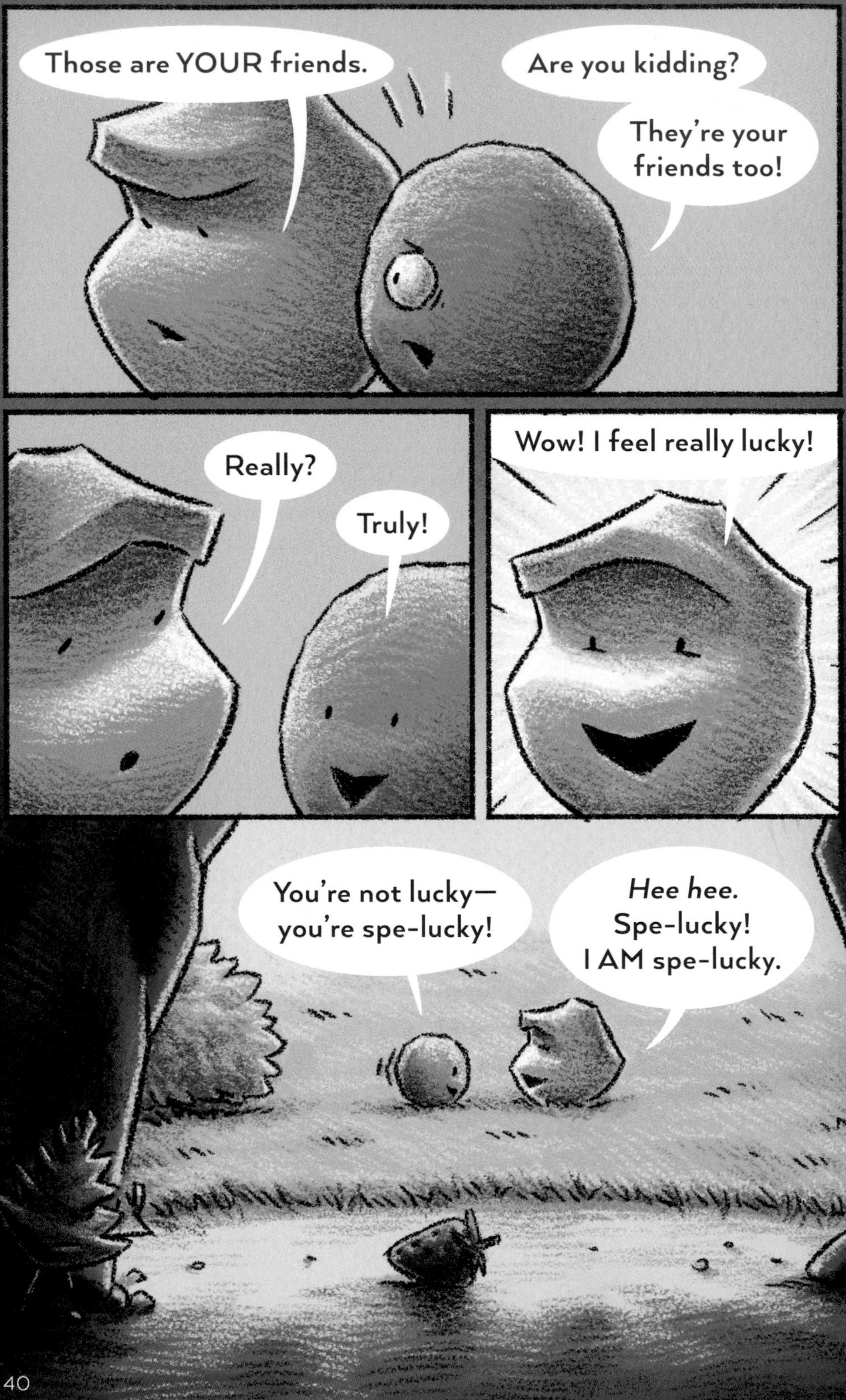
Those are YOUR friends.
Are you kidding?
They're your friends too!
Really?
Truly!
Wow! I feel really lucky!
You're not lucky— you're spe-lucky!
Hee hee. Spe-lucky! I AM spe-lucky.

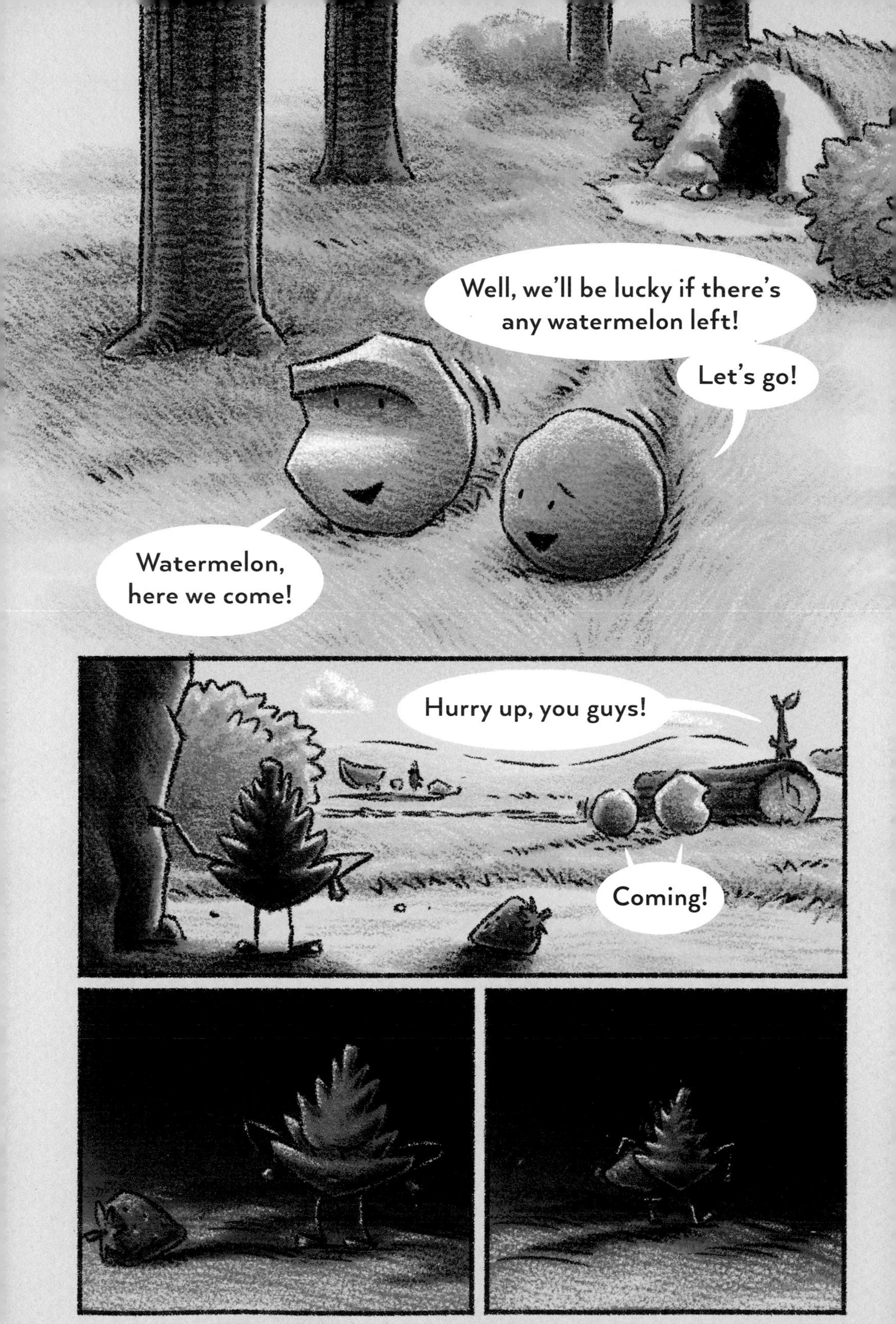
Well, we'll be lucky if there's any watermelon left!
Let's go!
Watermelon, here we come!
Hurry up, you guys!
Coming!

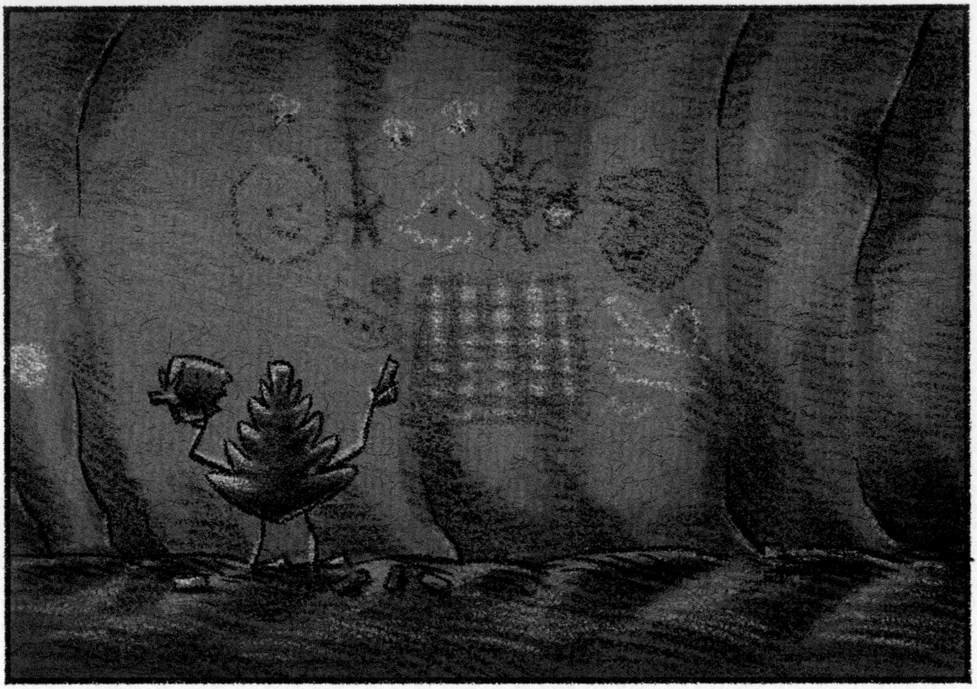

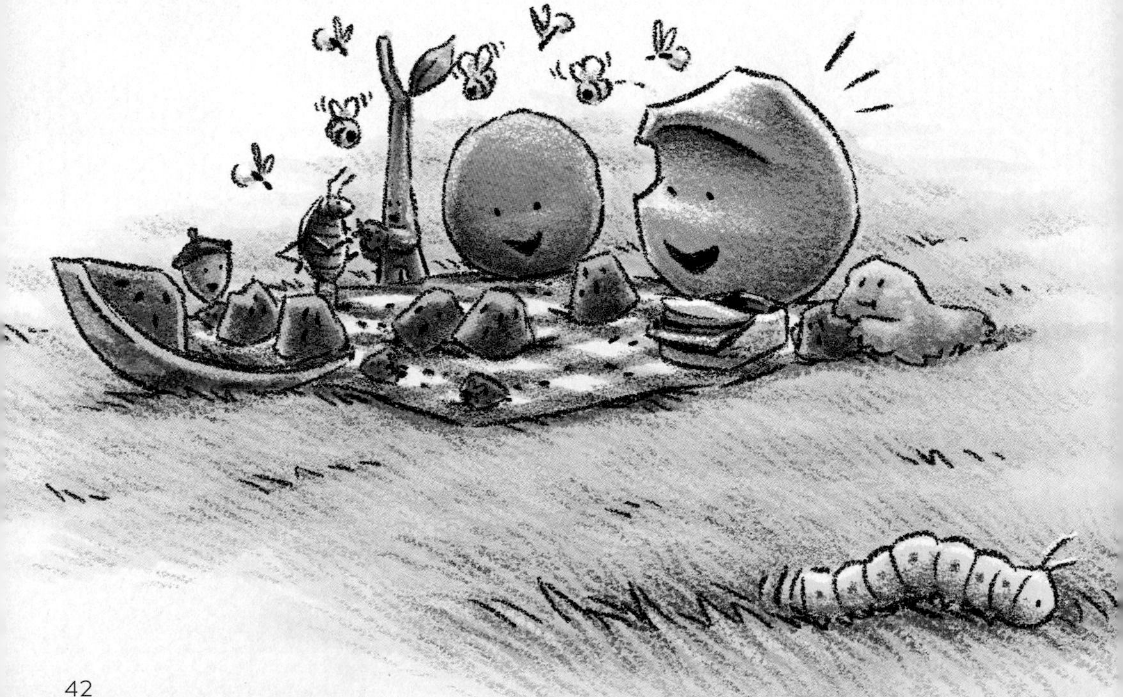

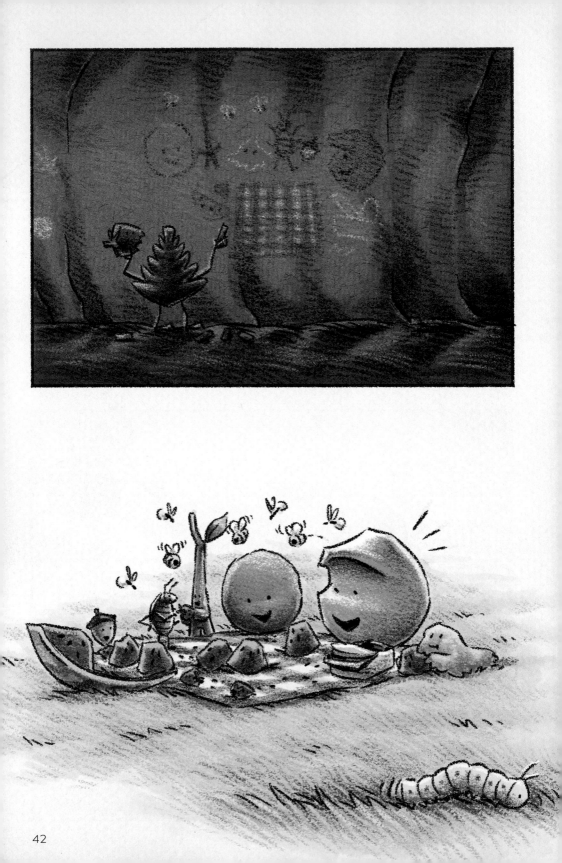

CAVE ART ACTIVITY

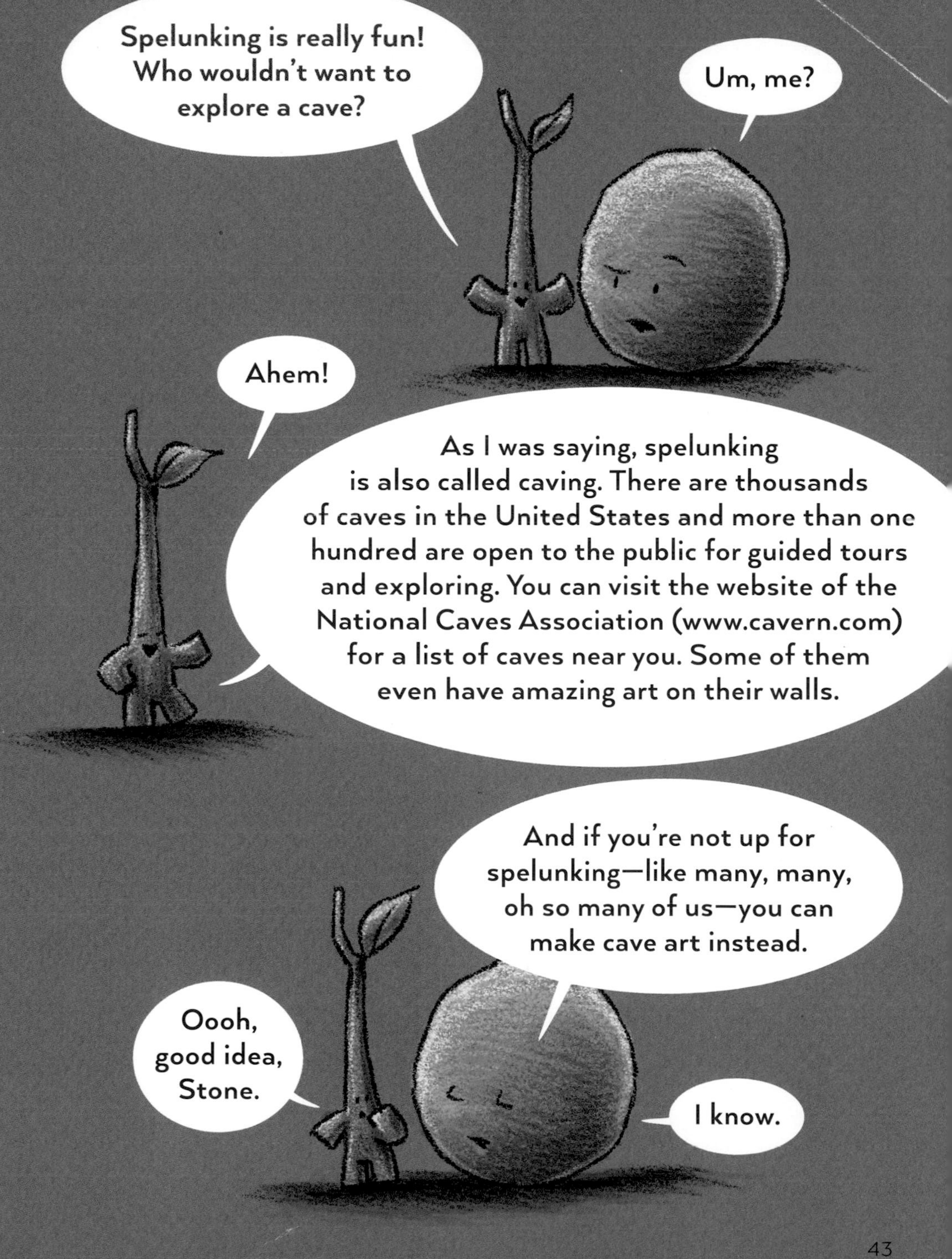
Spelunking is really fun! Who wouldn't want to explore a cave?
Um, me?
Ahem!
As I was saying, spelunking is also called caving. There are thousands of caves in the United States and more than one hundred are open to the public for guided tours and exploring. You can visit the website of the National Caves Association (www.cavern.com) for a list of caves near you. Some of them even have amazing art on their walls.
And if you're not up for spelunking—like many, many, oh so many of us—you can make cave art instead.
Oooh, good idea, Stone.
I know.

Cave Art

What you'll need:

- Brown craft paper or brown grocery bag
- Colored chalk or pastels
- Red tempera paint
- Spray bottle
- Pencil

Directions:

1. Tear off a large piece of craft paper or a large part of your grocery bag and crumple it into a ball, then smooth it out as flat as you can. This will create a texture like the cave wall.
2. Draw Stick, Stone, and Pinecone or any animal that you like.
3. Outline those drawings in chalk or pastels.
4. Color in with any color you like for their eyes and mouths.
5. Dilute the red paint with water and add it to the spray bottle.
6. Place your hand on your work, in the corner, and spray the diluted paint over your hand to create an outline of your hand. This is how cave artists signed their work.
7. Enjoy your new cave art!

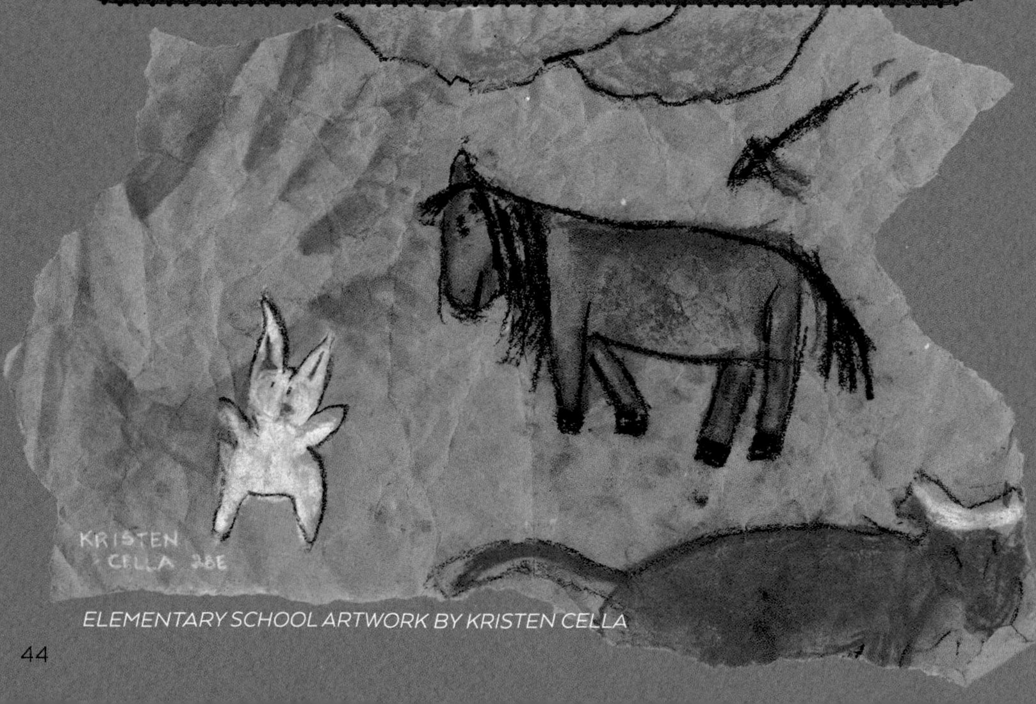
KRISTEN
CELLA 2BE

ELEMENTARY SCHOOL ARTWORK BY KRISTEN CELLA

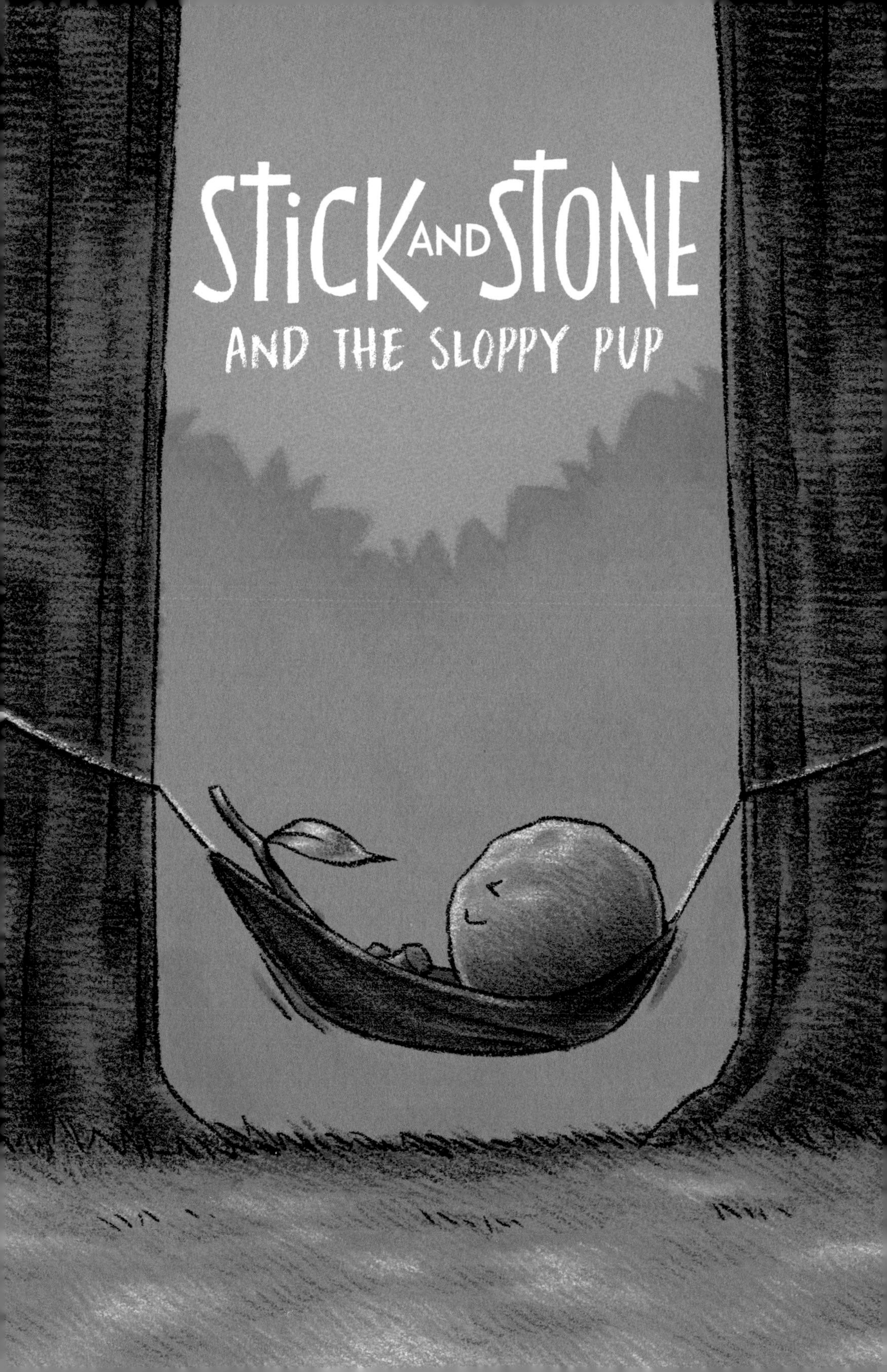
STICK AND STONE
AND THE SLOPPY PUP

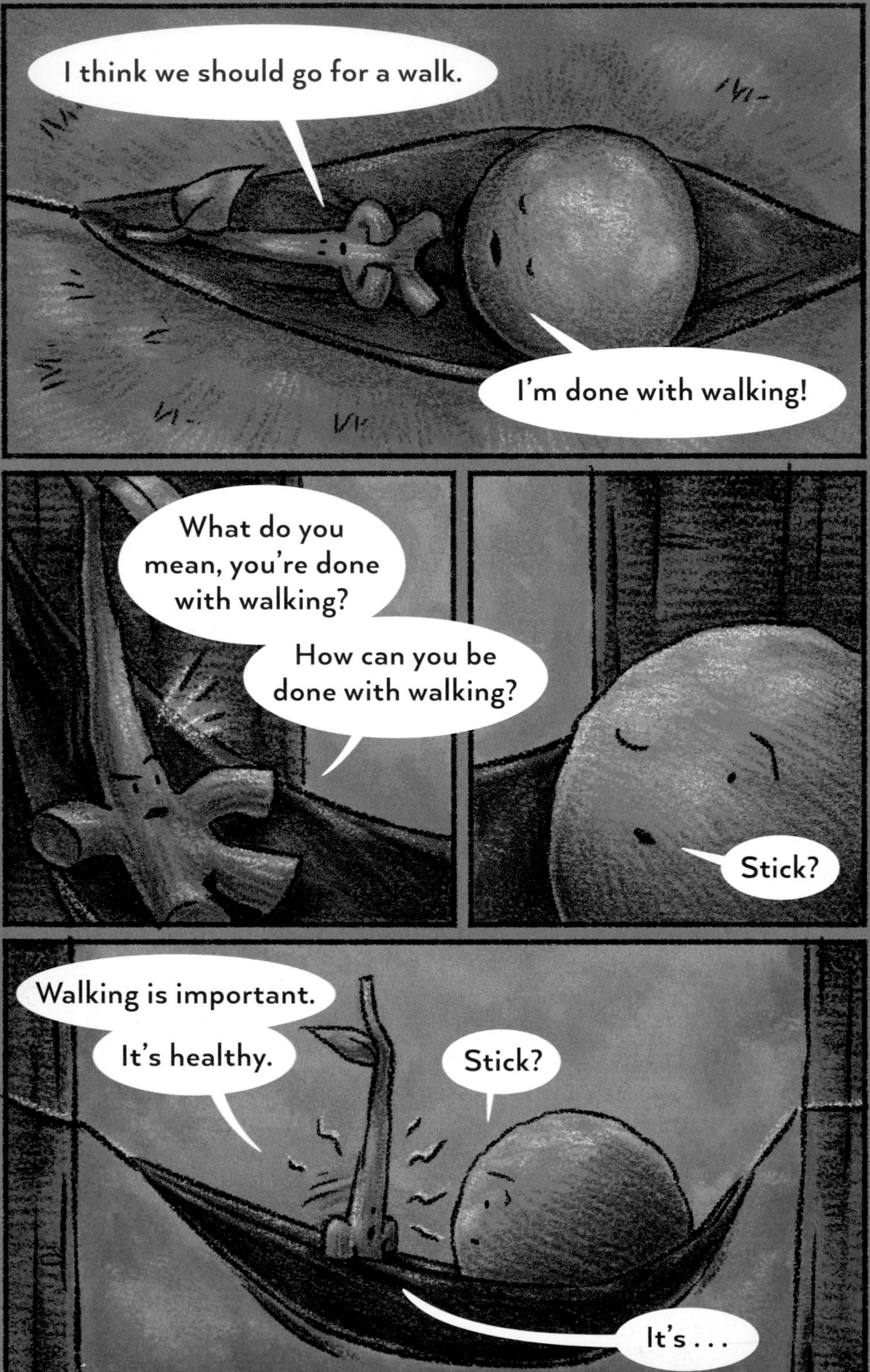
I think we should go for a walk.
I'm done with walking!
What do you mean, you're done with walking?
How can you be done with walking?
Stick?
Walking is important.
It's healthy.
Stick?
It's . . .

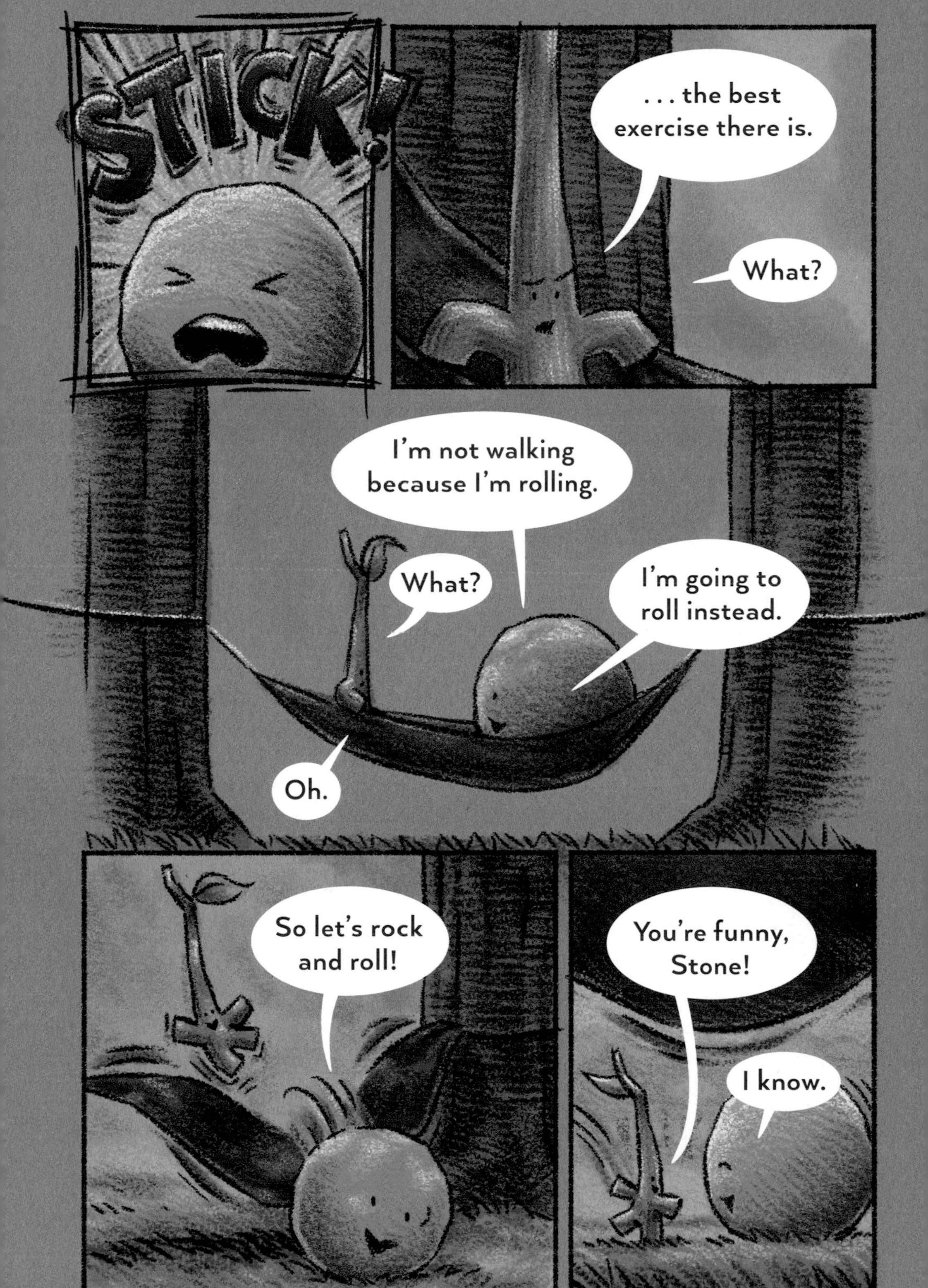
STICK!
. . . the best exercise there is.
What?
I'm not walking because I'm rolling.
What?
I'm going to roll instead.
Oh.
So let's rock and roll!
You're funny, Stone!
I know.

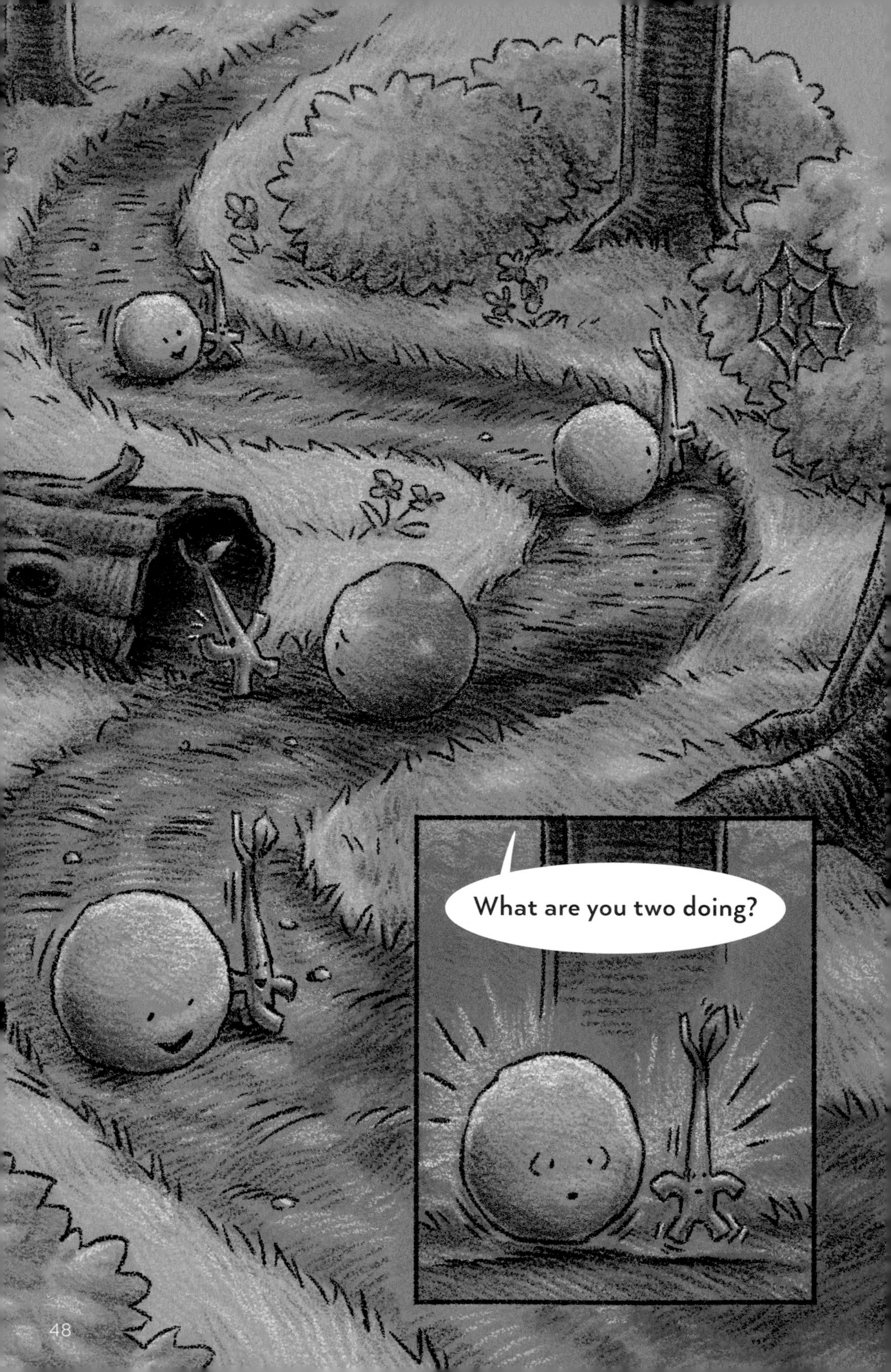
What are you two doing?

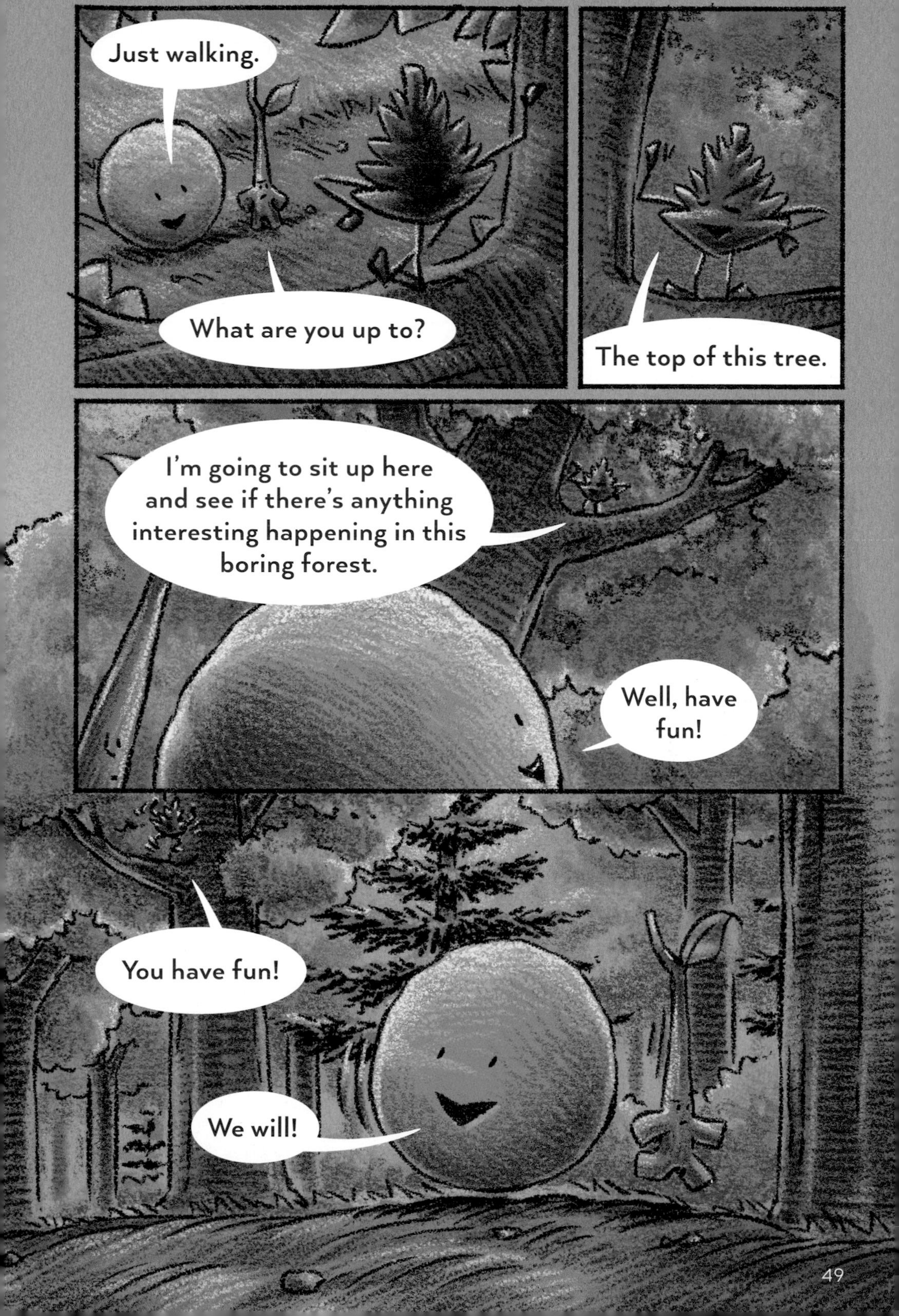
Just walking.
What are you up to?
The top of this tree.
I'm going to sit up here and see if there's anything interesting happening in this boring forest.
Well, have fun!
You have fun!
We will!

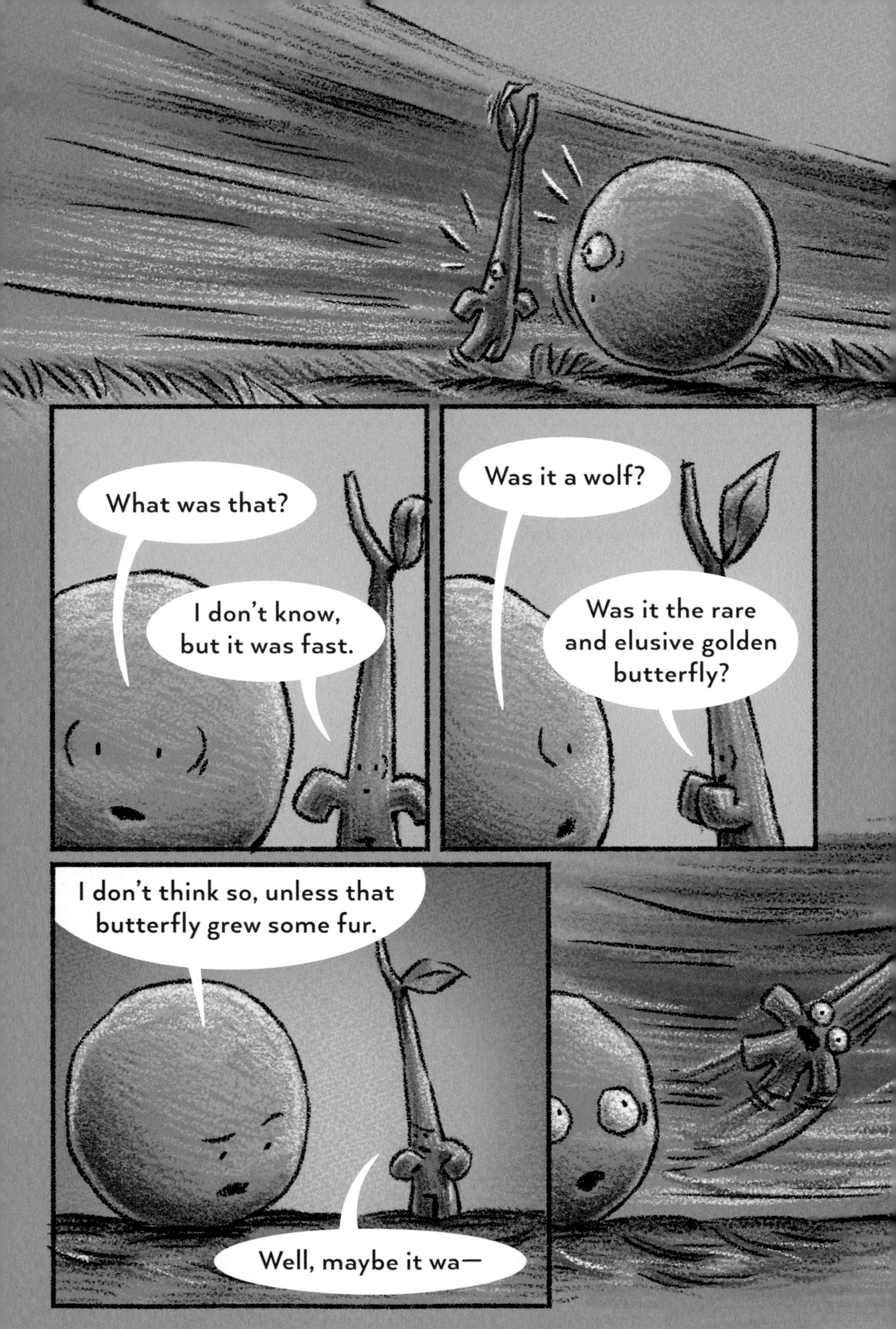
What was that?
I don't know, but it was fast.
Was it a wolf?
Was it the rare and elusive golden butterfly?
I don't think so, unless that butterfly grew some fur.
Well, maybe it wa—

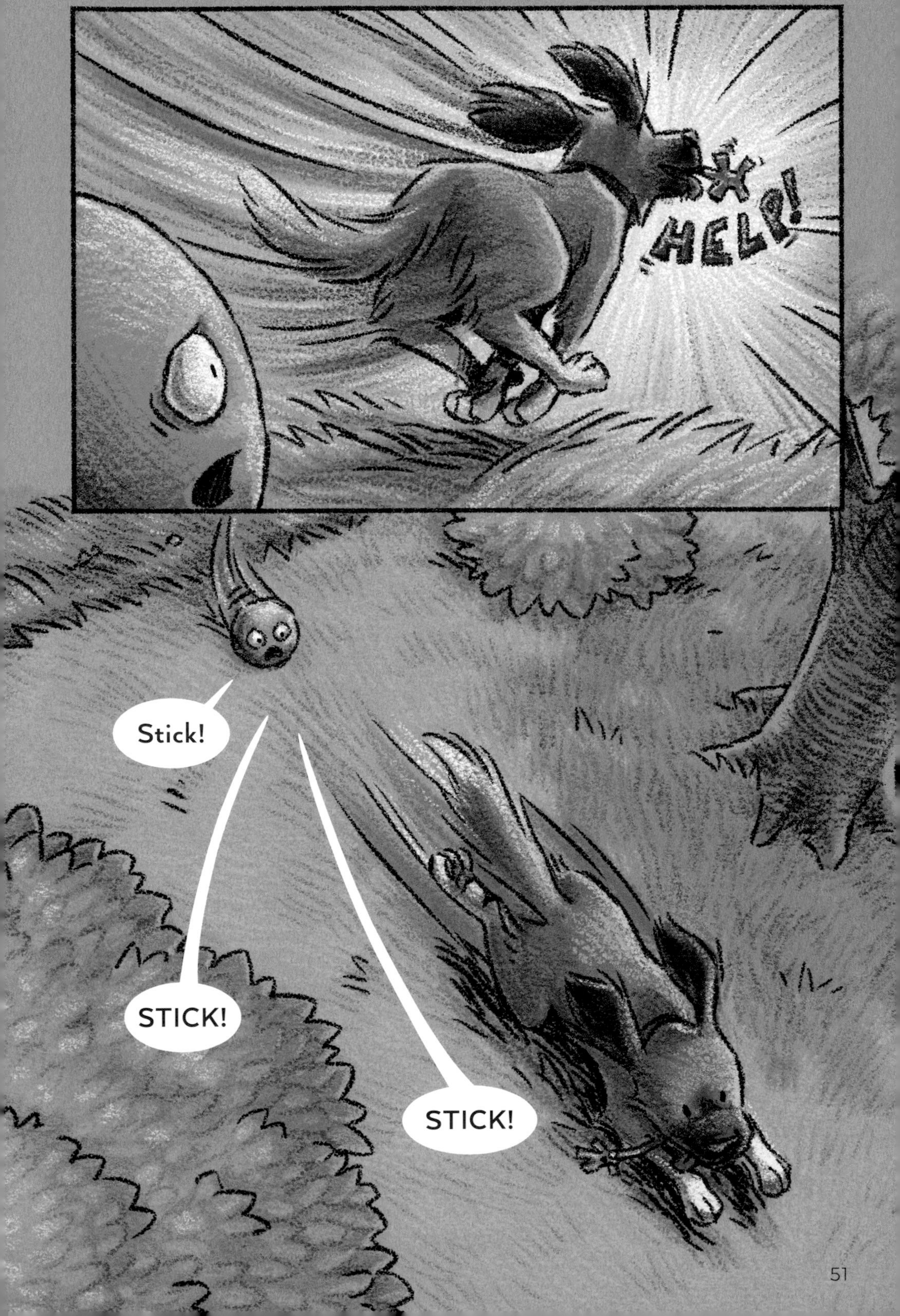
HELP!
Stick!
STICK!
STICK!

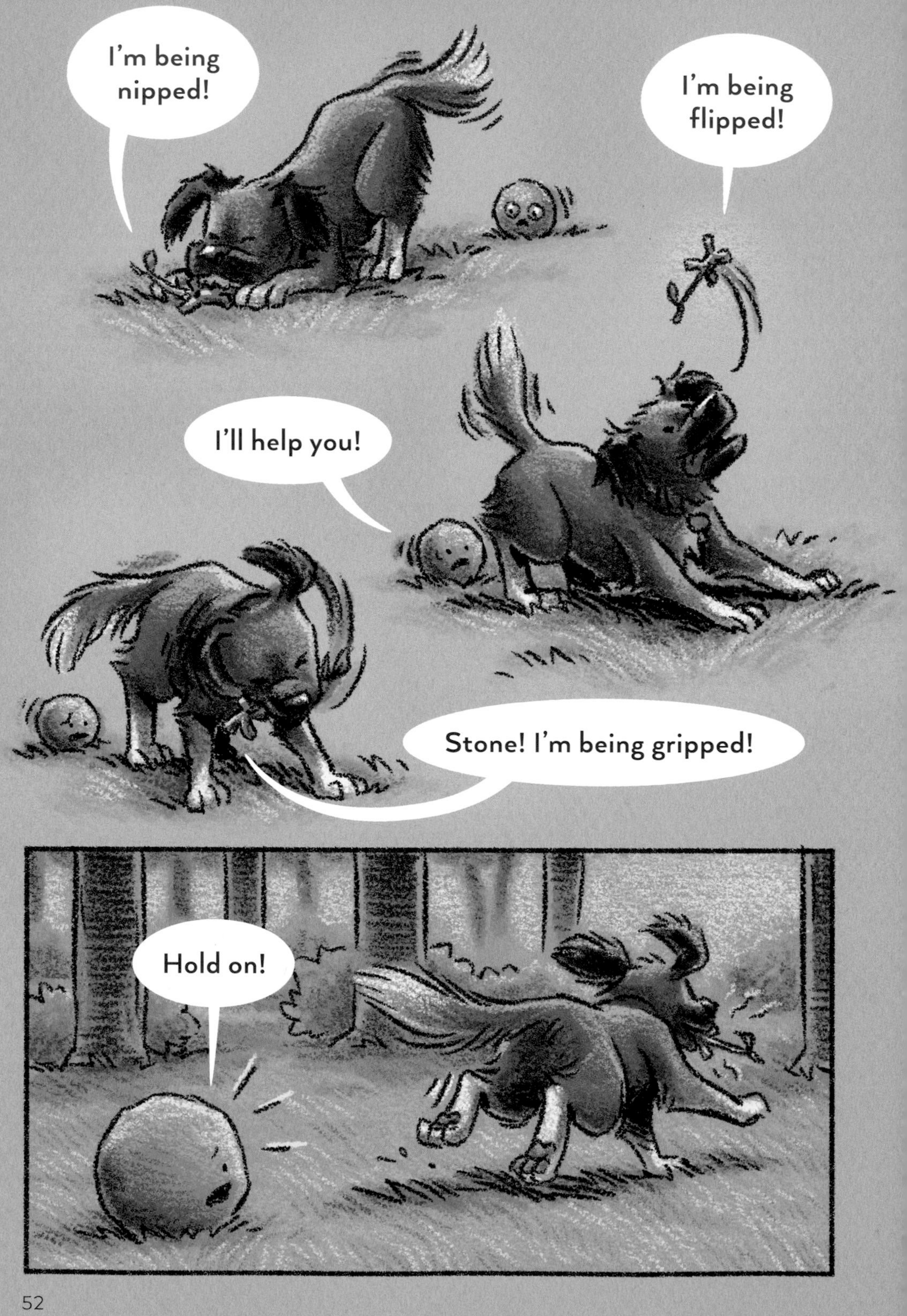
I'm being nipped!
I'm being flipped!
I'll help you!
Stone! I'm being gripped!
Hold on!

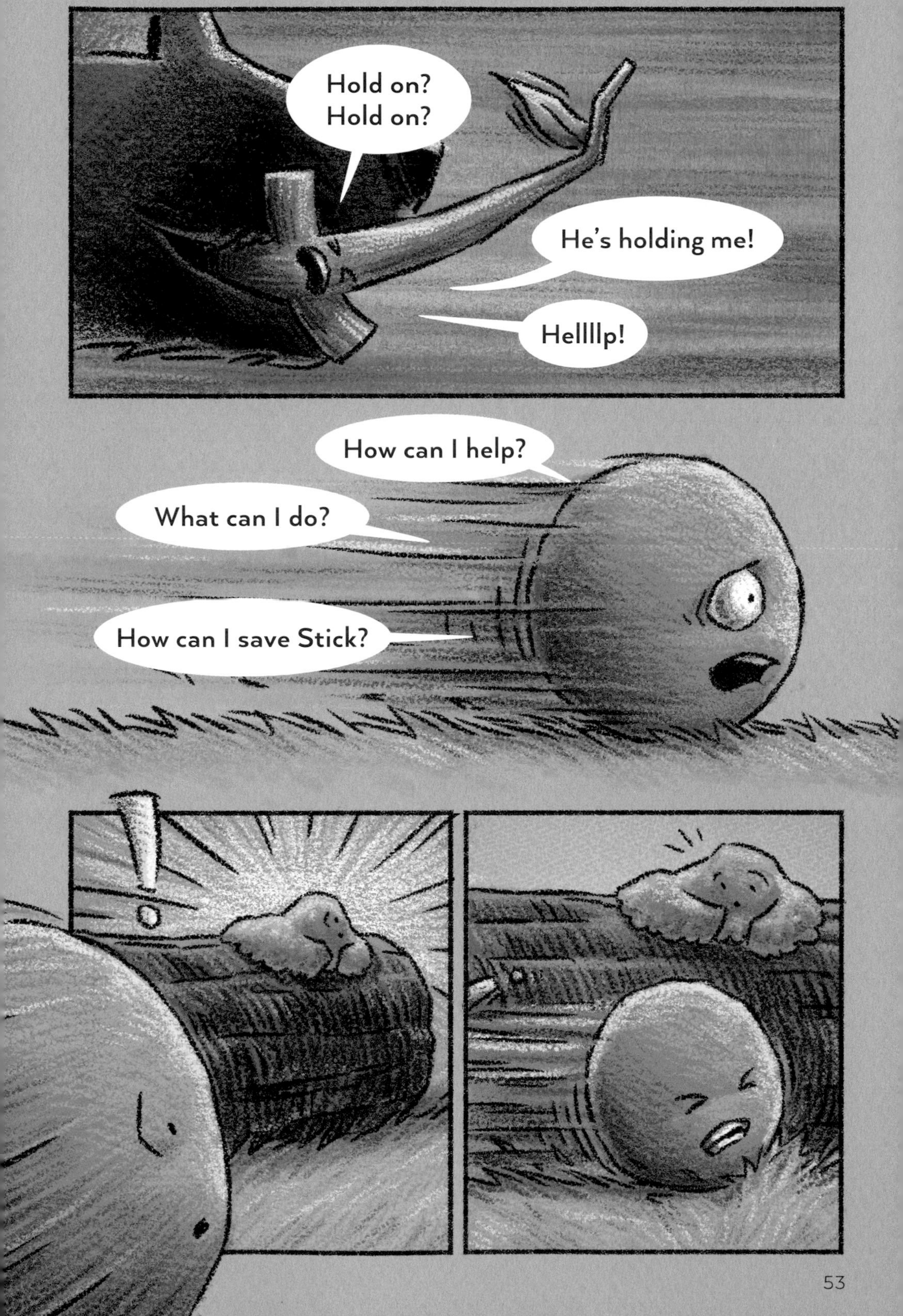
Hold on?
Hold on?
He's holding me!
Hellllp!
How can I help?
What can I do?
How can I save Stick?

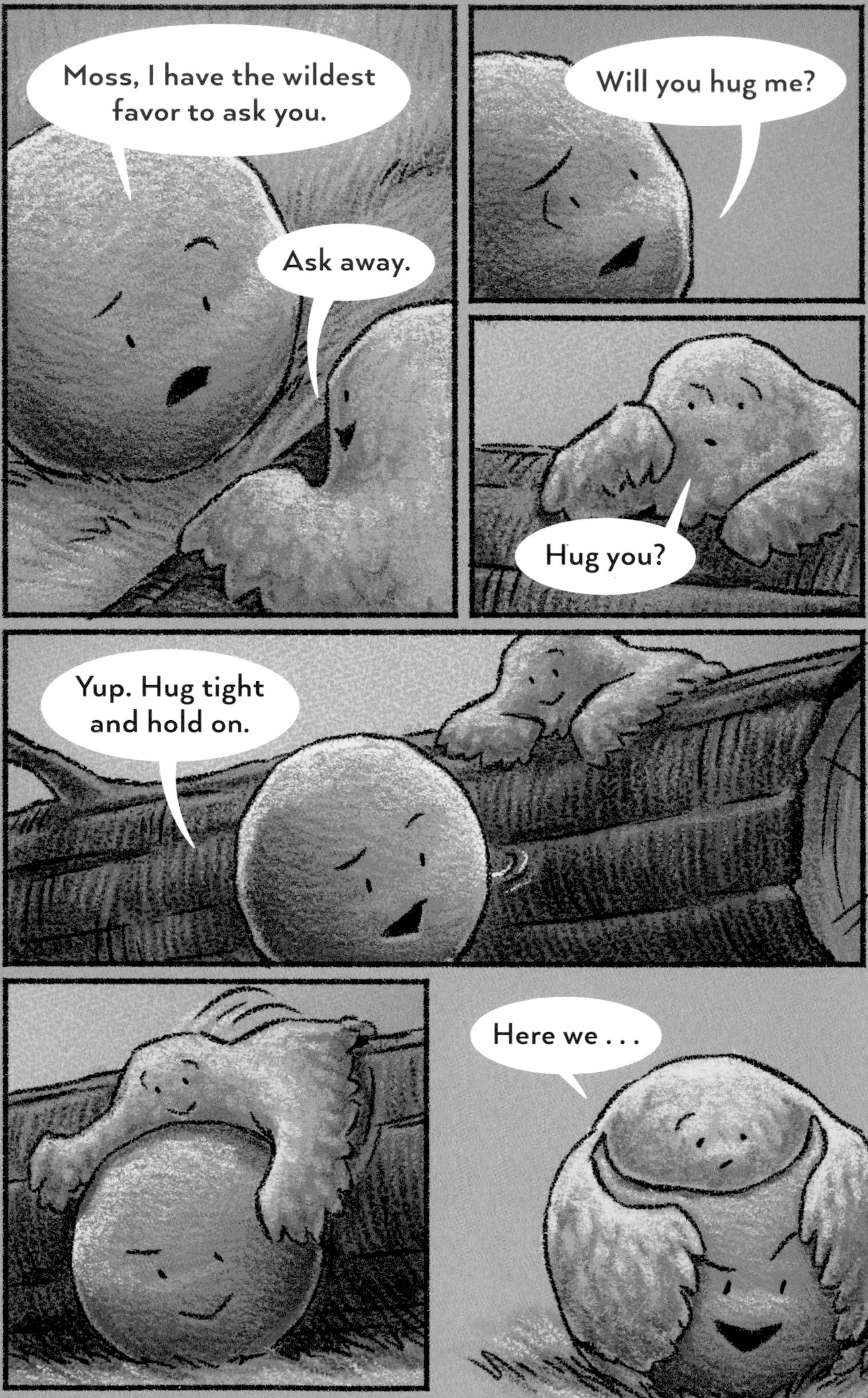
Moss, I have the wildest favor to ask you.
Ask away.
Will you hug me?
Hug you?
Yup. Hug tight and hold on.
Here we . . .

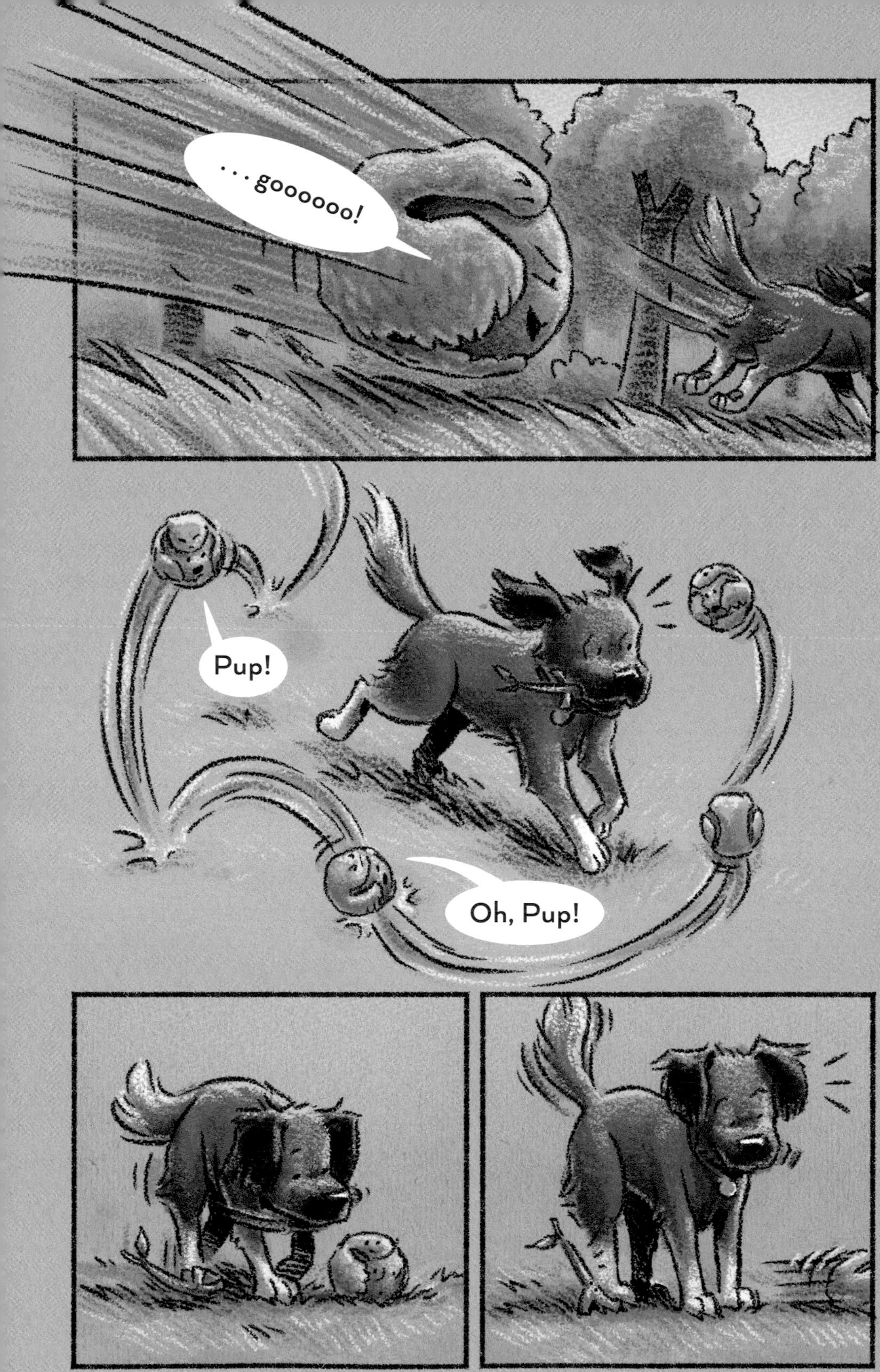
. . . goooooo!
Pup!
Oh, Pup!

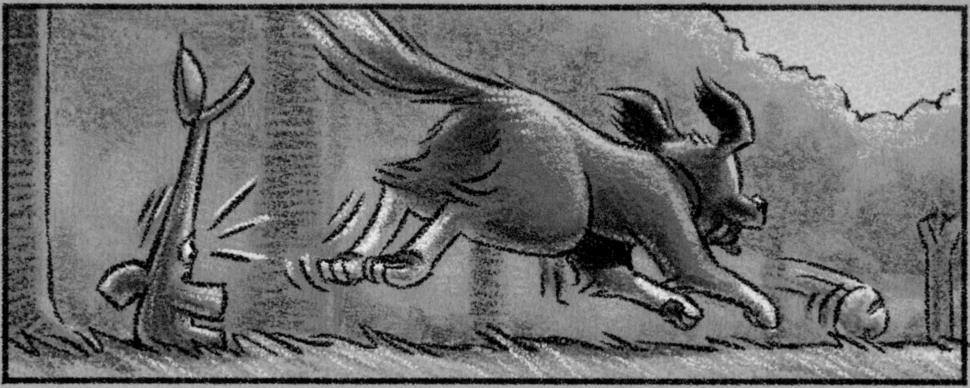

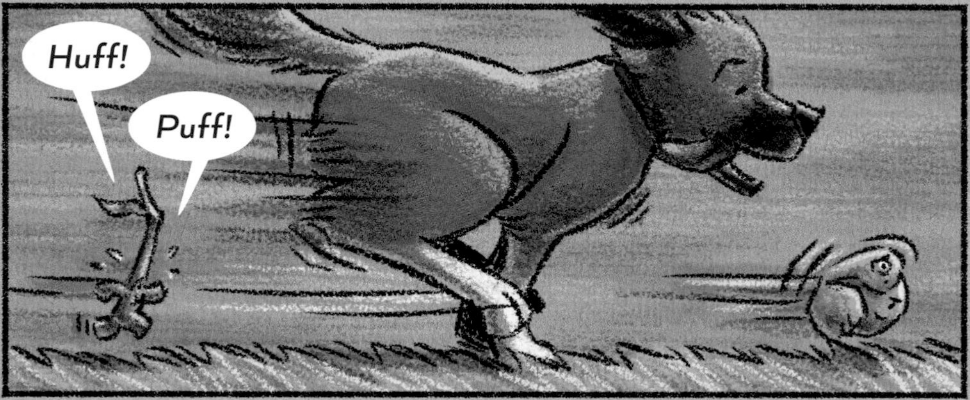
Huff!
Puff!

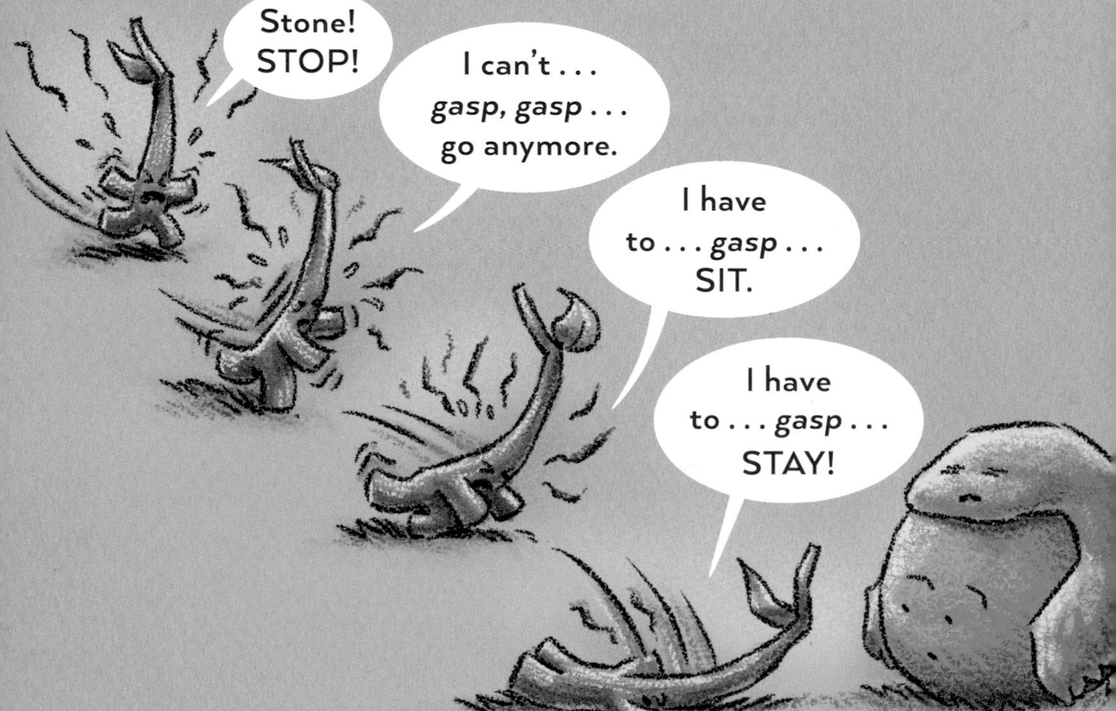
Stone! STOP!
I can't . . . *gasp, gasp* . . . go anymore.
I have to . . . *gasp* . . . SIT.
I have to . . . *gasp* . . . STAY!

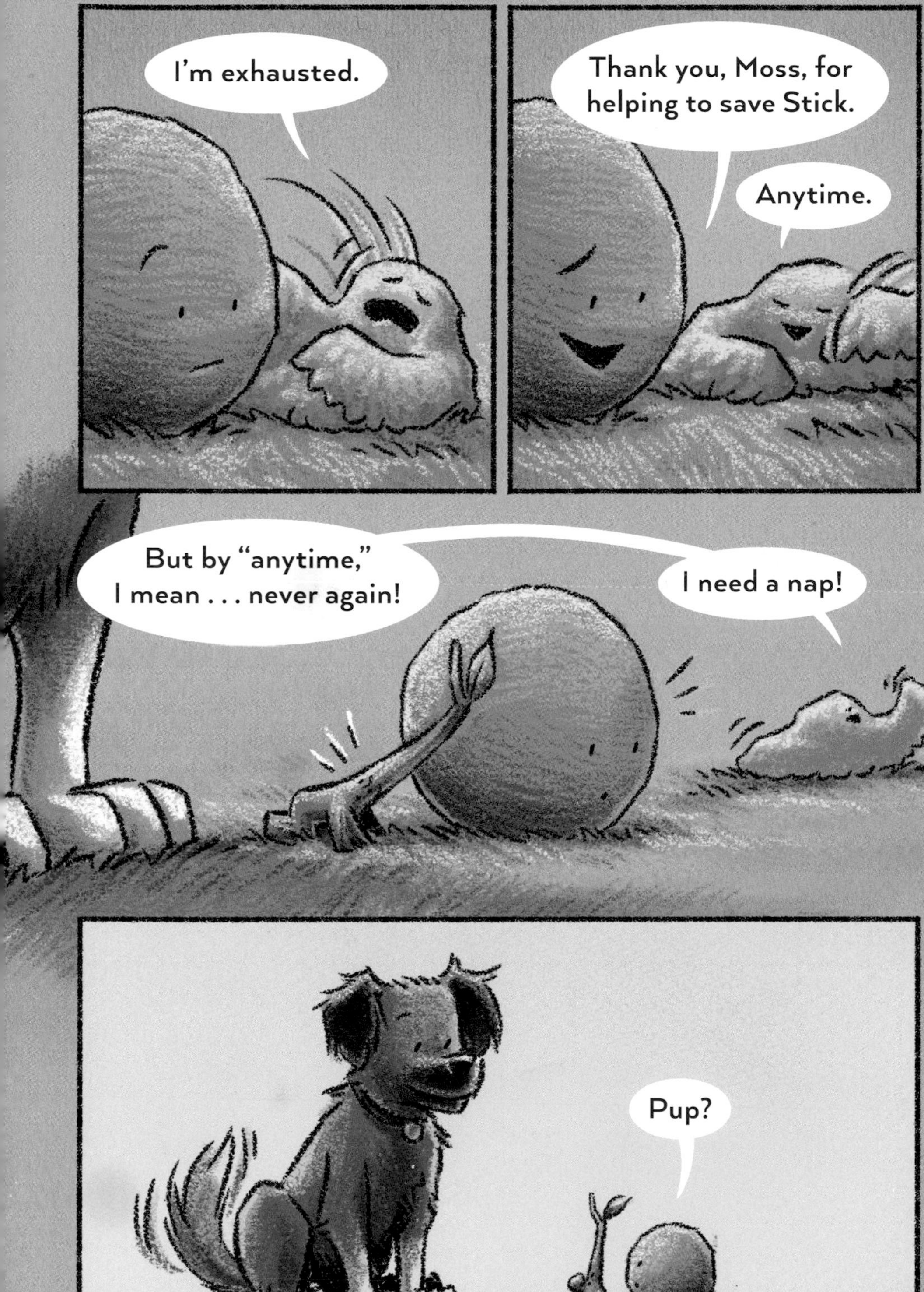
I'm exhausted.
Thank you, Moss, for helping to save Stick.
Anytime.
But by "anytime," I mean . . . never again!
I need a nap!
Pup?

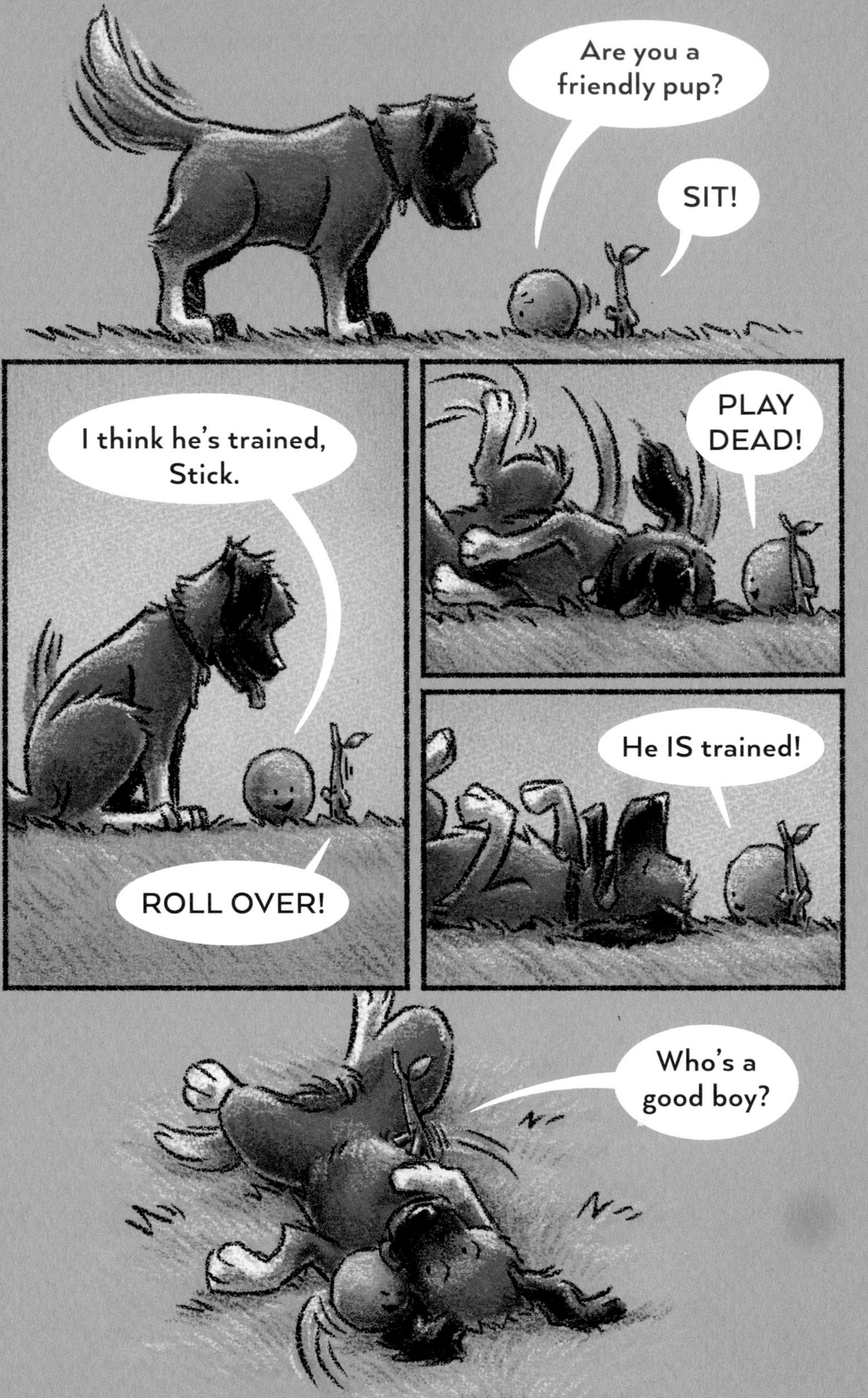
Are you a friendly pup?
SIT!
I think he's trained, Stick.
ROLL OVER!
PLAY DEAD!
He IS trained!
Who's a good boy?

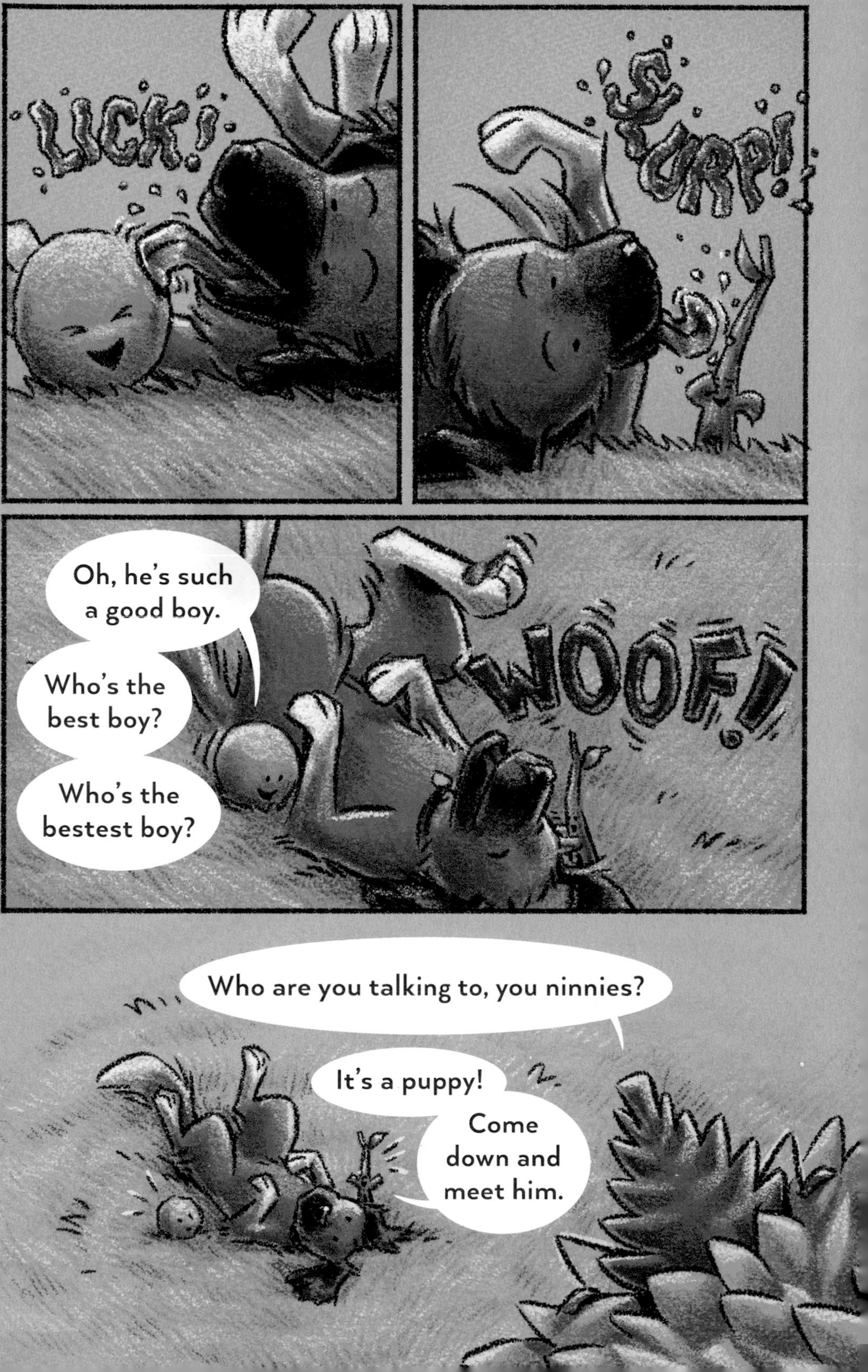
LICK!
SLURP!
Oh, he's such a good boy.
Who's the best boy?
Who's the bestest boy?
WOOF!
Who are you talking to, you ninnies?
It's a puppy!
Come down and meet him.

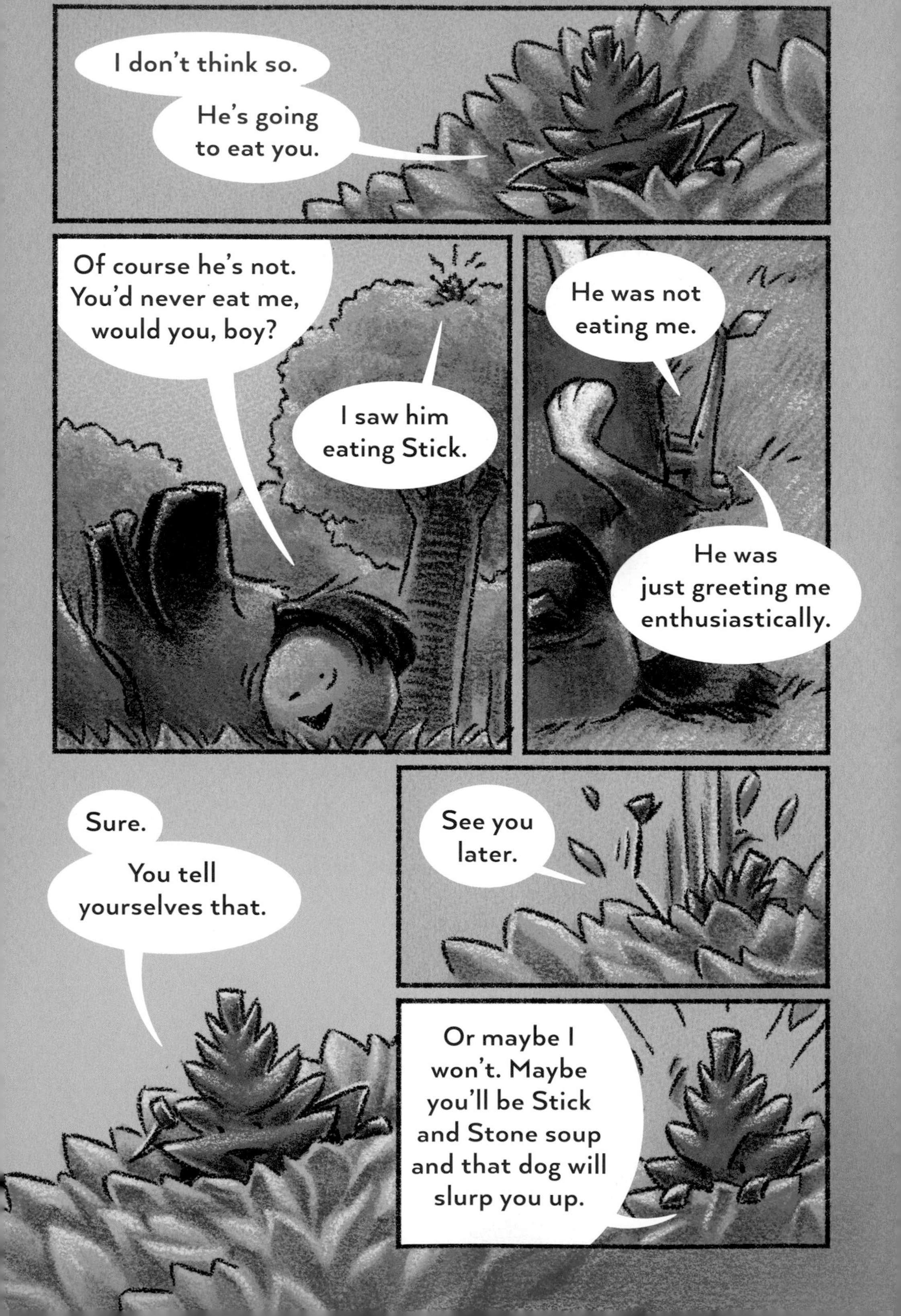
I don't think so.
He's going to eat you.
Of course he's not. You'd never eat me, would you, boy?
I saw him eating Stick.
He was not eating me.
He was just greeting me enthusiastically.
Sure.
You tell yourselves that.
See you later.
Or maybe I won't. Maybe you'll be Stick and Stone soup and that dog will slurp you up.

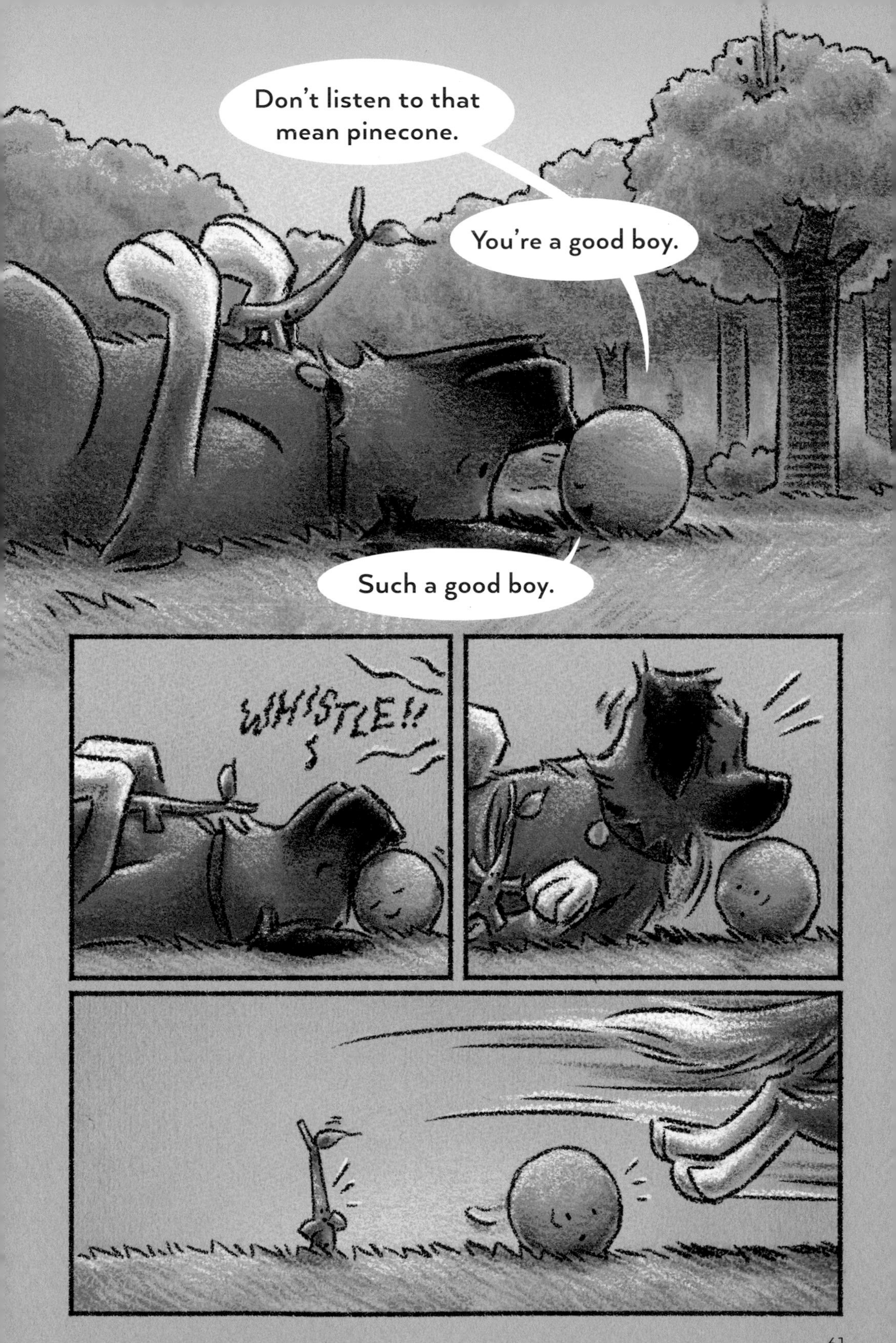
Don't listen to that mean pinecone.
You're a good boy.
Such a good boy.
WHISTLE!!

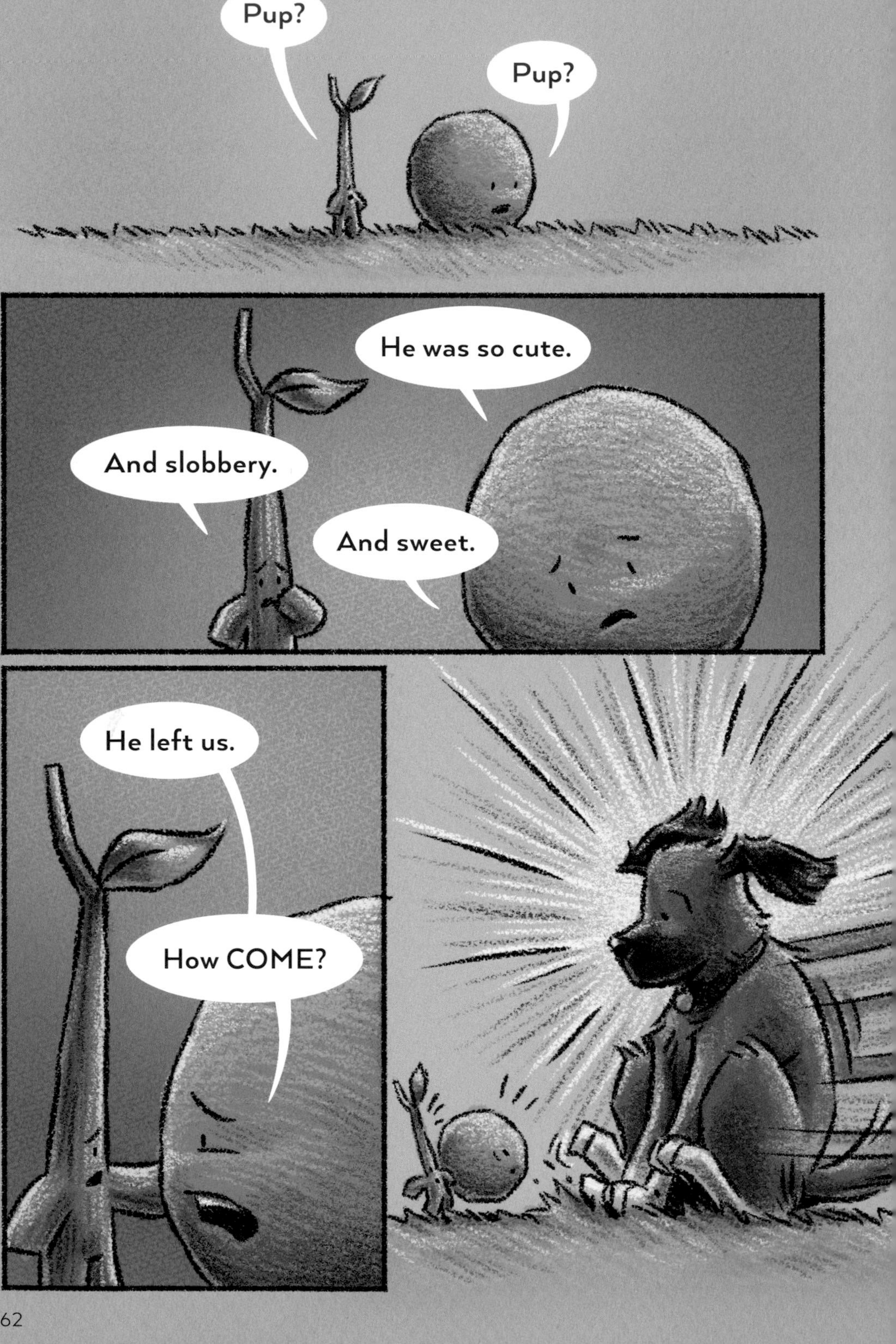
Pup?
Pup?
He was so cute.
And slobbery.
And sweet.
He left us.
How COME?

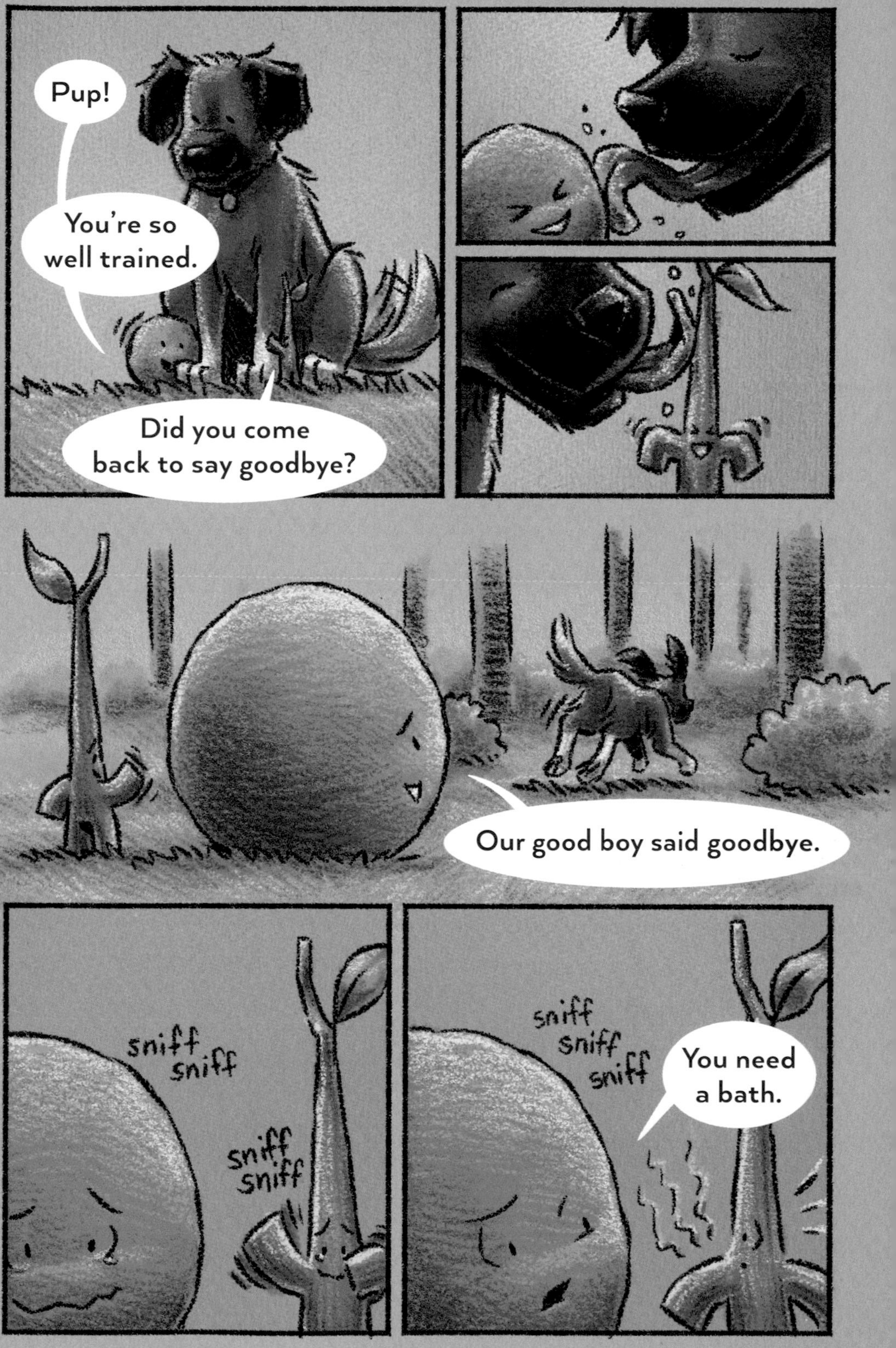
Pup!
You're so well trained.
Did you come back to say goodbye?
Our good boy said goodbye.
sniff sniff
sniff sniff
sniff sniff sniff
You need a bath.

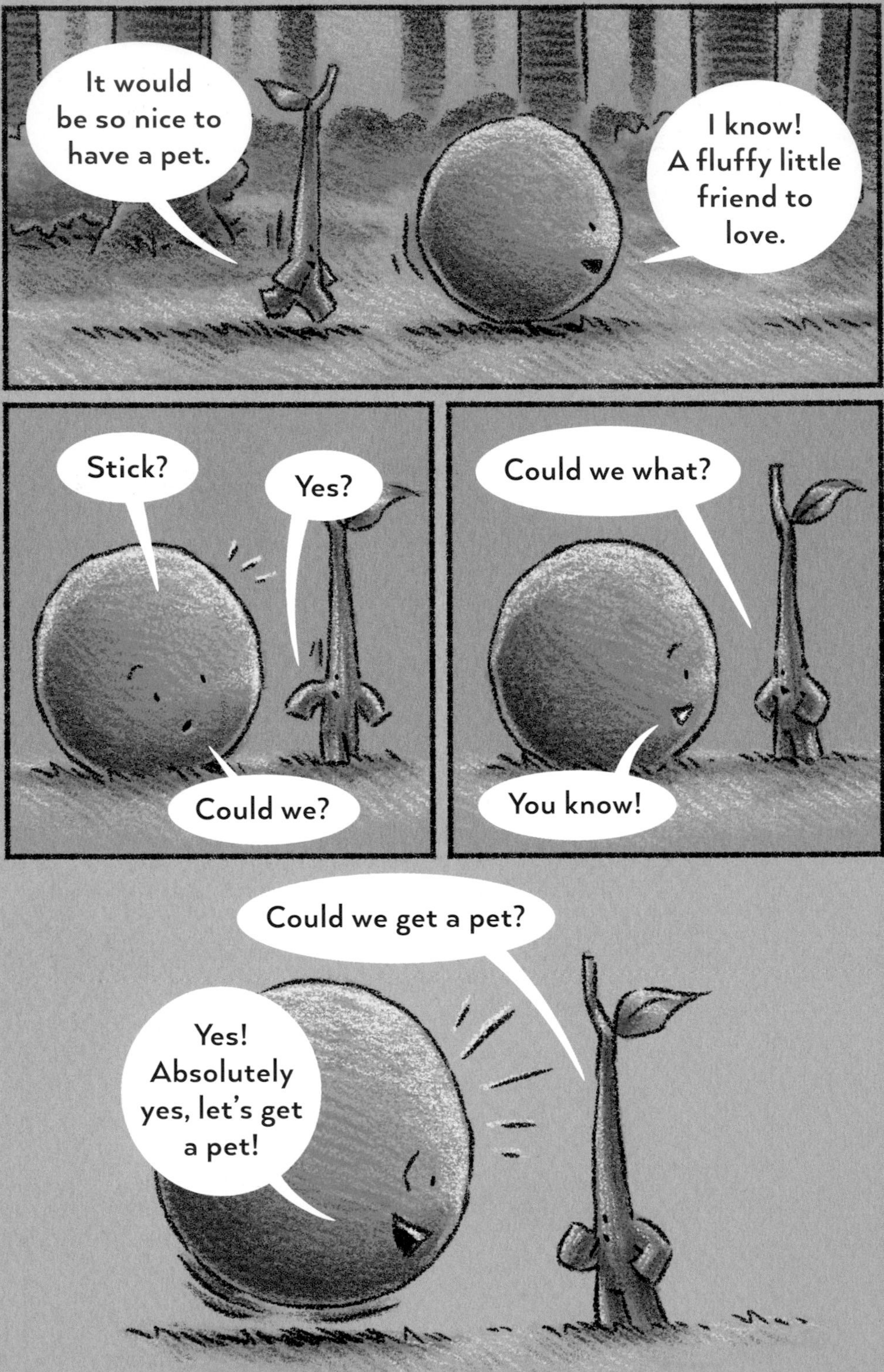
It would be so nice to have a pet.
I know! A fluffy little friend to love.
Stick?
Yes?
Could we?
Could we what?
You know!
Could we get a pet?
Yes! Absolutely yes, let's get a pet!

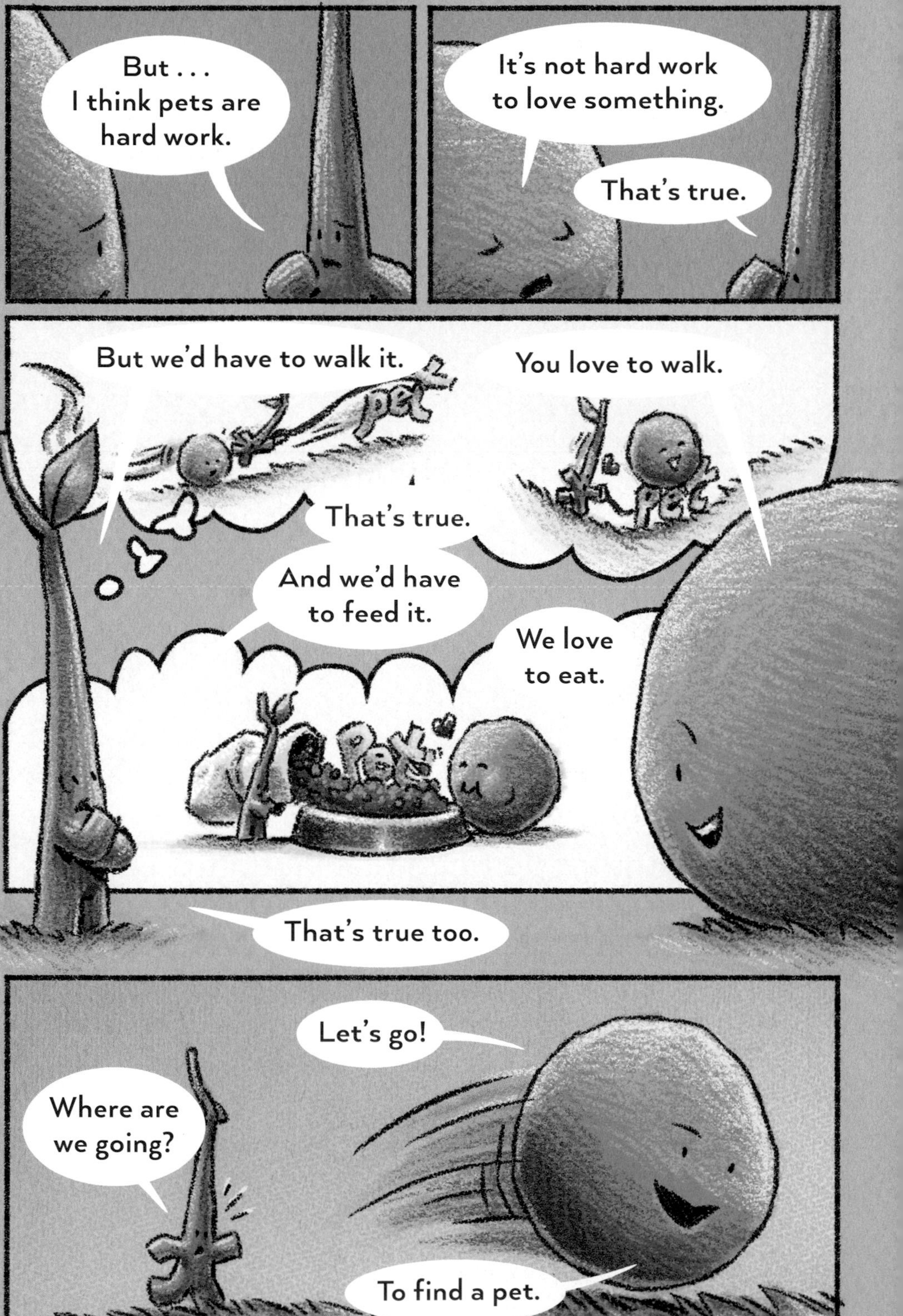
But . . .
I think pets are
hard work.
It's not hard work
to love something.
That's true.
But we'd have to walk it.
pet
You love to walk.
pet
That's true.
And we'd have
to feed it.
We love
to eat.
pet
That's true too.
Let's go!
Where are
we going?
To find a pet.

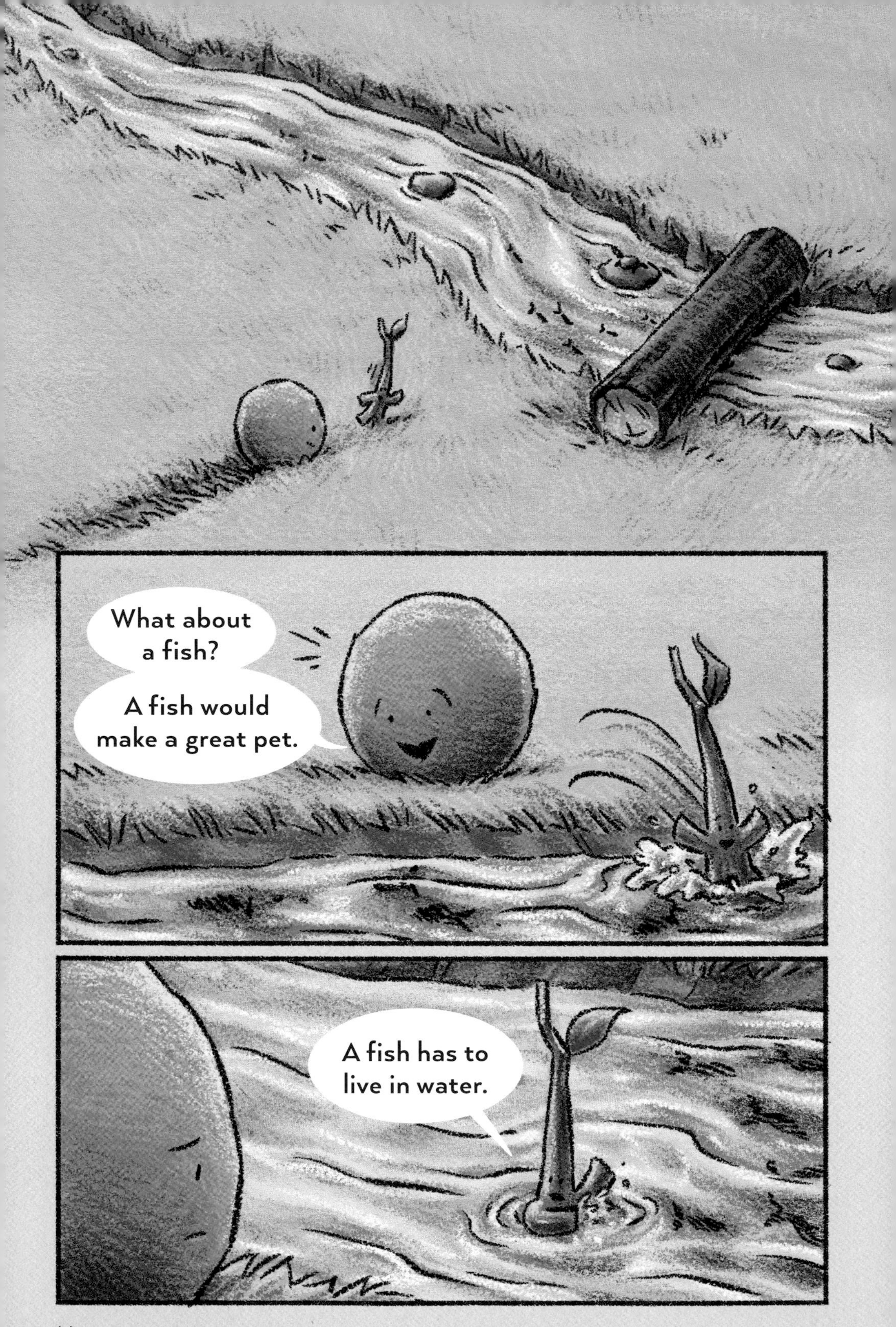
What about a fish?
A fish would make a great pet.
A fish has to live in water.

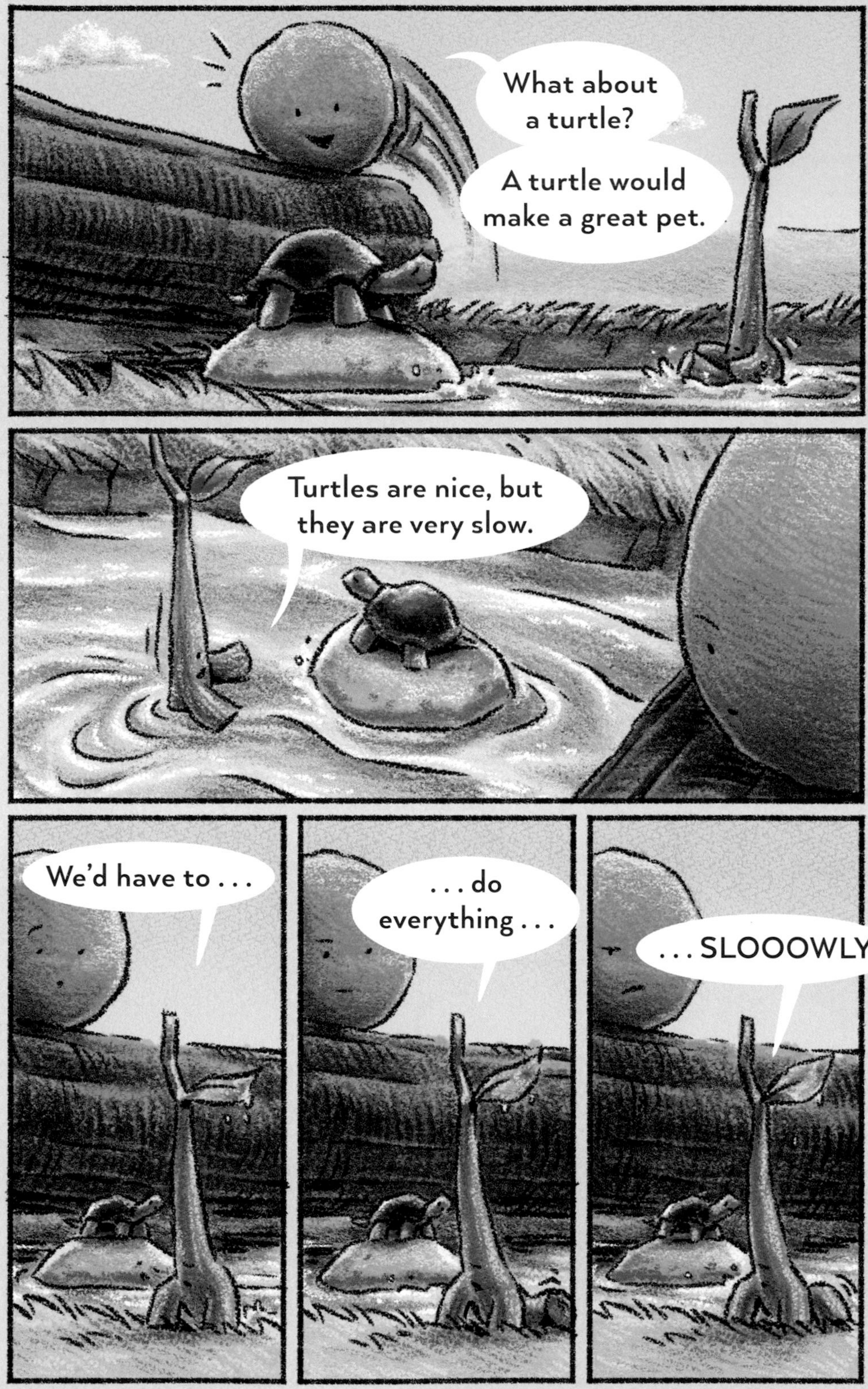
What about a turtle?
A turtle would make a great pet.
Turtles are nice, but they are very slow.
We'd have to . . .
. . . do everything . . .
. . . SLOOOWLY.

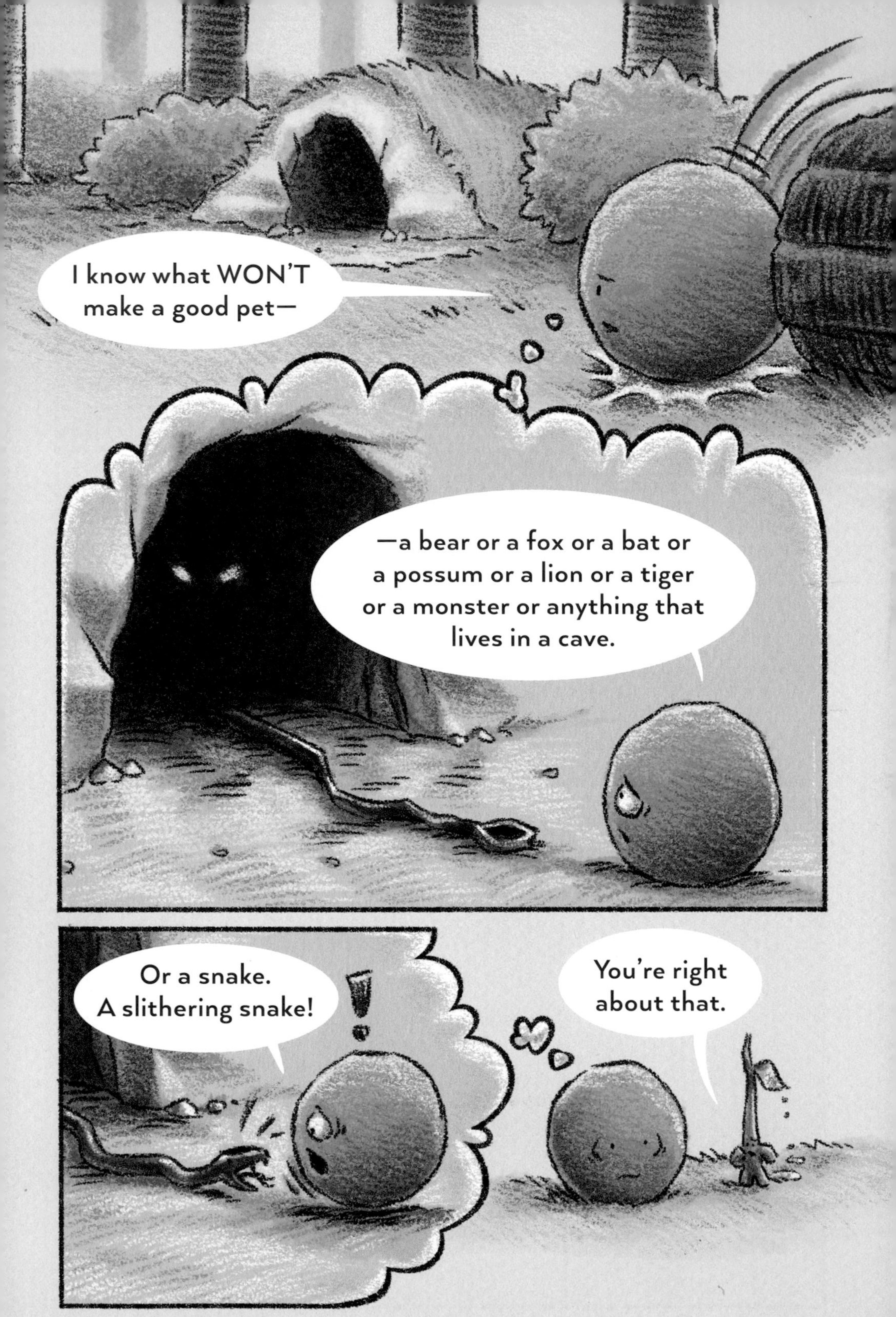
I know what WON'T make a good pet—
—a bear or a fox or a bat or a possum or a lion or a tiger or a monster or anything that lives in a cave.
Or a snake. A slithering snake!
You're right about that.

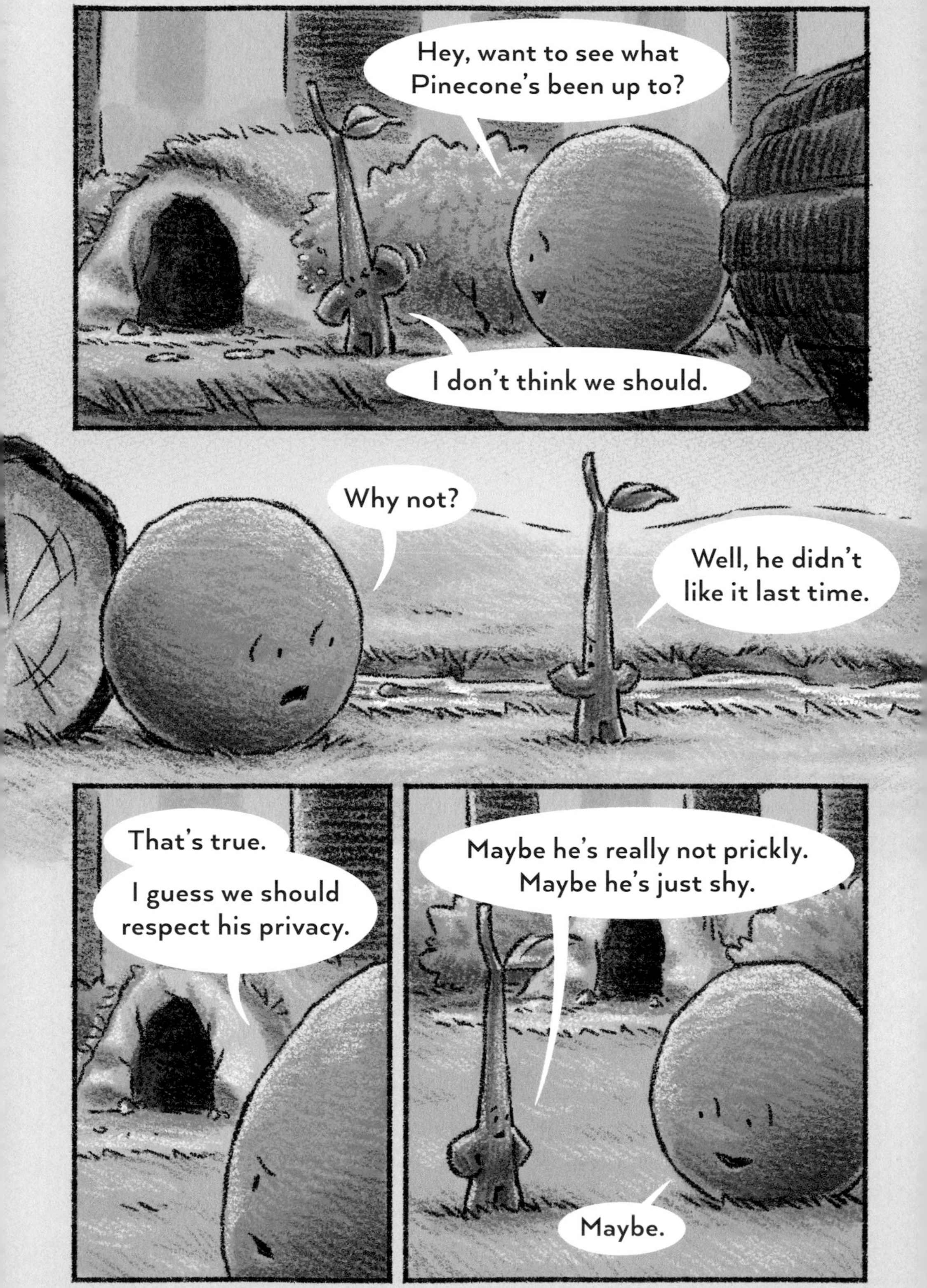
Hey, want to see what Pinecone's been up to?
I don't think we should.
Why not?
Well, he didn't like it last time.
That's true.
I guess we should respect his privacy.
Maybe he's really not prickly. Maybe he's just shy.
Maybe.

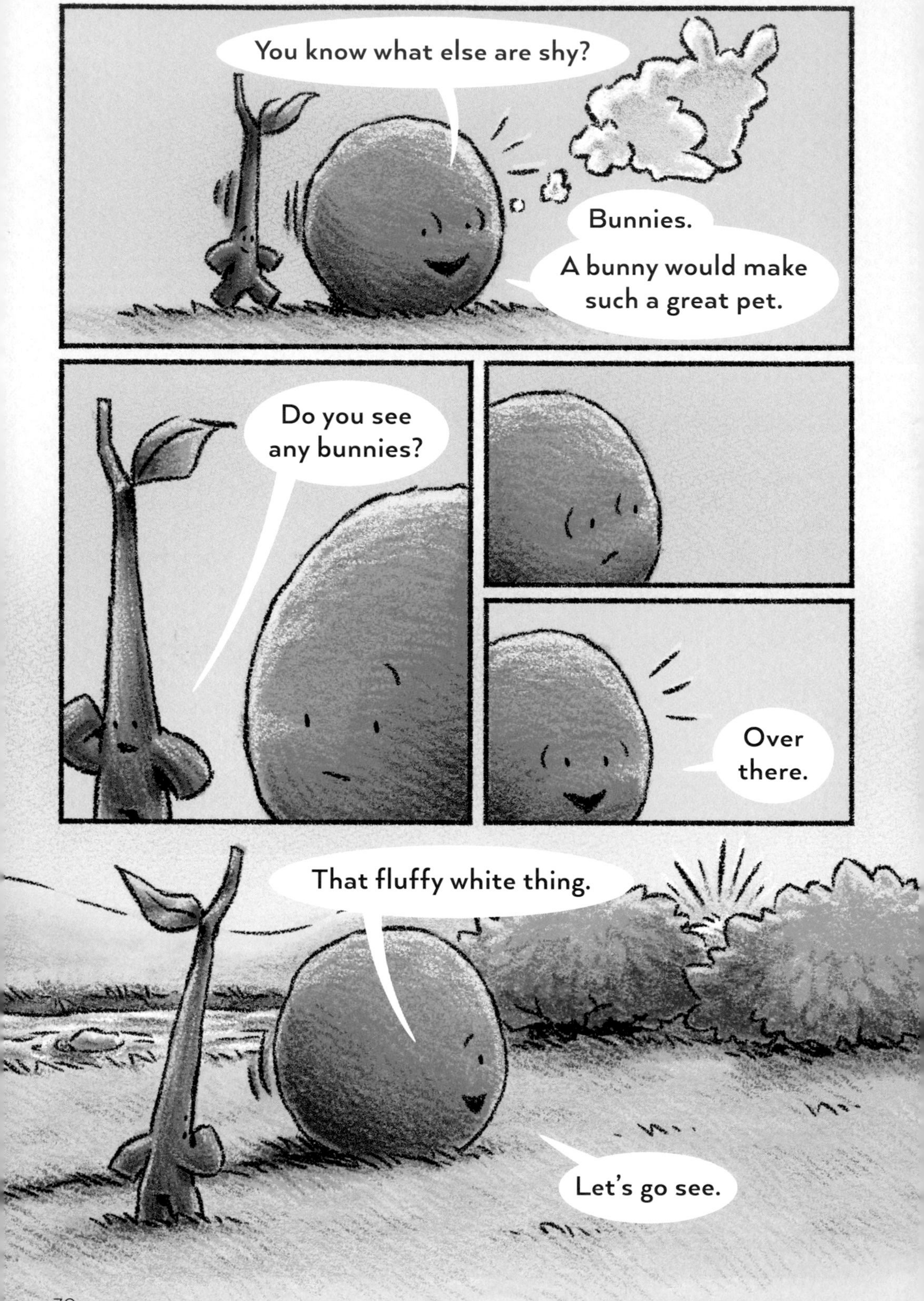
You know what else are shy?
Bunnies.
A bunny would make such a great pet.
Do you see any bunnies?
Over there.
That fluffy white thing.
Let's go see.

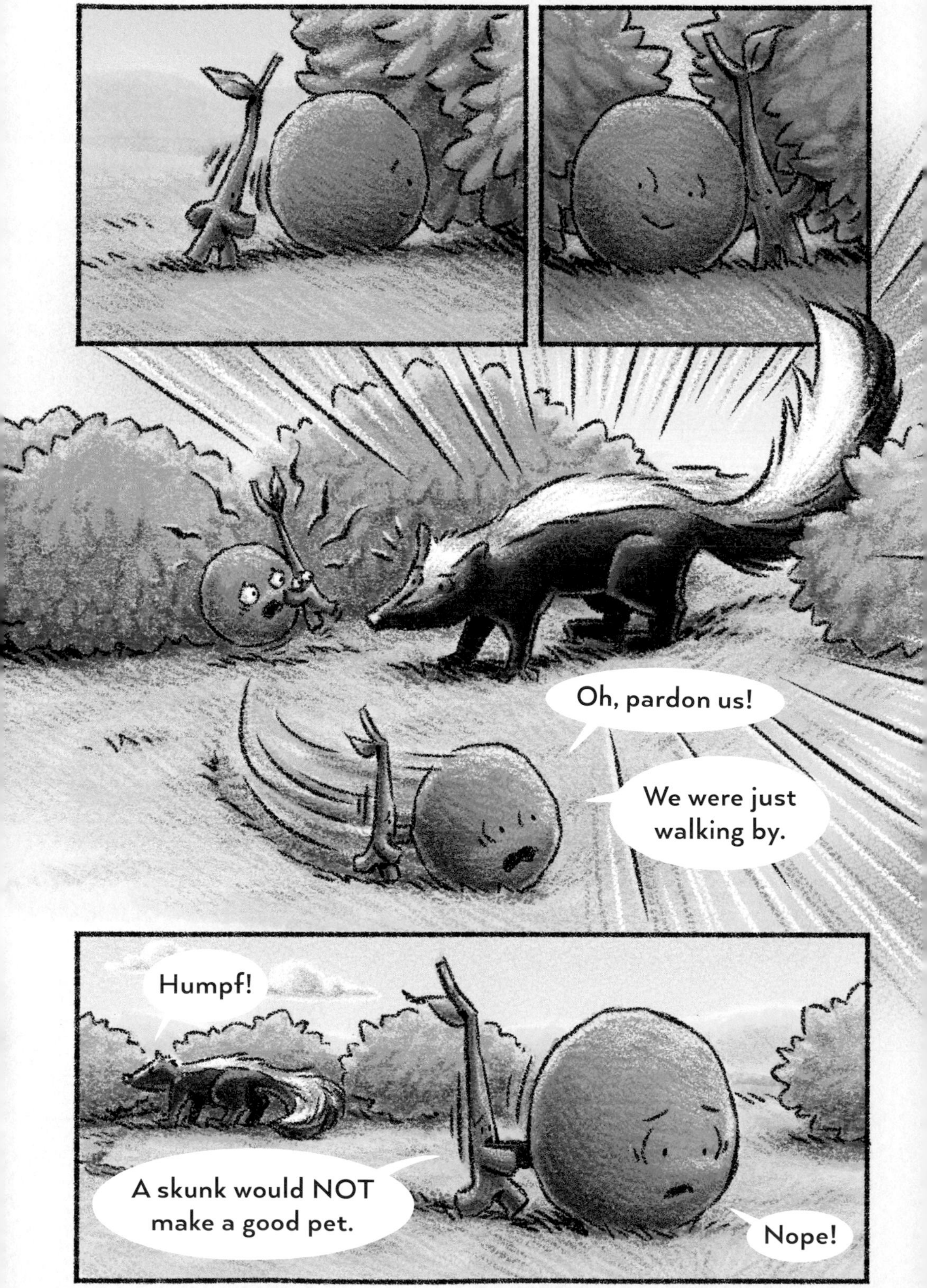

Oh, pardon us!
We were just walking by.
Humpf!
A skunk would NOT make a good pet.
Nope!

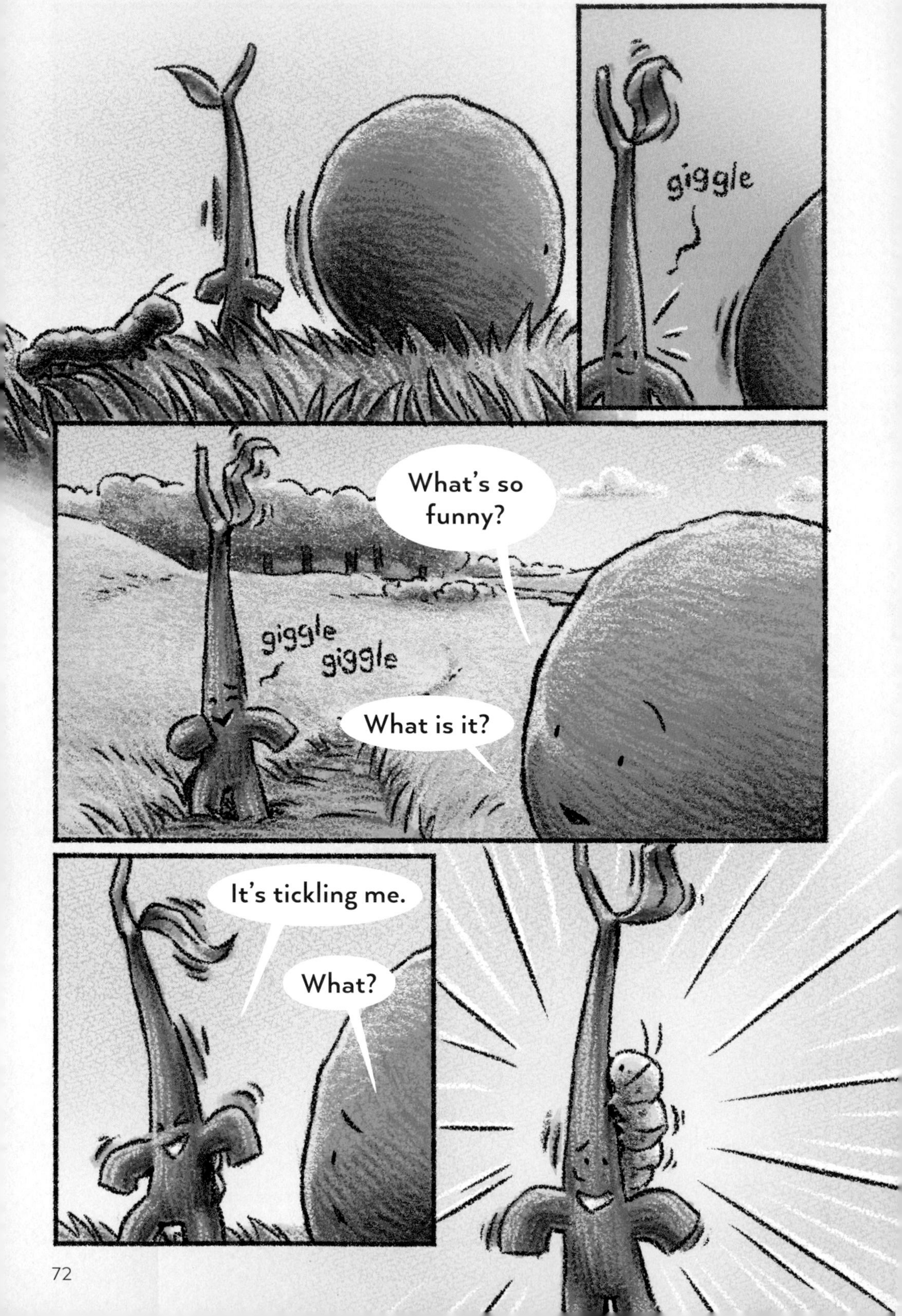
giggle
What's so funny?
giggle giggle
What is it?
It's tickling me.
What?

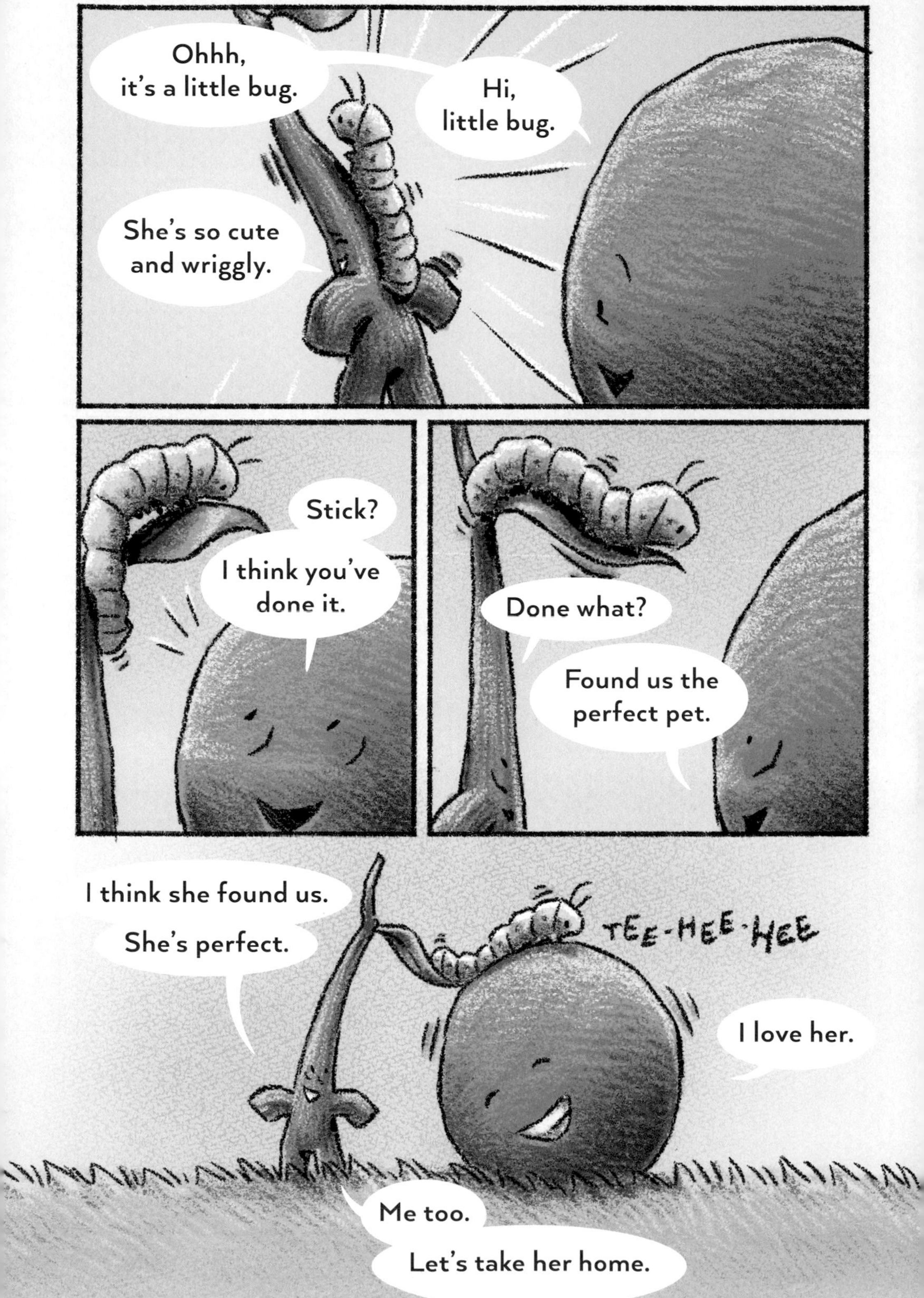

Ohhh, it's a little bug.
Hi, little bug.
She's so cute and wriggly.
Stick?
I think you've done it.
Done what?
Found us the perfect pet.
I think she found us.
She's perfect.
TEE-HEE-HEE
I love her.
Me too.
Let's take her home.

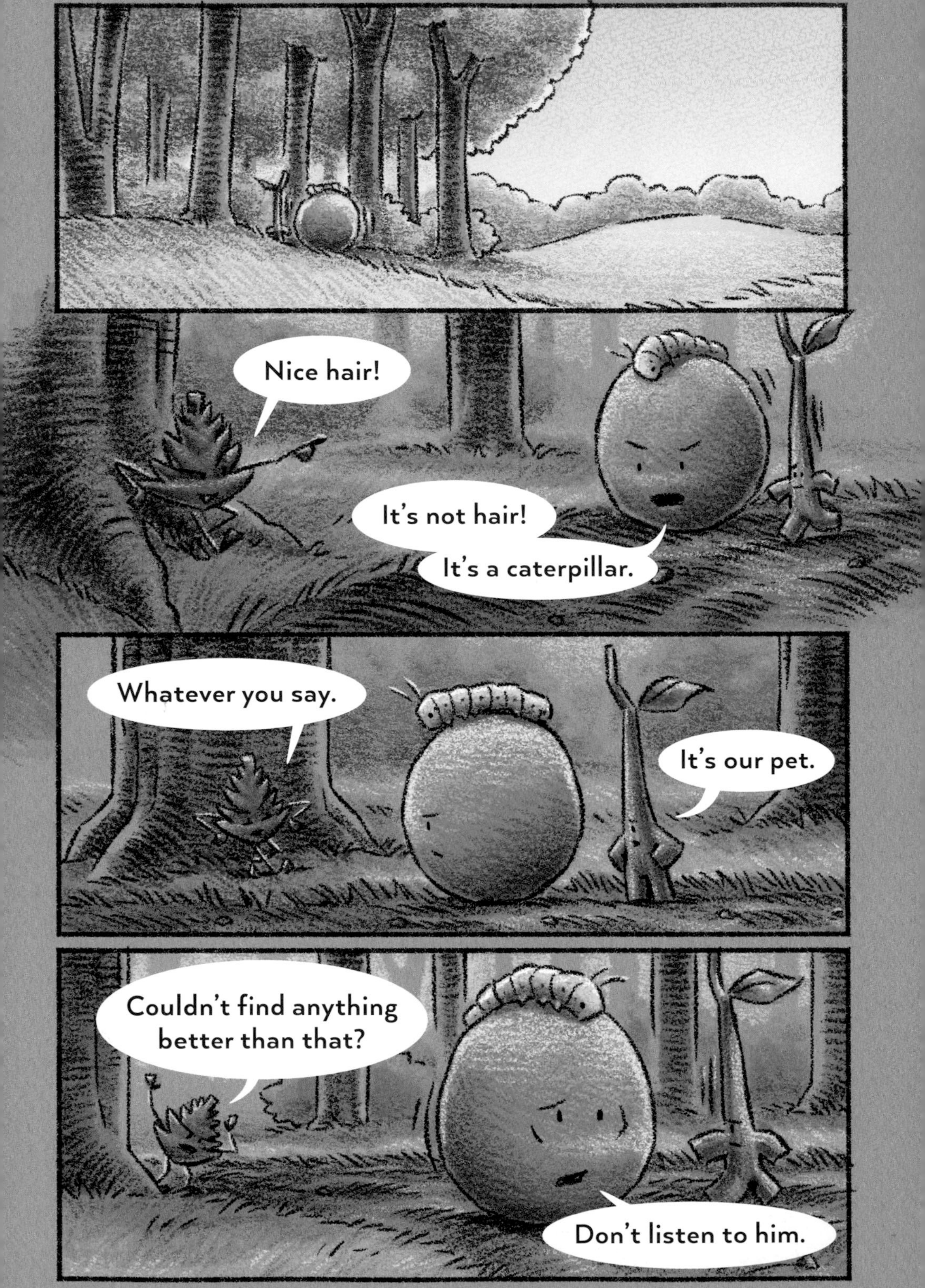
Nice hair!
It's not hair!
It's a caterpillar.
Whatever you say.
It's our pet.
Couldn't find anything better than that?
Don't listen to him.

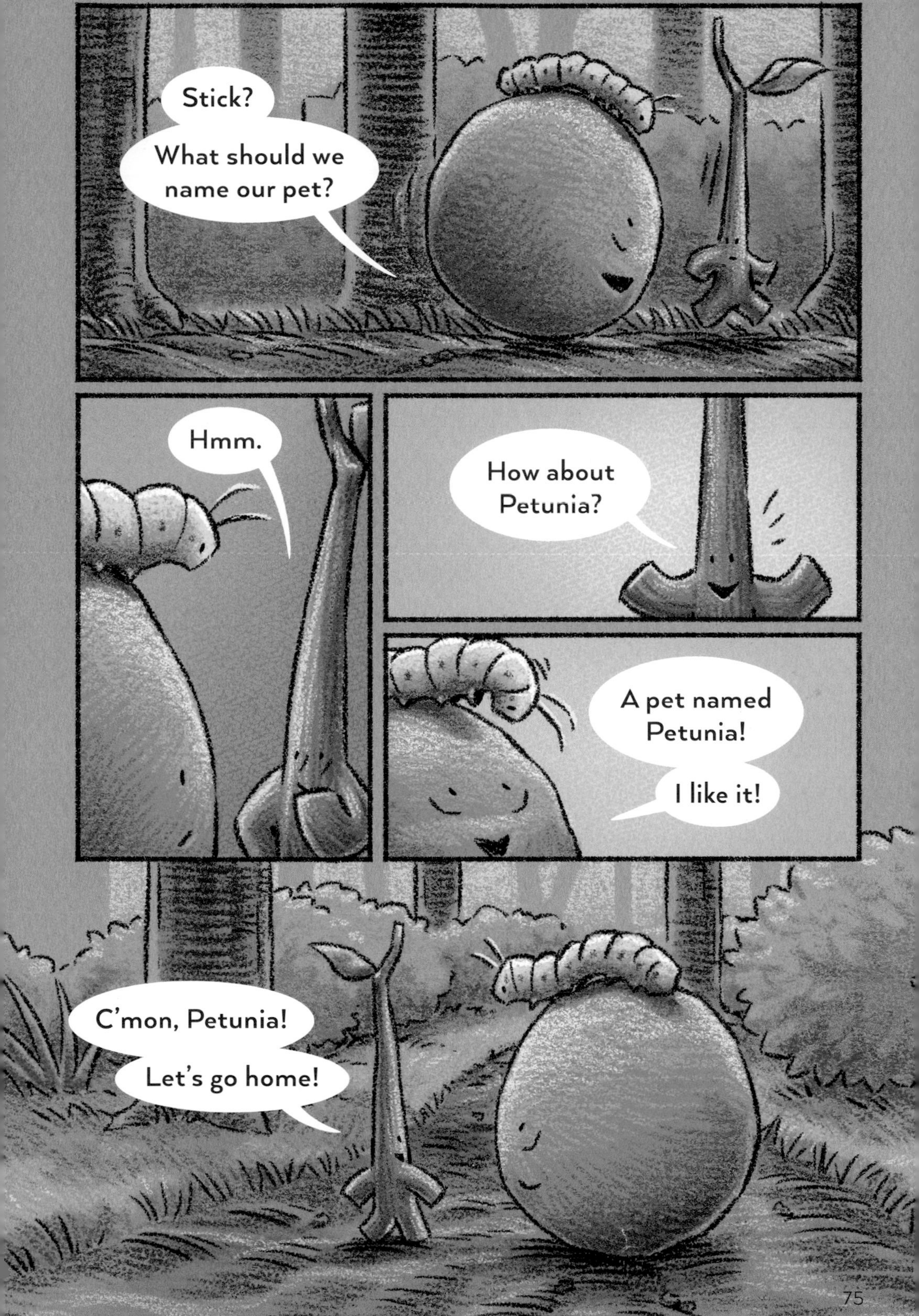
Stick?
What should we name our pet?
Hmm.
How about Petunia?
A pet named Petunia!
I like it!
C'mon, Petunia!
Let's go home!

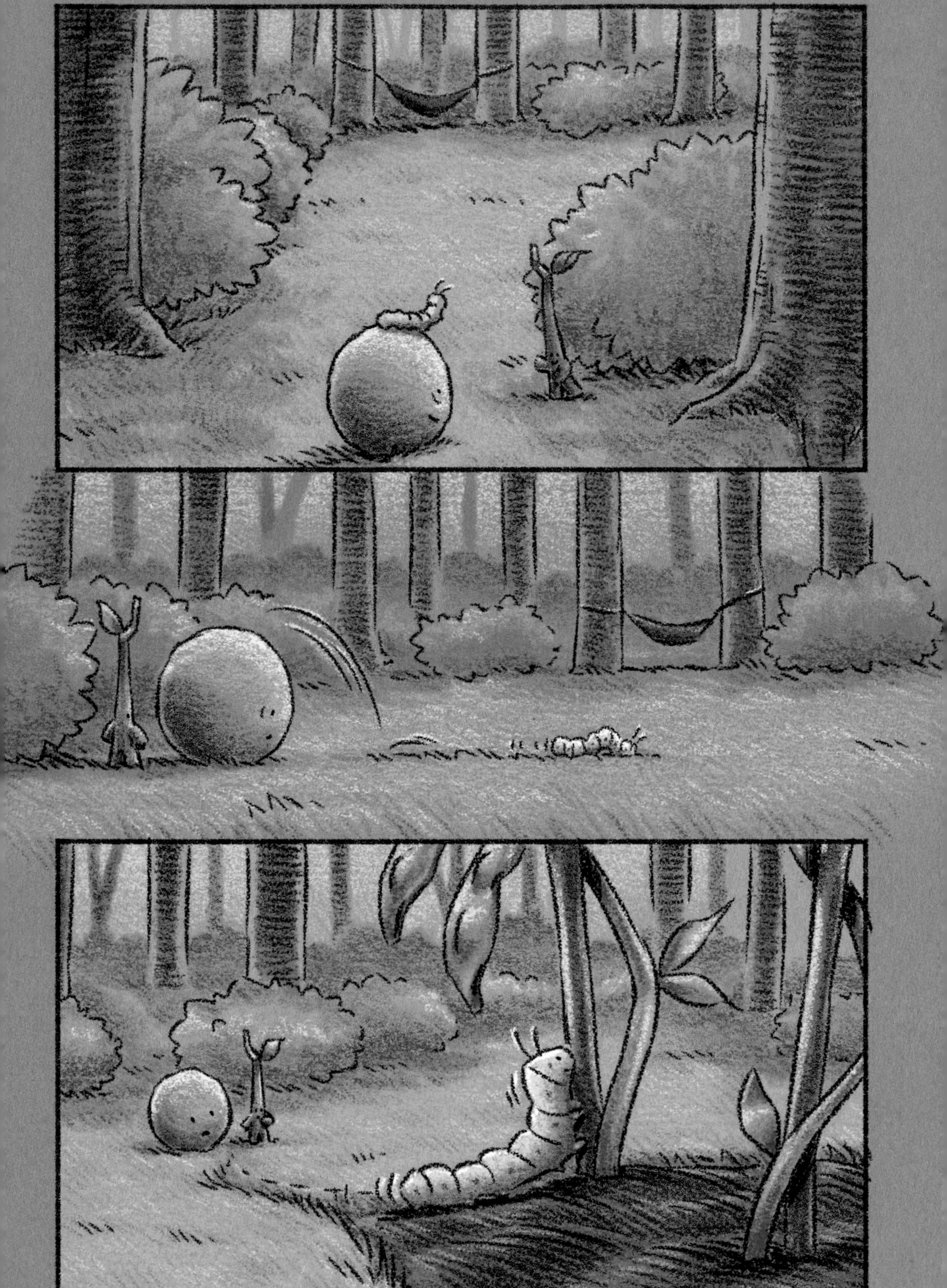

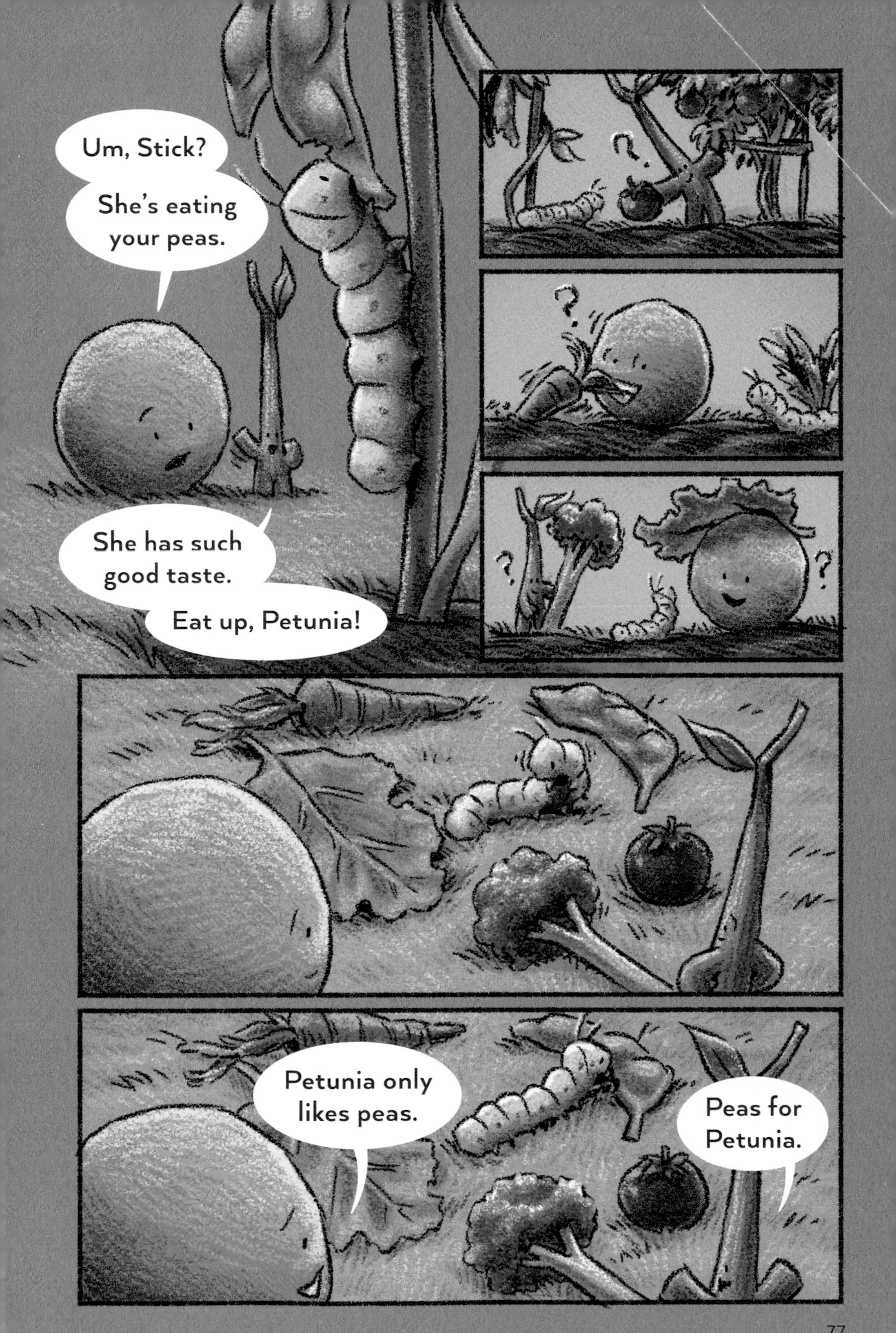
Um, Stick?
She's eating your peas.
She has such good taste.
Eat up, Petunia!
Petunia only likes peas.
Peas for Petunia.

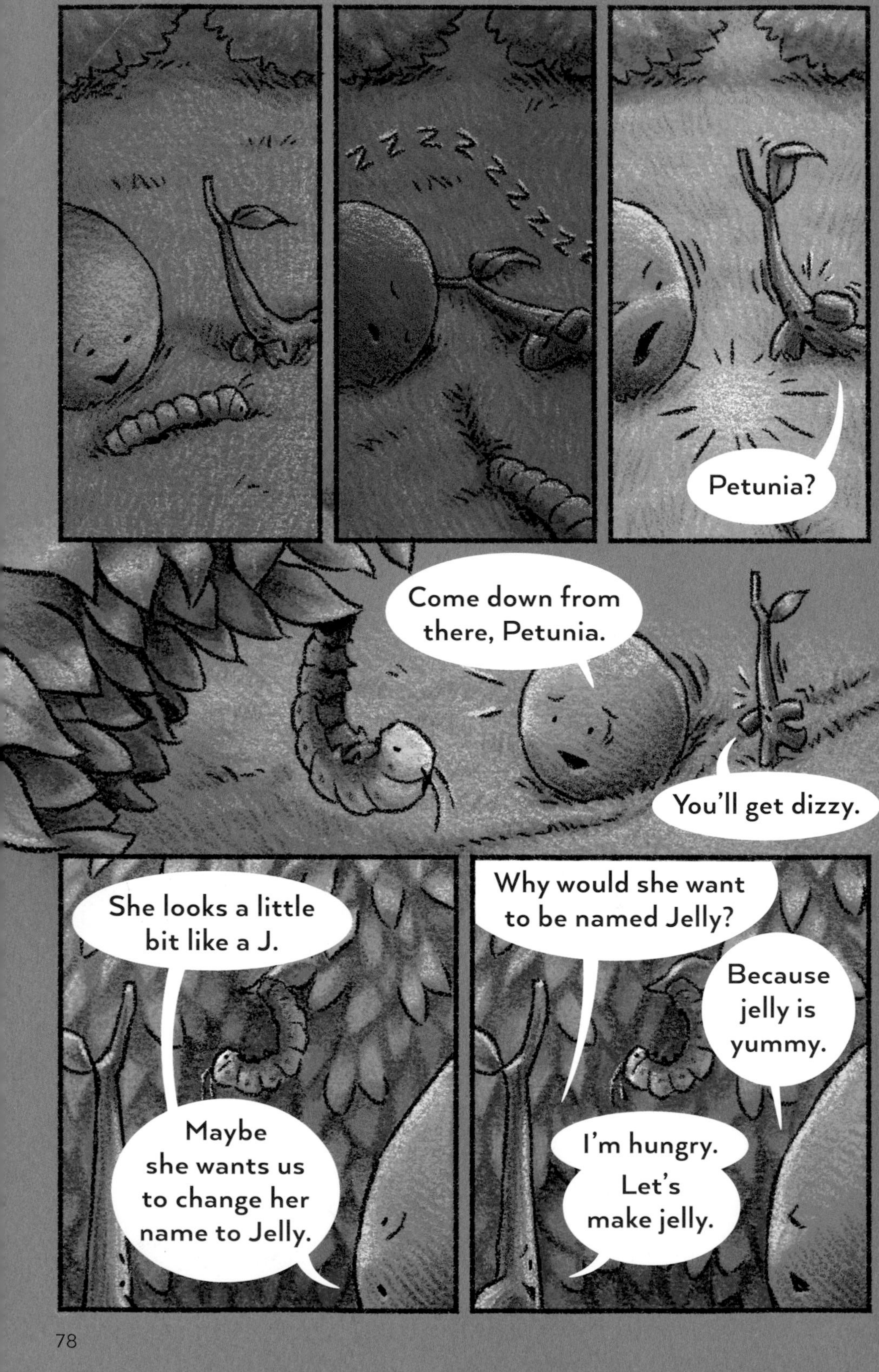

ZZZZZZZZZ
Petunia?
Come down from there, Petunia.
You'll get dizzy.
She looks a little bit like a J.
Maybe she wants us to change her name to Jelly.
Why would she want to be named Jelly?
Because jelly is yummy.
I'm hungry. Let's make jelly.

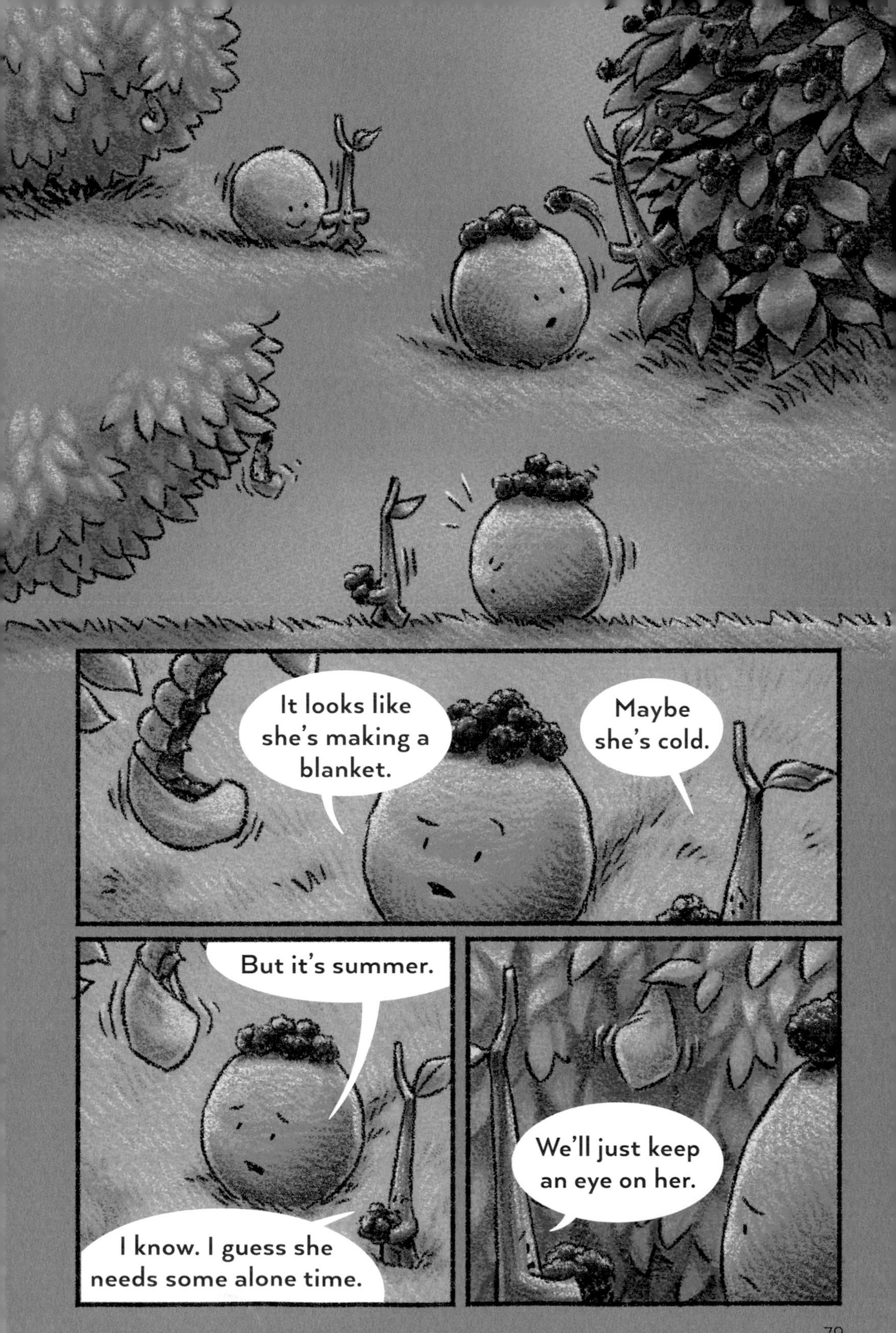
It looks like she's making a blanket.
Maybe she's cold.
But it's summer.
I know. I guess she needs some alone time.
We'll just keep an eye on her.

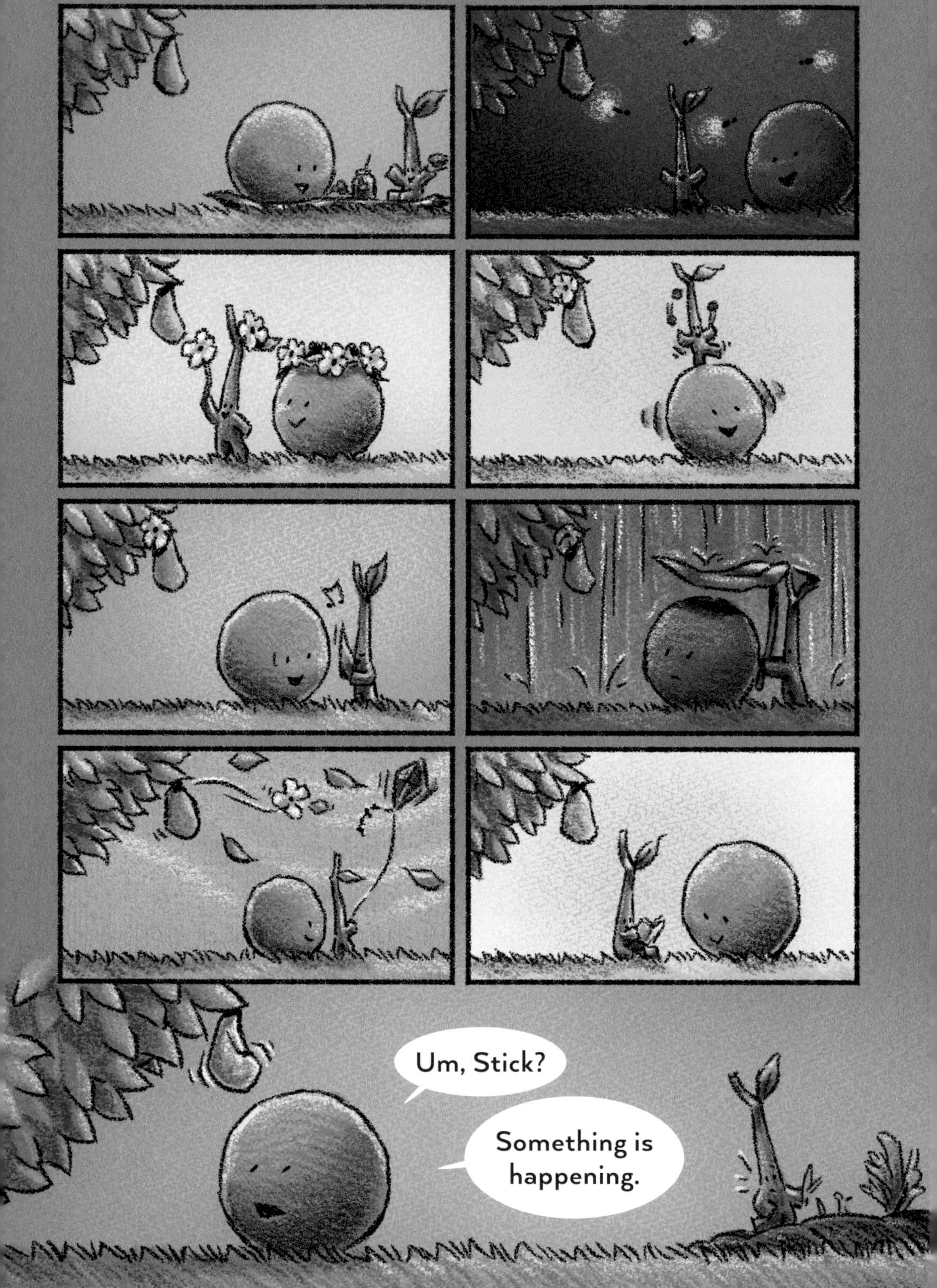
Um, Stick?
Something is happening.

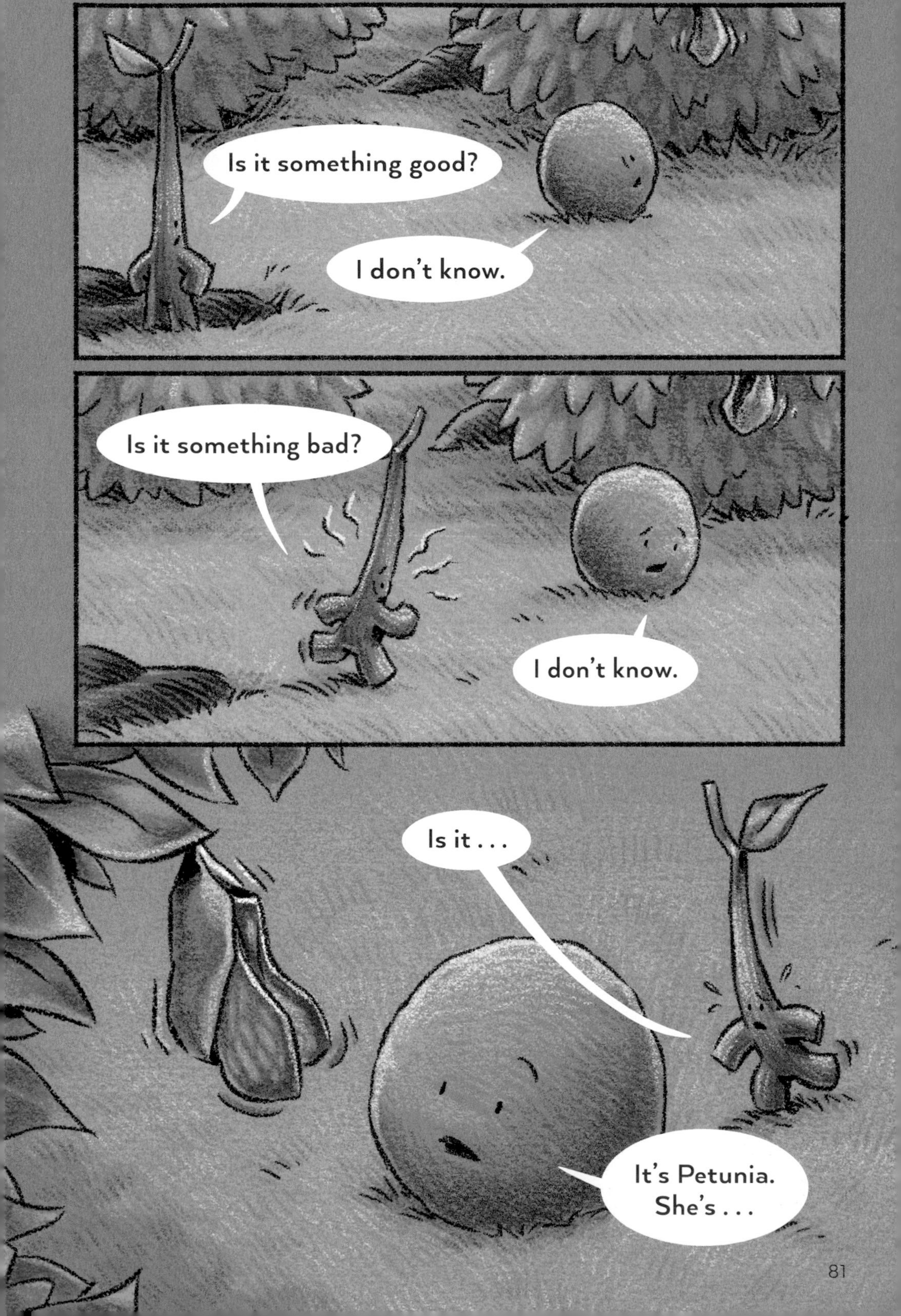
Is it something good?
I don't know.
Is it something bad?
I don't know.
Is it . . .
It's Petunia. She's . . .

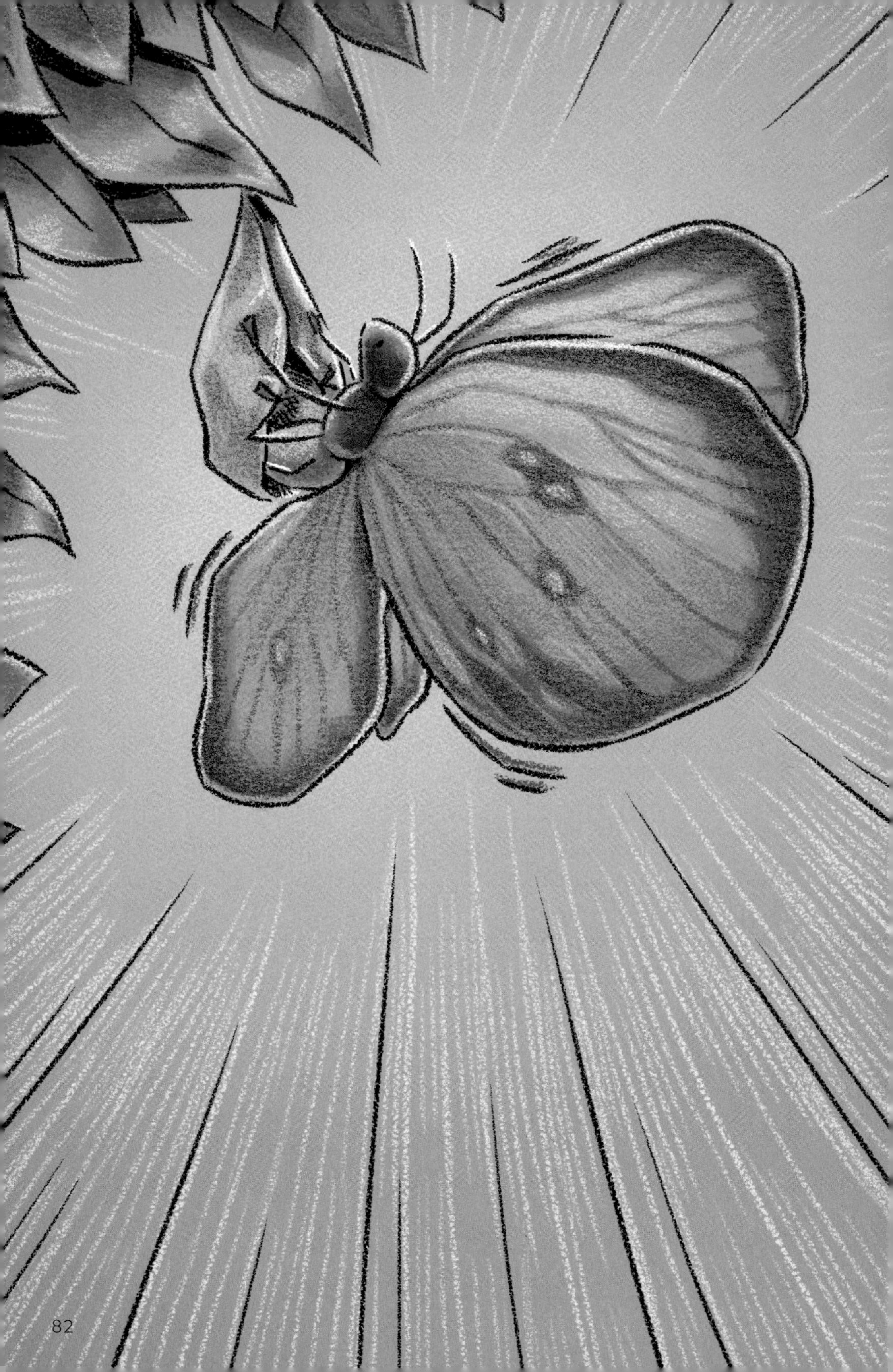

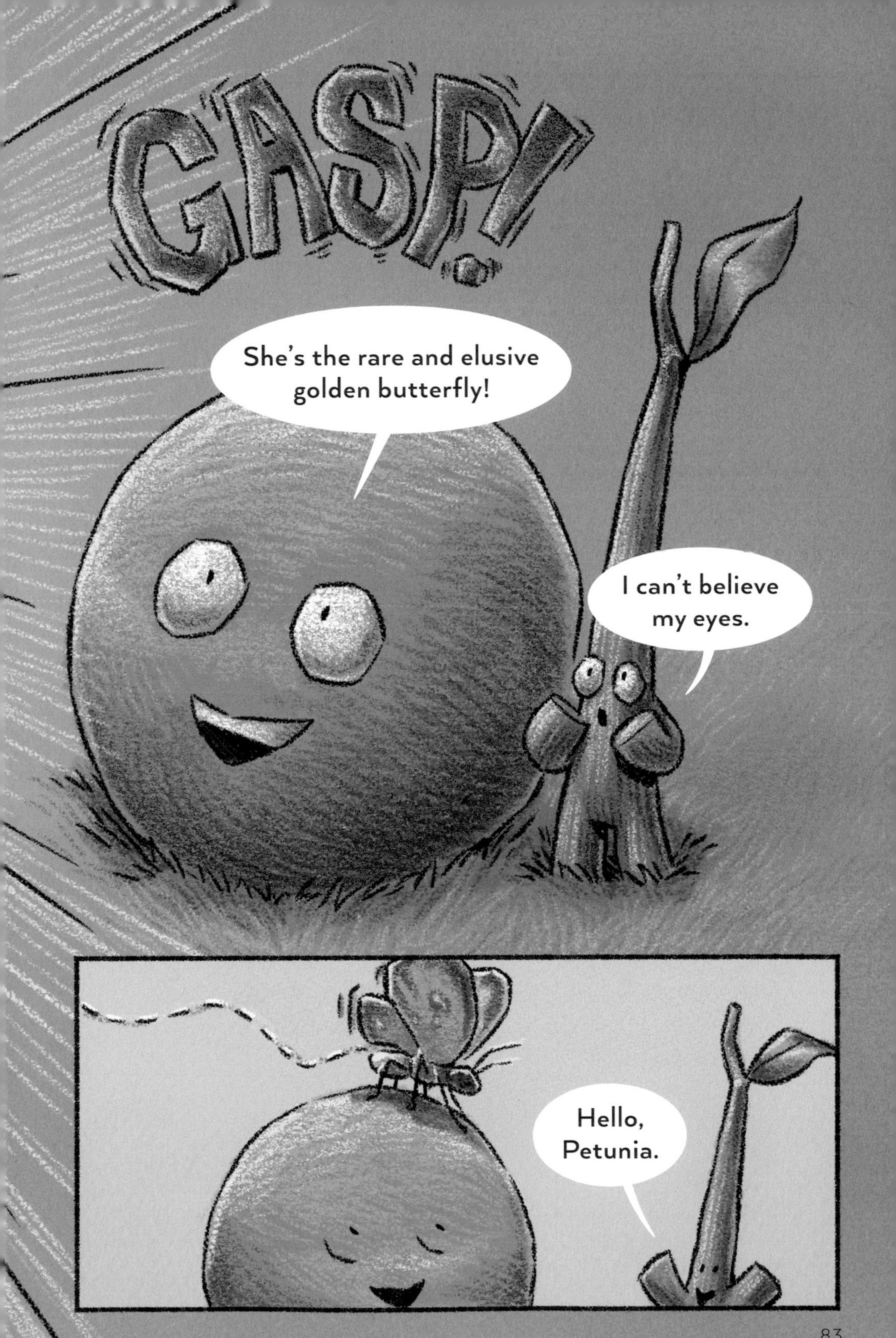
GASP!
She's the rare and elusive golden butterfly!
I can't believe my eyes.
Hello, Petunia.

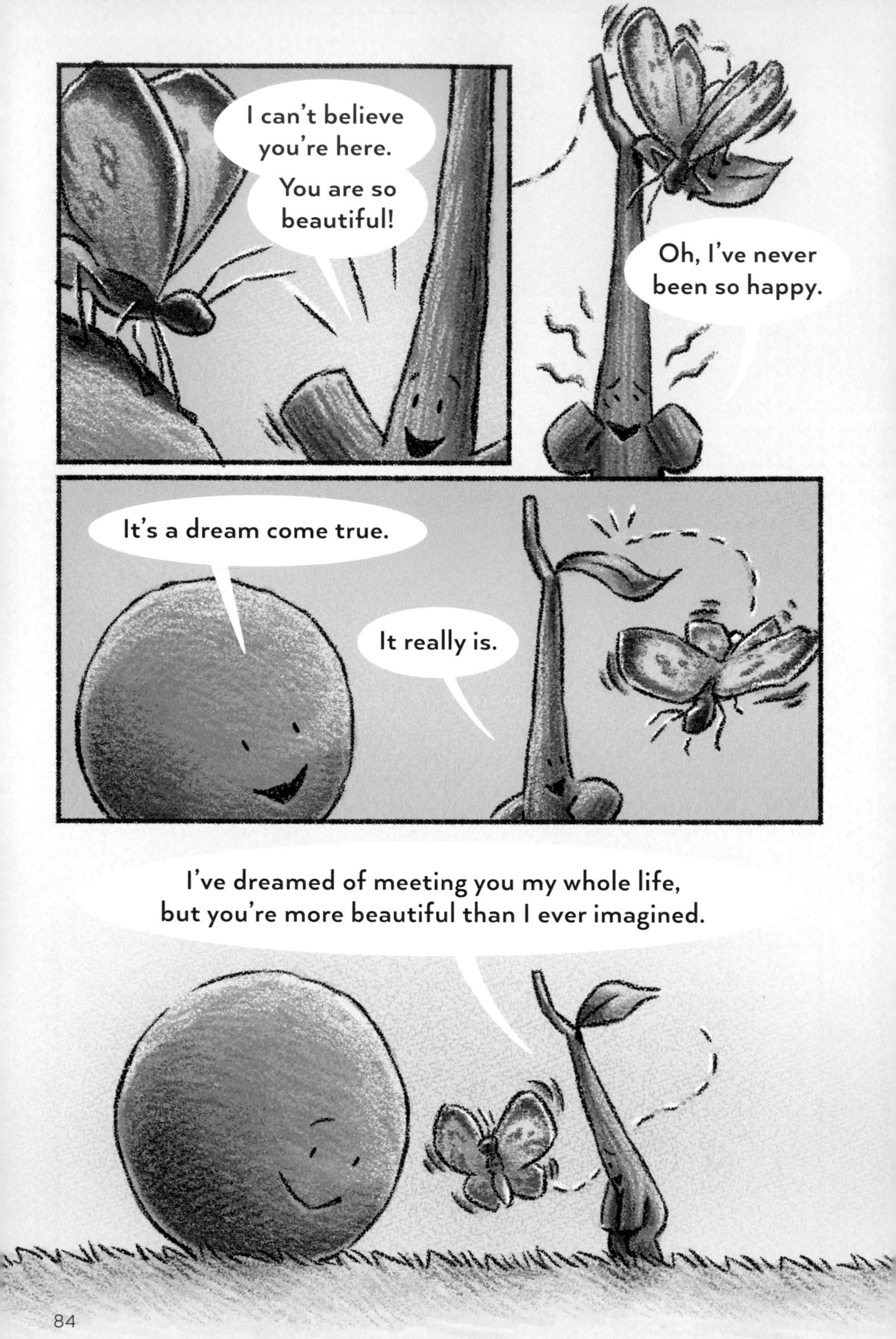
I can't believe you're here.
You are so beautiful!
Oh, I've never been so happy.
It's a dream come true.
It really is.
I've dreamed of meeting you my whole life, but you're more beautiful than I ever imagined.

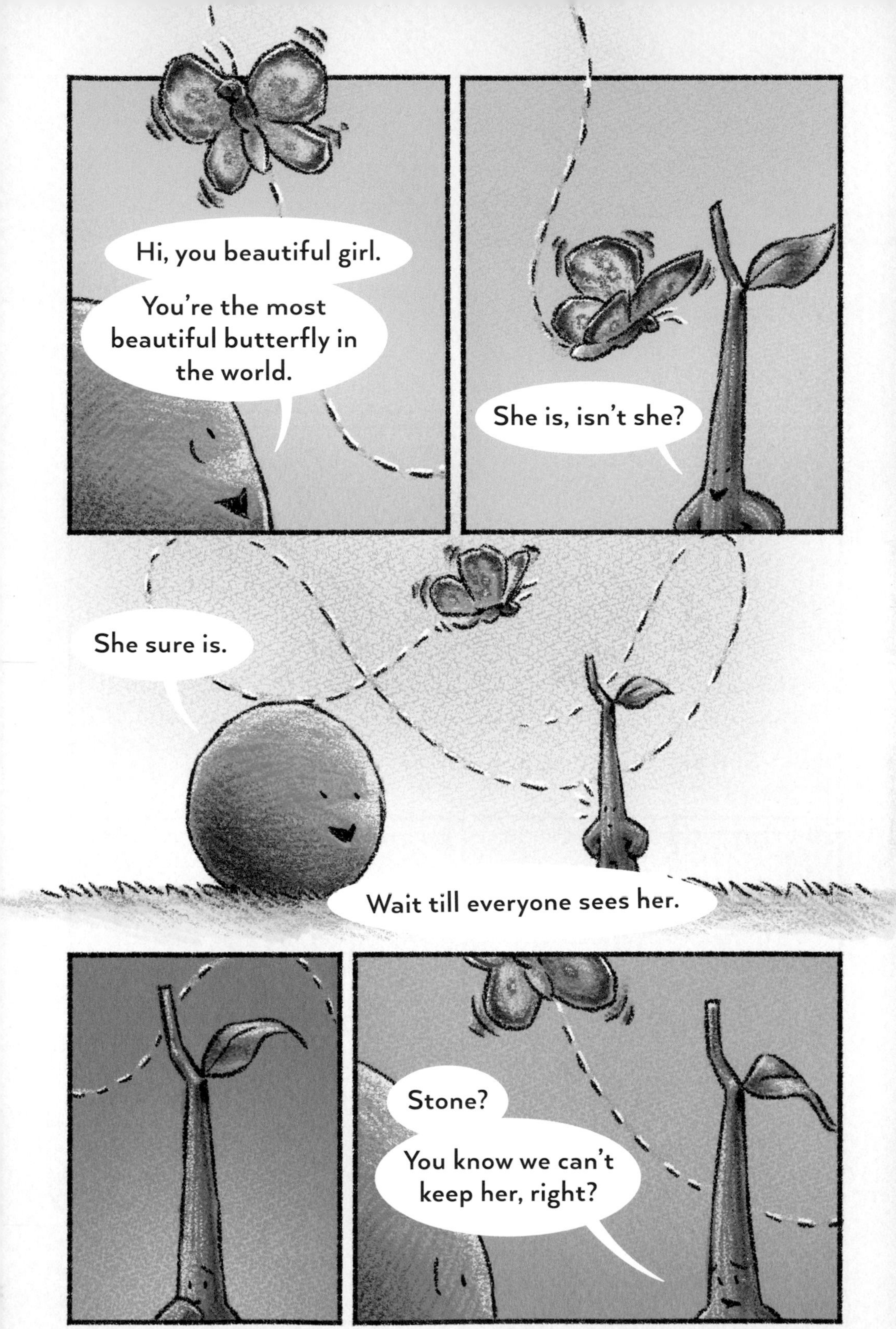
Hi, you beautiful girl.
You're the most beautiful butterfly in the world.
She is, isn't she?
She sure is.
Wait till everyone sees her.
Stone?
You know we can't keep her, right?

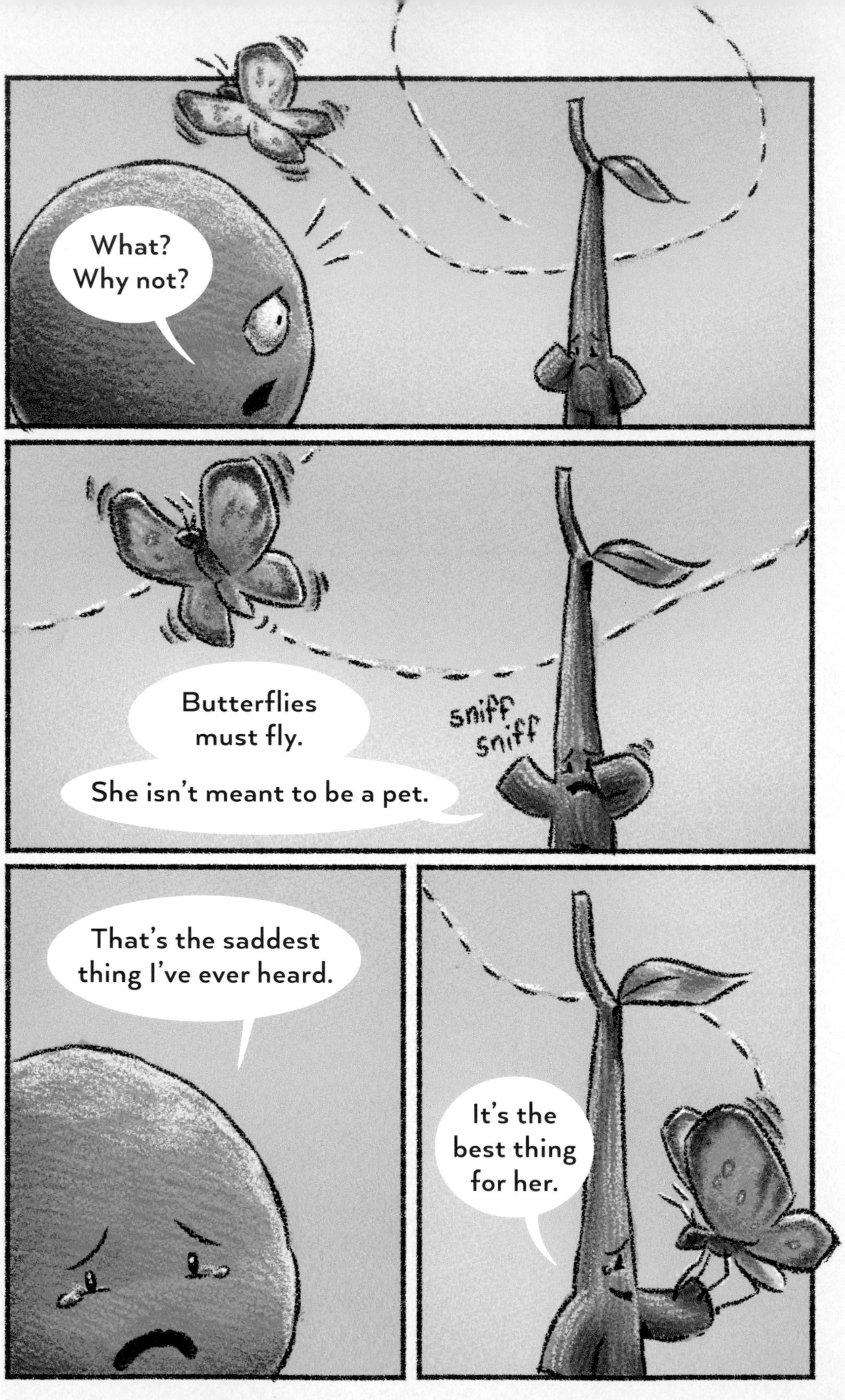
What? Why not?
Butterflies must fly.
She isn't meant to be a pet.
sniff sniff
That's the saddest thing I've ever heard.
It's the best thing for her.

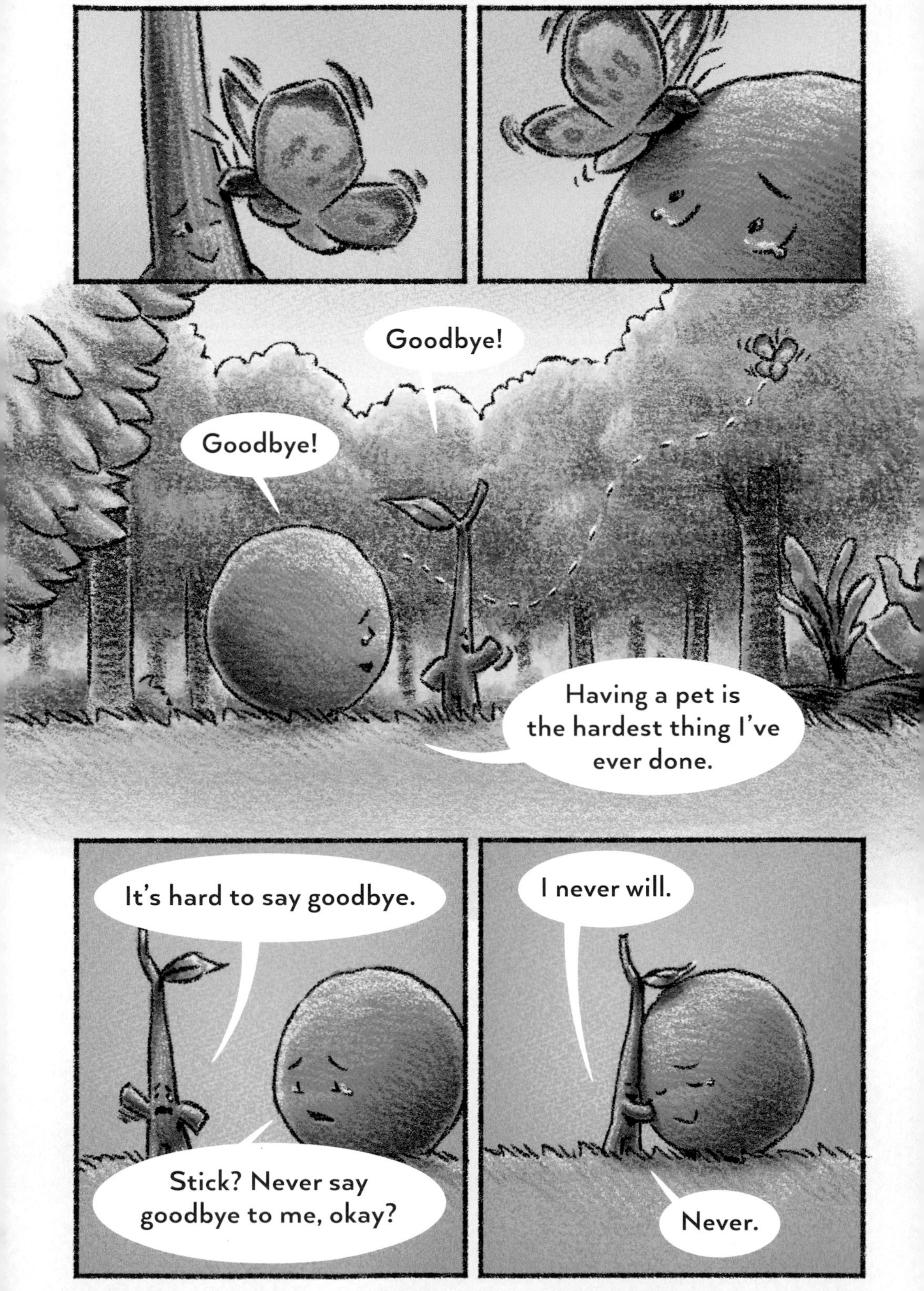
Goodbye!
Goodbye!
Having a pet is the hardest thing I've ever done.
It's hard to say goodbye.
Stick? Never say goodbye to me, okay?
I never will.
Never.

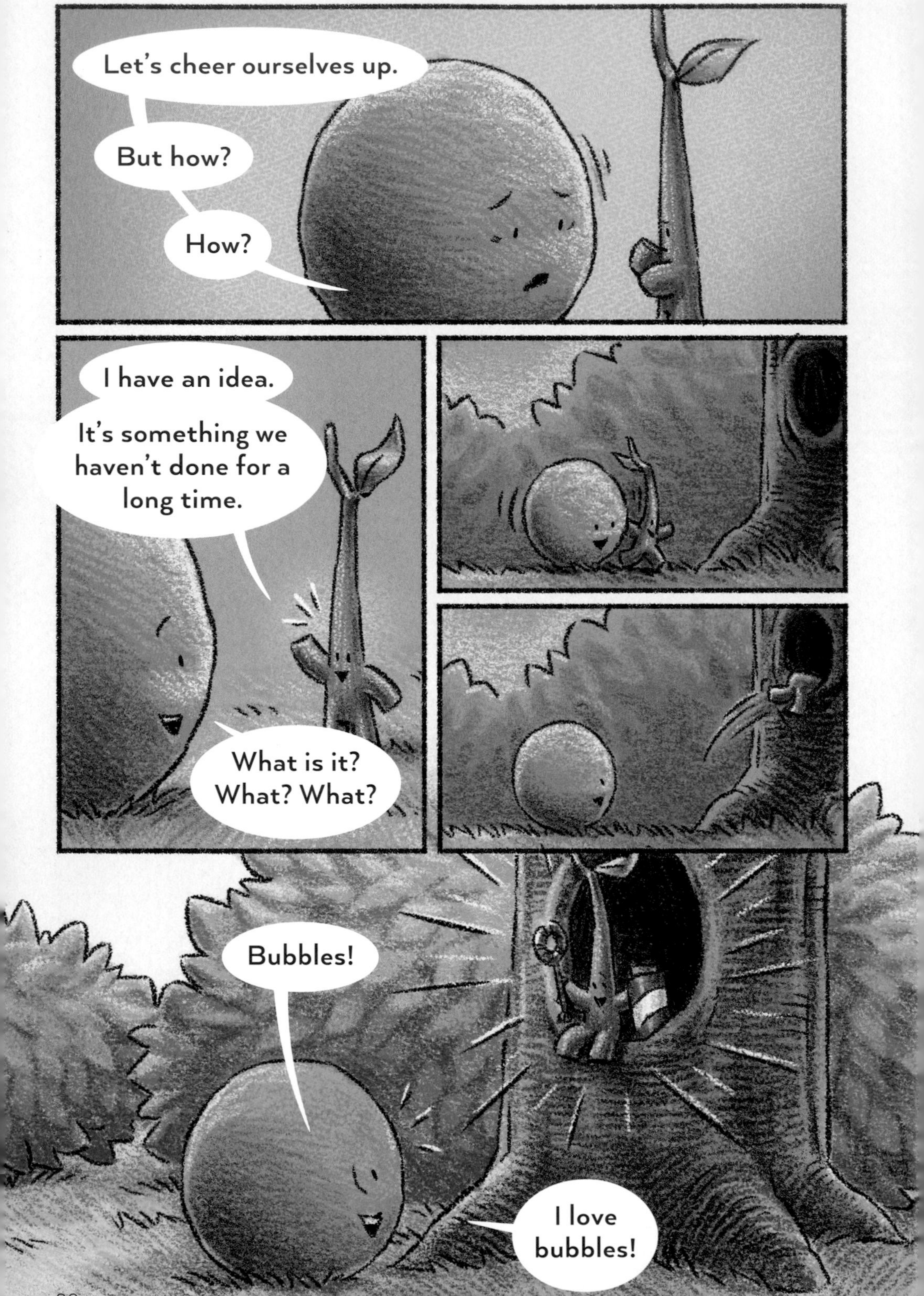
Let's cheer ourselves up.
But how?
How?
I have an idea.
It's something we haven't done for a long time.
What is it? What? What?
Bubbles!
I love bubbles!

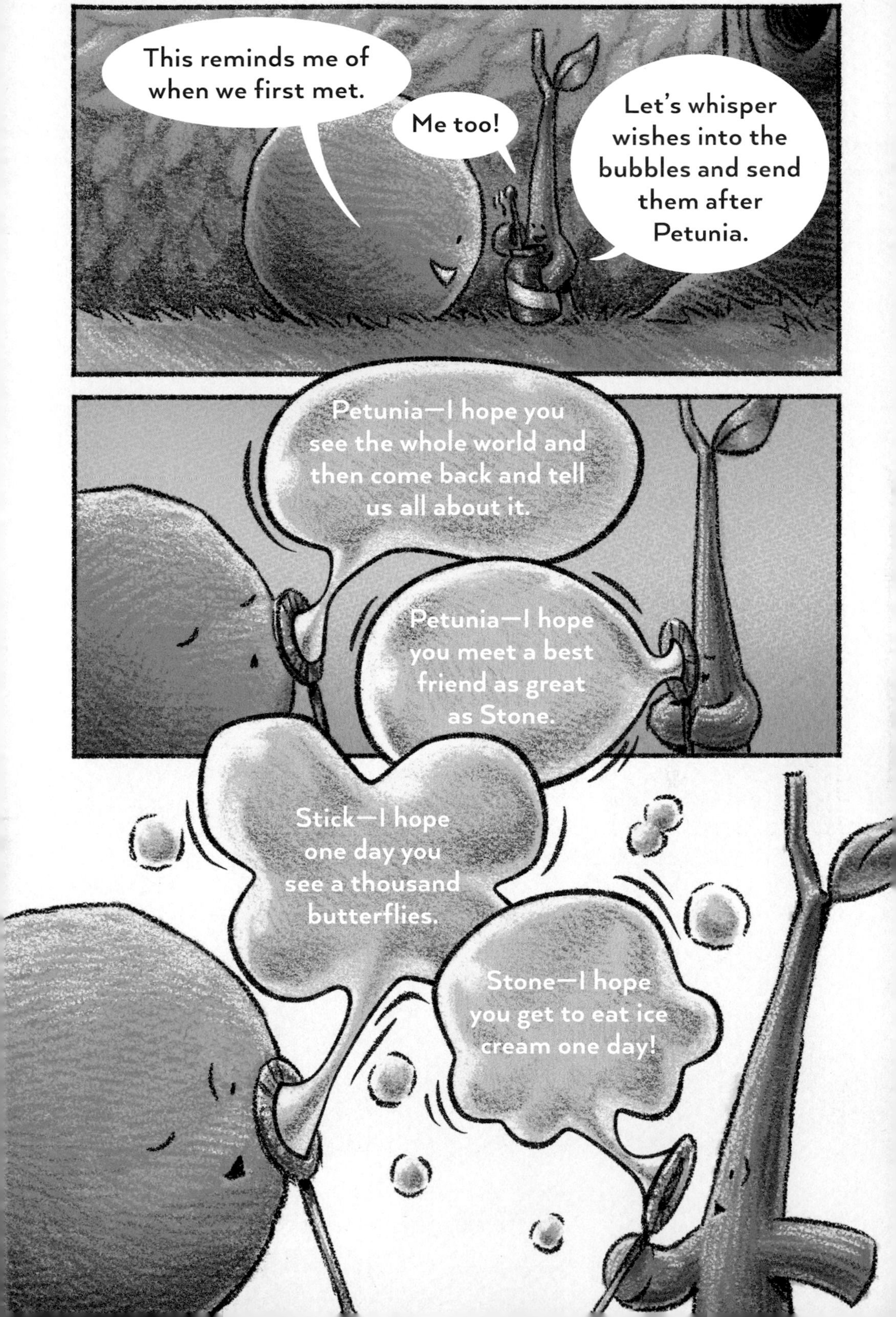
This reminds me of when we first met.
Me too!
Let's whisper wishes into the bubbles and send them after Petunia.
Petunia—I hope you see the whole world and then come back and tell us all about it.
Petunia—I hope you meet a best friend as great as Stone.
Stick—I hope one day you see a thousand butterflies.
Stone—I hope you get to eat ice cream one day!

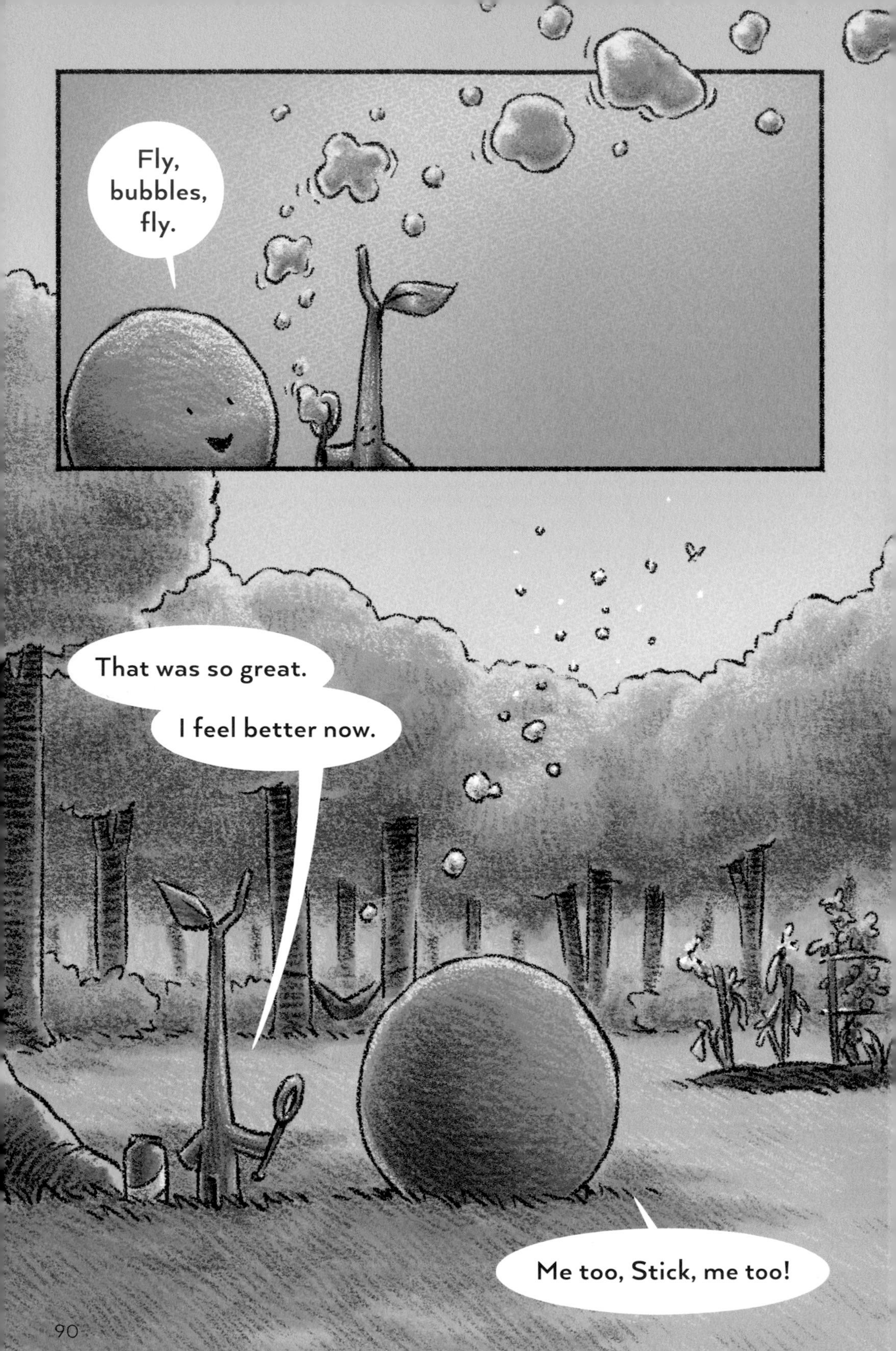
Fly, bubbles, fly.
That was so great.
I feel better now.
Me too, Stick, me too!

BUTTERFLY AND BUBBLE ACTIVITIES

Stick and Leaf Golden Butterfly Craft

What you'll need:

- Sticks (1 per butterfly)
- Leaves (4 per butterfly, preferably 2 larger and 2 smaller)
- Clothespins (1 per butterfly)
- Scissors
- Glue gun
- Black marker
- Gold permanent marker or paint pen

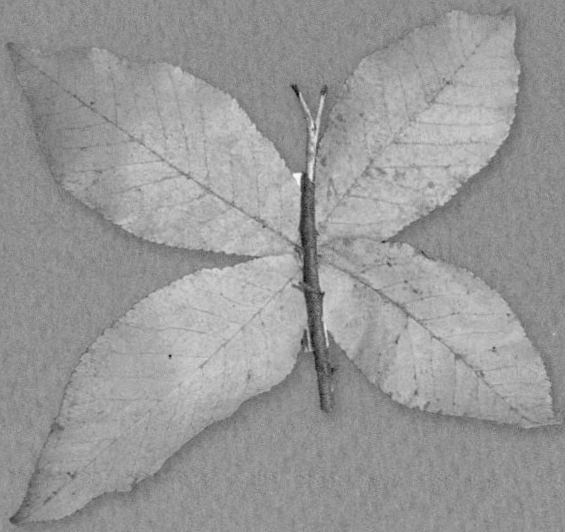

Directions:

1. Go on a nature walk and collect sticks and rounded leaves in any color. If it's fall, try to find some yellow leaves.
2. If you have time, press the leaves in a thick book overnight.
3. If yellow leaves are hard to find, use the gold permanent marker or paint pen to color your leaves.
4. Vertically snip the very top of your stick to split it and make two antennae. Color the tips black with your marker.
5. Using a glue gun, glue the two larger leaves to the top of the clothespin to form the top wings of the butterfly.
6. Next, glue on the two smaller leaves to make the bottom wings.
7. Finally, glue the stick on top of the leaves for the butterfly's body with the antennae at the top.

Rainbow Bubble Snakes

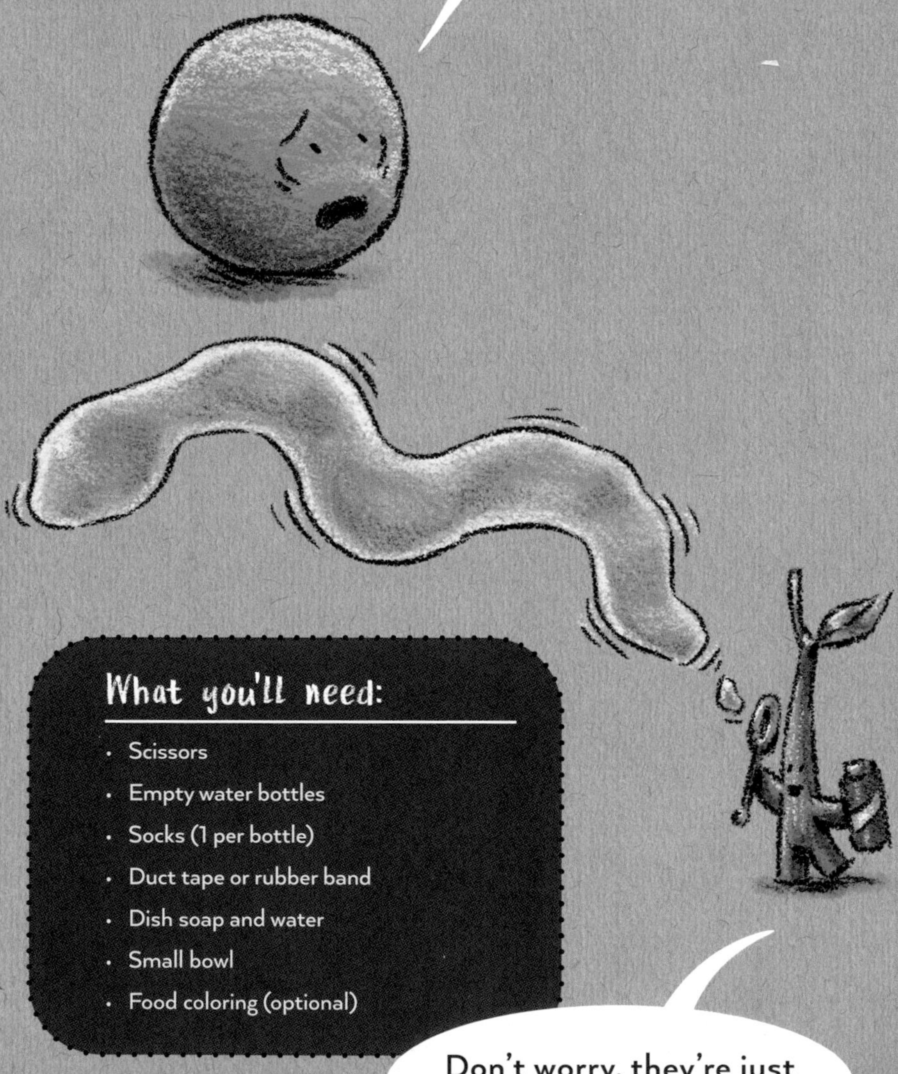
Snakes? Yikes! I don't think this is a good idea, Stick.
Don't worry, they're just made out of bubbles.

What you'll need:

- Scissors
- Empty water bottles
- Socks (1 per bottle)
- Duct tape or rubber band
- Dish soap and water
- Small bowl
- Food coloring (optional)

Directions:

1. Cut the bottom off a water bottle so that the entire bottom is gone.
2. Stretch out a sock and slide it over the open bottom, pulling it all the way up and then folding it down.
3. Use a rubber band or duct tape to secure the sock to the bottle.
4. Put a big squirt of dish soap into a shallow bowl. Add a small splash of water to make it a little bit more liquid.
5. Dip the sock end of the bubble maker into the mixture until it is soaked. (It should not be dripping. If it is dripping, you've added too much water.)
6. Blow on the mouthpiece of the bottle to make the bubble snake. The harder you blow, the longer the snake will be.
7. Once you've mastered the snake, you can add some color to make a rainbow snake. Drip a few drops of food coloring directly onto the part of the sock that will be dipped, trying to keep the colors from mixing with each other. Then follow steps 5 and 6. You may wish to do this snake outside.

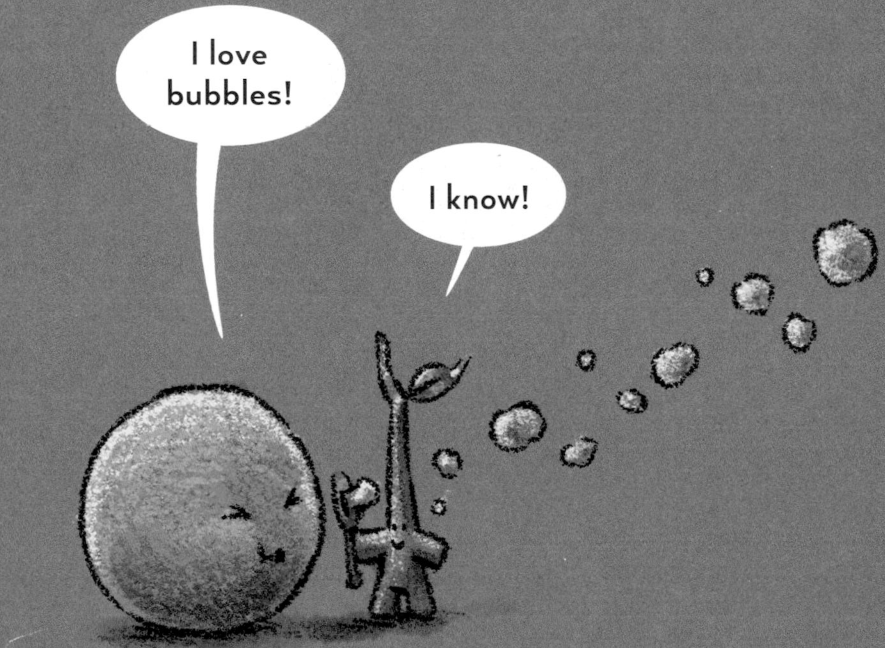
I love bubbles!
I know!

For Tom: illustrator, collaborator, and most important, friend. —B.F.
For Walley, Lua, and Sophie—our perfect pets in greener pastures.
And for Matt, with love, another butterfly story. —K.C.

Clarion Books is an imprint of HarperCollins Publishers. • HarperAlley is an imprint of HarperCollins Publishers. • Stick and Stone On the Go • Text copyright © 2023 by Beth Ferry • Illustrations copyright © 2023 by Kristen Cella • All rights reserved. Manufactured in Bosnia and Herzegovina. No part of this book may be used or reproduced in any manner whatsoever without written permission except in the case of brief quotations embodied in critical articles and reviews. For information address HarperCollins Children's Books, a division of HarperCollins Publishers, 195 Broadway, New York, NY 10007. • www.harperalley.com • ISBN 978-0-35-854938-3 • The artist used a drawing tablet, digital brushes simulating pencils and watercolors, and scans of drawing paper to create the digital illustrations for this book. • Typography by Michelle Cunningham • 23 24 25 26 27 GPS 10 9 8 7 6 5 4 3 2 1 • First Edition